IMPOSTOR'S LURE

CARLA NEGGERS

IMPOSTOR'S LURE

mira

mira

ISBN-13: 978-0-7783-5997-5

Impostor's Lure

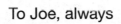

To Joe, always

IMPOSTOR'S
LURE

1

London, England

What's happening?

The room is spinning and I can't keep my eyes open. Jet lag? But my heart is racing, beating so fast I can hardly breathe. I gulp for air but it's useless.

I stumble…

Where am I?

"London, Verity. You're in London."

I narrow my eyes to focus through blurred vision. I'm in a suite at Claridge's, meeting Wendell Sharpe. He's flying in from Dublin. He's a private art detective.

Why do I want to meet with a private art detective?

Forgeries…

"My name is Verity Blackwood, and I'm just back in London from Maine and Boston and I'd like to talk to you about forgeries."

That's what I told Mr. Sharpe. I don't know if I repeat my words out loud or silently, but I can't bring myself to care.

I sway, sliding into a pool of warm water that I know, somewhere deep inside me, isn't there. I fall onto the bed in my well-appointed hotel room—Claridge's is lovely…an iconic London hotel… Wendell Sharpe's choice…

I sink into the soft duvet.

"Graham?"

He's not here. My husband. He didn't fly home with me.

He gave me the micronutrient tablets, didn't he? They're supposed to help with jet lag, but they didn't agree with me. Maybe if I sleep I'll be all right.

I open my eyes and see Jacob Marley dragging his chains above the bed. "For your sins, Verity," he says. "For your sins."

He shuffles away, but it's not the Charles Dickens character. It's Stefan. Hot tears stream down my temples and into my duvet. "Dear Stefan, it wasn't me. I promise you. It wasn't me."

He's dripping in blood as he must have been the night he was killed. It's as if nothing's changed in the two weeks since then, but Graham and I attended his funeral. We saw his coffin. He can't be here.

He's a ghost. My imagination.

My guilt.

I try to lift my hand to place it on my racing heart, but I can't move. "Help me."

I speak in the barest whisper. No one will hear me, but it doesn't matter. All I want is to slide deeper and deeper into the warmth and sleep.

2

An antique Maine lobster boat was bound to draw attention at a Boston Harbor marina, but Emma Sharpe hadn't recognized any of the onlookers until now. She pulled off her work gloves and peered out the window of her apartment, located on the ground floor of a former produce warehouse that shared the wharf with the marina.

What was Tamara McDermott doing here?

Emma tossed her gloves into the sink. She'd been cleaning since midmorning. It was after lunch now—she'd grabbed a chickpea salad out of the fridge—but she was almost finished. Kitchen, living room, bedroom, bathroom. All in four hundred square feet. Plenty of space when it'd been just her, but now she shared the apartment with her husband. Emma smiled at the thought. She and Colin Donovan, also an FBI agent, had been married ten weeks. She hoped she felt this way in ten years. Twenty. Fifty. He was and always would be the love of her life.

But he hated chickpea salad, and he'd been mystified when she'd opted to stay home and clean instead of join him and his three brothers, down from Maine, at their annual Red Sox game.

She took her keys and exited the apartment, ignoring the blast of mid-August heat. Tamara McDermott was in her late forties, a prominent federal prosecutor based in Washington, DC. Emma hadn't worked directly with her but definitely recognized her. It was Sunday, and Tamara hadn't called ahead to meet. She wore a casual marine-blue knit dress with diamond stud earrings, a simple gold watch and sturdy sandals. Little or no makeup, sweat dripping down her temples and matting her gray-streaked dark hair at her nape. She must have walked at least a couple of blocks. She wouldn't be sweating this much if she'd been dropped off by a cab. It was, though, a stiflingly hot day. Emma had on a shapeless linen sundress that didn't do her any favors, flip-flops, no makeup. She'd pinned up her hair haphazardly, thinking she wouldn't be seeing anyone until she'd had a shower and put on fresh clothes.

"Hello, Emma." Tamara squinted in the early-afternoon sun. "This is Colin's boat, isn't it?"

"It's his younger brother Andy's boat. He's a lobsterman in Maine."

"Who's Julianne?"

Julianne was the name of the classic wooden boat. "Andy's fiancée. She's a marine biologist. It was her grandfather's boat, and he named it after her."

"But it's Andy's boat now?"

Emma smiled. As a prosecutor, Tamara was known for her thoroughness, solid preparation and relentless focus. Of course she'd pick up on the nuances of the lobster boat's history. "Andy bought it from Julianne's grandfather. She objected. It was a source of tension."

"All worked out now, one can assume. Well, it's a beautiful boat—not that I know anything about boats."

"I didn't realize you were in Boston," Emma said.

"My daughter turned twenty-one yesterday. We're celebrating tonight. She's a student here in town. She's studying archives preservation. I came up for the weekend. I start vacation tomorrow. Unless I get cold feet," she added with a wry smile.

"It's been a while, has it?"

"It's been several years since I took a proper break, yes. I'm scheduled to be away for three weeks. I get clammy hands thinking about it." She laughed, glancing again at the *Julianne*, which bobbed in the quiet harbor water between two recreational powerboats. Few working boats used the marina. "I wonder what it'd be like to jump on a gorgeous old lobster boat and take off, see where I ended up." She turned back to Emma and smiled. "Drowned, probably."

Her voice had taken on an edge that belied her laugh and smile. "What brings you here, Ms. McDermott? How can I help you?"

"Tamara. Please. My daughter—Adalyn—started a new job with an art conservationist in Cambridge. Jolie Romero. I understand you know her."

"I'm familiar with her name," Emma said. "I don't know her personally."

"Have you had anything to do with her since you joined the FBI, or did you deal with her when you were a nun?"

"I've never dealt with Jolie Romero. What's this about?"

Tamara waved a hand. "Sorry. I don't mean to interrogate you. Adalyn moved into the apartment above Jolie's studio. I got the grand tour this morning. It's in Porter Square. It's nice. I suppose I'm being an overprotective mother. That's what Adalyn would say. You remember being twenty-one. Or were you in the convent then?"

Emma didn't take offense at the blunt question. "I was a novice with the Sisters of the Joyful Heart in southern Maine for a short time, but I never made my final vows."

"So you were never a real nun?"

Fishing for something. Definitely. "Not in the way you mean."

"The convent specializes in art conservation, doesn't it?"

"As well as art education," Emma said.

"Now you're an art crimes expert on Matt Yankowski's elite team here in Boston. Quite a change. Why didn't you stay with your family's art recovery business?"

"Yank recruited me out of the convent. That's the short answer. Ms.—Tamara, would you like to go inside? I have iced tea, water—"

"No, no, I won't keep you. Forgive me. I swear I've lost the ability to have a normal conversation. Adalyn is just back from three months in London, and all of a sudden she's interested in art crimes. She'd love to meet you. We're having dinner at Stephanie's on Newbury Street. Why don't you and Colin join us? Yank will be there. We're old friends."

"Thank you, I'd love to join you. I don't know what Colin's plans are with his brothers. I can let you know."

"No need. Just come." Tamara touched the thick rope that secured the *Julianne*—Donovan style—to a post. "I made a reservation for six o'clock, but I'm meeting Adalyn at the bar around five thirty. She wants Irish whiskey for one of her first legal drinks. Yank says he knows what to recommend thanks to Colin."

"I imagine she'll have her own ideas, too."

"Ha, she always does. We'll see you tonight, then."

"I look forward to it," Emma said.

Tamara relaxed visibly. "A belated congratulations on your wedding. Colin's a keeper."

Emma smiled. "I think so, too."

"I'll bet you do."

Tamara headed toward the street, her ankles swollen, no doubt from the heat and humidity, as she crossed the brick-paved wharf, passing more boats and empty slips. She took a water bottle from her tote bag, and when she reached the street, turned left, picking up her pace and quickly disappearing from view.

Emma returned to her apartment and pulled on her gloves. She and Colin did certain tasks together and took turns on the rest, but she was quite content not being at Fenway Park on a hot Sunday afternoon. She'd finally convinced him she was sincere when she said cleaning had a meditative effect on her, a product of her years in the convent. To him, cleaning was work. Get in, get it done, then have a beer.

He *was* a keeper.

She glanced out the window as new onlookers stopped to admire the *Julianne*.

Whatever else tonight's dinner was about, it wasn't just to celebrate Adalyn McDermott's twenty-first birthday.

When the four Donovan brothers descended after the game, the Red Sox had won, Emma had finished cleaning except for the oven, and Colin had been in touch with their boss about tonight's dinner. "Yank says he'll mop our floors for a month if we both go tonight."

"What about these guys?" Emma asked, referring to Mike, Andy and Kevin Donovan.

Mike grinned. "*These guys* will be just fine. We're heading back up to Maine. Kevin's on duty in the morning. Andy's got lobster traps to check and I have two retirees from Florida to outfit for a weeklong kayak trip on the Bold Coast." He winked at Emma. "Things to do, places to go."

Mike was a former Special Forces soldier with a cabin on the Bold Coast of Maine and a fiancée, Naomi MacBride, in Nashville. He was a licensed wilderness guide and outfitter, and he did the occasional contract security job—with

Naomi, an intelligence consultant. An odd relationship, but it seemed to be working. Kevin, the youngest, a Maine marine patrol officer, was unattached. All four brothers were strongly built, with blue-gray eyes and a no-nonsense manner Emma found in concert with their upbringing in a rugged Maine fishing village.

They'd arrived on the *Julianne* late yesterday. Andy had slept on the boat. Mike and Kevin had camped out in Emma and Colin's tiny living room. It was enough family time for now. They were packed up and out the door in thirty minutes.

Colin slipped his arm around Emma as they watched the lobster boat glide across the harbor. "Does part of you wish you were going with them?" she asked.

"All of me, provided you were with us."

"Mike would throw me overboard."

"Hey, he likes you now."

"I know he does, but he'd still throw me overboard. He gets restless. It'd be something to do. You guys used to do stuff like that as kids, didn't you?"

"Always wearing life vests."

Emma laughed, leaning into him. "Tamara says you're a keeper."

"She's insightful and smart as well as tough."

"You worked with her?"

"Once. My first undercover mission."

Five years ago, when Emma had still been with the Sisters of the Joyful Heart, Matt Yankowski had come up to Maine to meet with Colin as his contact agent. He'd stopped at the convent to talk to Emma about *not* making her final vows. About joining the FBI instead. She'd taken a detour to work with her grandfather at the Dublin offices of Sharpe Fine Art Recovery, but within a year, she was getting put through her paces at the Academy. She'd been in Boston for seventeen months, again recruited by Yank, this time for HIT, a small team that specialized in transnational criminals and criminal networks. HIT stood for high-impact target. Yank's idea.

Colin was a relative newcomer to HIT, shoehorned in as much for Yank to keep tabs on him as anything else. He'd had a rough landing after a major deep-cover mission. Of course, that was exactly when he and Emma met, and here they were, not quite a year later, in love, married.

"Do you think Tamara is working an investigation and that's what tonight's about?" he asked.

"Using her daughter's birthday as cover to talk to us?"

"What if it's about the daughter?"

"I don't know. Something was off about her visit. Why not just have Yank invite us if they're friends? Spend the day with her daughter. Sometimes family needs to be your sole focus."

Colin drew her closer. "We should have stayed in Ireland longer."

"An extended honeymoon. I'd have liked that."

He kissed the top of her head. "Save any cleaning for me?"

"The oven."

He laughed. "How appropriate."

3

Tamara stepped out of her rental car and breathed in the Maine air, cooler, fresher here by the sea. It was hot here, too, though. She nearly froze on the drive up from Boston when she'd turned on the air-conditioning and it cooled her sweat. *Dumb* to have walked up and down the Boston waterfront. She liked to walk and she had a lot on her mind, but she knew better. Boston could get just as hot and humid in August as Washington did.

She hadn't thought this little adventure through. It wasn't like her, but Adalyn...

What had she got herself into?

"Maybe nothing," Tamara said aloud as she looked out at the sea, waves washing over sand and rocks. A good place to kayak, Graham Blackwood had told her. Then he'd promptly admitted he didn't know anything about kayaking. He wanted to try while he was in Maine.

Kayak, get past a friend's murder. Why the hell not?

Tamara spotted a seagull that on another day, under different circumstances, would have enthralled or at least amused her. Patrick, her ex-husband, considered them rats with wings. Killjoy. Good riddance to him.

Twenty-two years of marriage up in smoke.

"Blah. Don't think about it."

Except she'd been thinking about it most of the ninety-minute drive up to Maine. They'd told Adalyn it'd been an amiable split. Different paths now that they were in their late forties.

No mention of the cute young girlfriend.

Tamara didn't like herself for giggling when she'd heard they broke up.

"More like cackling with joy."

She didn't want Patrick to be miserable, but she didn't want him to find true love or whatever he was looking for with a shallow paralegal who looked good on his arm. Tamara didn't want to think about what the gold digger was like in bed. Maybe she wasn't being very evolved, but there it was. Good, maybe, for a prosecutor who'd never had much bad happen to her in her life to experience such raw emotion.

She shook off her thoughts. She needed to focus on why she was here.

Where was Graham Blackwood?

She'd pulled into a turnaround on a narrow road in front of his rental house—assuming she hadn't made a wrong turn. It was on an isolated section of the coast near the Sisters of the Joyful Heart convent. Graham's choice. He'd given her directions and asked her to keep their meeting private. *Verity wanted to talk to you before her flight, but she's already cutting it close. I'm staying in Maine for a few days. I'll explain everything tomorrow. It concerns Adalyn. Verity and I are both fond of her.*

Tamara didn't see another soul, hear any cars—just the breeze and the wash of the sea. That's what she wanted on her vacation. She'd return to Boston for dinner and be on her way for three weeks of bliss as soon as possible. She might even get a head start and leave tonight. She'd packed after her unnerving brunch with Adalyn.

Who are these Blackwoods, Adalyn?

*They're friends. I met them in England. I know Verity better
than I do Graham. She worked at the National Gallery in London.*

Why did they come here?

*They needed a change of pace. A friend of theirs died. Actually, he
was murdered two weeks ago on his way home from London.*

Tamara had pounced. *Wait. What friend? Murdered how?
Have the police made an arrest? Did you know him?*

Mom…will you stop? Please. I shouldn't have said anything.

Tamara managed to pry the name of the dead man from
her daughter. Stefan Petrescu. He was a Romanian linguist
who'd lived near the Blackwoods in Oxford. He'd been shot.
No leads, witnesses or arrests as far as Adalyn knew.

Adalyn insisted the Blackwoods weren't involved. *It's just
one of those random, awful things that happen. I wish I hadn't
brought it up.*

Why did you?

*Because you asked why Graham and Verity are here, and Stefan
is why. They have a friend who lives in southern New Hampshire,
an hour north of Boston. He's an artist. A painter. They decided to
visit him and then spend a few days in Maine.*

Well, *that* was bullshit, only Adalyn didn't see through it.

Once Tamara picked her jaw up off the floor, she was convinced she had to keep her meeting with Graham Blackwood
and find out if his concerns about Adalyn had anything to
do with this linguist's murder—how it had affected her emotionally, whether she was being straight about it, whether it
was the catalyst for the Blackwoods' visit to the US. Who this
artist was and how they knew him.

Why Heron's Cove of all the many places to visit in Maine.
Sharpe country.

Whatever. Tamara needed to know what was going on. Period. After brunch, she drove to the HIT offices on the harbor and walked the few blocks to Emma and Colin's place.

She'd resisted asking too many questions until she could talk to Graham Blackwood, but she hadn't gotten any sense that Matt Yankowski and his art crimes specialist or the rest of his team were involved in or even aware of the Petrescu murder investigation. She doubted they knew anything about the Blackwoods and their visit to New England. Yank, of course, knew Adalyn. They hadn't seen each other in a few years, but he'd been at her party for her very first birthday.

The Sharpe connection was more worrisome. Had Adalyn gotten mixed up in some kind of art crime? How on earth would the death of a linguist be related to an art crime?

Jolie Romero, art conservation, a meeting near Emma's former convent—Tamara didn't know how or if they were connected to Stefan Petrescu's murder, but they were enough to get her in a rental car and up to Maine. She needed information. She'd hear what Graham Blackwood had to say and then, if warranted, talk to the FBI agents tonight.

A reasonable plan of action.

She hoped she was just being a burnt-out, paranoid prosecutor who needed a vacation, but no way was she going off to Nova Scotia and leaving Adalyn here on her own. Tamara knew herself. She had to be satisfied her daughter wasn't in trouble. She wouldn't relax otherwise. Twenty-one was a milestone but it was still very young, and Adalyn spent her days fooling with musty documents and digital archives— she didn't have her mother's experience with the dark side of the world.

Tamara stepped back toward her car. Maybe she was in the wrong parking area. Could Graham be waiting for her at the convent entrance? There was a trail, too, that hugged the rocks and water. It led into the woods onto the small peninsula where the convent was located and in the opposite direction, toward the village of Heron's Cove. Ordinarily she would appreciate the solitude and the scenery, but right now she wanted to get on with this meeting and return to Boston.

Graham hadn't initiated contact. Verity, his wife, had. Tamara had arrived in Boston around the time the Blackwoods were to check in for their return flight to London. Adalyn had told her Verity wanted to meet her at check-in—only Graham was there, not Verity.

He wasn't a bad-looking guy. In his early fifties, balding, maybe ten pounds overweight, rumpled clothes, he was a former UK diplomat, a bit self-important. He'd struck Tamara as concerned but not panicked. They'd had a brief conversation. He couldn't talk long now, needed to sort out his rental car since he'd decided to extend his stay, why not meet tomorrow in Maine? Not that far. Beautiful weather. Tamara had figured there was more to it, but murder hadn't entered her mind. She'd thought, okay, maybe he and his wife aren't wild about this Jolie Romero and they're worried Adalyn jumped in with this woman too soon. I'll have a nice drive to Maine, get this off my brain and then enjoy our birthday dinner and my vacation.

Tamara had debated inviting Yank to join her in Heron's Cove, but she knew Graham would disappear or clam up with an FBI agent present, and nothing about the Englishman's demeanor had suggested he was dangerous. Obviously, he had concerns, or he wouldn't have suggested this meeting. That didn't mean they involved the murder of his linguist friend.

Tamara's rental car was a nondescript, four-door gray sedan. She pulled open the back door on the driver's side. She'd get her tote bag, drink some water, think. Her phone was dead. It'd died while she was at the HIT offices. She'd let herself get so worked up she'd left her charger at the restaurant where she had taken Adalyn for brunch. She couldn't call Graham and ask him where he was.

She heard a sound behind her. The crunch of gravel, foot-steps...

A hood—a blanket—dropped over her. She gasped, suck-ing in hot fabric.

Felt a pinprick in her upper arm.

"No!"

She kicked and flailed, but her attacker shoved her into the back seat, onto the floor.

She couldn't breathe.

The key to averting an attack is situational awareness.

Her self-defense instructor, a million years ago. She'd trained for just this sort of attack. She *never* should have come here alone. She'd expected cars, people, houses.

She felt herself sinking, slipping. The drug was already tak-ing effect. Morphine? What?

She heard a car door shut. Hers. Then another car door open and shut. The driver's.

My key.

She didn't have it. "I have three FBI agents waiting for me."

Did she speak out loud? She couldn't tell. She was sinking deeper, each breath more shallow than the last. She couldn't keep herself awake.

She went limp, drifting.

Adalyn. My sweet baby...

4

Oliver York was sipping a rare Islay Scotch at Claridge's, his favorite London hotel, and arguing opera with Henrietta Balfour, an MI5 officer and sometimes garden designer. Or was it a garden designer and sometimes MI5 officer? He shuddered. He didn't like thinking about the British Security Service. He'd been in trouble with them for years.

Henrietta sat across from him at a cozy table in a quiet corner of the elegant art-deco bar, under dim light that made her skin seem even milkier. He wasn't winning their argument. He knew less about opera than she did. Her grandfather Freddy Balfour, an MI5 legend, had been an opera buff, and she'd picked up a few tidbits from him before his death.

"Most operas are elaborate confession stories with music," Oliver said.

Henrietta rolled her lovely blue-green eyes. "That is simplistic, Oliver."

Probably so. He and Henrietta had known each other since childhood but had only decided they were in love, or might be in love, earlier that summer. They'd been discussing an old flowerpot she'd unearthed at his farm in the Cotswolds when he'd noticed her reddish-brown curls, her spray of freckles, her long flowered skirt and muddy Wellingtons and had thought…*dear Henrietta*. What had happened to the lonely, outspoken seven-year-old who'd marched up to him, then only ten himself, and demanded to know who'd killed his parents? What had happened to the gangly teenager who'd liked to see how many sheep droppings she could clear in one leap?

She'd followed in her grandfather's footsteps was what had happened to her.

Last winter, she'd told everyone in the village she'd quit her dull London office job—which had never existed—to design gardens in the Cotswolds. She'd inherited a house from a great-aunt, finally making a career change possible. That was her story, at least. Oliver remained convinced MI5 had taken advantage of her connection to him and sent her to the Cotswolds to keep an eye on him.

Unlike his actual MI5 handler, whose name Oliver didn't like to think never mind utter, Henrietta had never threatened to toss him in prison. A fate he deserved, he supposed. He'd been making amends for his thieving ways. Bit by bit, day by day. It wasn't just to satisfy the authorities. It was to satisfy himself. He hadn't hurt or killed anyone, but he had helped himself to a considerable fortune in art—all of it now returned, intact, to its owners.

Well, except for the one unsigned landscape he'd kept for sentimental reasons. Its owner, an Irish artist in love with a priest self-exiled to a parish on the Maine coast, had tacitly gifted it to him.

Within days of their flowerpot discussion, he and Henrietta had confronted a vicious killer and finally, after thirty years, learned the truth about his traumatic past—the murder of his parents in front of him when he was eight and his own kidnapping to a Scottish ruin.

That incident proved to him she was MI5, no question, although she did know her way around a garden.

They'd driven in together from the Cotswolds that morning, but Henrietta had booked a room at Claridge's, a short walk from Oliver's London apartment, where he was staying, alone. She'd given up her own London apartment—which he'd never seen—last winter to move full-time to her great-aunt's house, not far from his Cotswolds farm. She'd stayed with him at the farm multiple times since June, but never in London. She wouldn't discuss the details of her MI5 status with him, but he suspected her superiors were leery of their relationship. He'd coped with his childhood trauma by studying mythology, which MI5 didn't mind, and by becoming an art thief, which they did mind. That he was of occasional use to British intelligence in thwarting far worse criminals hadn't yet freed him from their clutches.

"Have you ever listened to or attended an entire opera?" Henrietta asked him, a note of challenge in her voice.

"Is that a requirement for an opinion?"

"For an informed opinion, certainly."

"I listened to *Madama Butterfly* while feeling sorry for myself one rainy night at the farm. I was drinking Scotch. I was alone." He noticed she'd narrowed her eyes on him, and he knew she was picturing him by the fire in the rambling old stone house he'd inherited from his grandparents. "I suppose it's not a surprise to you that *Madama Butterfly* has a sad ending."

"No way out for the poor dear Butterfly."

Oliver ordered another Scotch. He and Henrietta often had this sort of rambling, open-ended conversation on a range of subjects in which they had interest but not necessarily a great deal of knowledge or expertise. He recalled a profound discussion about various types of sheep when he was fourteen and she was eleven, a city girl and only child dropped off at her great-aunt's house while her parents went to Paris. Posey

Balfour had been a keen gardener. Hence, Henrietta's passion for gardening.

Oliver tuned back in to the conversation and realized she'd meandered to something about Thor, explaining he was the Norse god of thunder. "I suppose you know that, though," she added.

He did. He was an Oxford and self-taught scholar of mythology, folklore and legends. He specialized in Celtic mythology but, of course, he knew a great deal about Thor.

"I've seen all the Thor movies," Henrietta pronounced.

"The Thor movies?"

"I thought we could watch them together one evening at the farm. Chris Hemsworth is a delight as Thor. Very hunky."

"Henrietta…"

"The stories are based on Norse mythology. The Hulk makes an appearance in one of the movies. I know that's a creative stretch since he isn't a Norse god or Norse anything, but the movie's loads of fun."

Hulk. Thor. Only Henrietta could get from opera to comic book heroes. "Shall I get a refill for your Scotch?"

She grinned. "You'll love Tom Hiddleston as Loki." Mercifully, she glanced past him toward the bar's entrance. "Here's our friend now, but he doesn't look happy. I wonder what's wrong?"

Oliver pivoted in his chair, rising when he recognized Wendell Sharpe making his way to their table. They exchanged a handshake. Wendell took Henrietta by the hand and kissed her on each cheek. He sat between them but refused Oliver's offer of Scotch. "Just water, please."

"What's going on, my friend?" Oliver asked, returning to his own seat. "What brings you to London?"

"I'm supposed to meet with a woman here at the hotel. My choice. I figured I could get you two here for a drink afterwards, only she didn't meet me in the lobby as agreed and doesn't answer her door." Wendell paused, as if contemplating how much to say. "She left the key for me at the front desk in case I arrived early and she was out. In fact, I was a few minutes late. I flew into Heathrow and took a taxi…hellish traffic for a Sunday…"

"Who is this woman you're to meet?" Henrietta asked, cutting through Wendell's preoccupied near-rambling.

He didn't seem to hear the question. He stared at Henrietta's Scotch, but clearly his mind was elsewhere. Henrietta had only recently met him. He was Oliver's friend and, for a time, his nemesis, a spry, wiry Dublin-based private art detective in his eighties. He wore a bow tie, a terrible jacket, somewhat frayed trousers, and walking shoes. He and Oliver had played cat and mouse for a decade. By unspoken agreement, Oliver didn't admit to any of his thefts and Wendell didn't press him to admit to them. Oliver had never profited from his heists, but he had, indisputably, broken the law in various cities and countries. Statutes of limitations, jurisdictional issues, evidence, the will and other considerations—namely, MI5 having him by the short hairs—had prevented his arrest and prosecution for any of his heists. Sympathy for his lonely plight since witnessing his parents' murders at age eight played no role. Countless people were rotting in prisons having faced even worse childhood traumas.

Wendell was semiretired now, and Oliver had lost any urge to slip into private homes, museums and businesses and make off with valuable art.

"Oliver and I are here as you asked," Henrietta said.

"Yes, thank you. It's good to see you. Apologies for being distracted." Wendell's water arrived, and he drained a quarter of it before he set the glass on the table and continued.

"Who knows how long I'll be able to make the trip. Dublin to London is a pop-fly, but I'm no spring chicken."

Oliver had no idea what a pop-fly was, but Henrietta seemed to. "It's barely a pop-fly," she said. "You'll be flying to London into your hundreds."

"Ever the optimist," Wendell said.

The old man's unusual melancholy mood had Oliver wanting to order his friend a Scotch. "Who is this woman? Can you tell us?"

"Her name's Verity Blackwood. She called me this morning and asked to meet with me as soon as possible. She said she's a former exhibit coordinator with the National Gallery here in London. She left the gallery eighteen months ago when she married a former diplomat—Graham Blackwood—and joined him at his home in Oxford."

"She offered up those details or did you look her up after your call?" Henrietta asked.

"Offered them. I didn't have time to look her up. She wants to talk to me about forgeries. No details. I was up for a trip to London, and we agreed on meeting this evening. I decided to bundle this trip with some other business and meet friends for a pint or two."

Oliver didn't know if he fell into either category, but Wendell had asked if he'd be at Claridge's tonight, presumably with Henrietta. "I don't know Graham Blackwood personally," he said. "But I'm familiar with his name. He has his own foreign policy think tank these days. It's small and uncontroversial—more to keep him busy than anything else, I suspect. His father was a keen investor who did well in the tech tool-up in the 1990s, adding to the already healthy Blackwood fortune."

"It's only Verity who wants to meet with you?" Henrietta asked. "Alone? Why? Why is she staying here instead of meeting you in Oxford? Where's her husband?"

Wendell drank more water, looking tired. He addressed Henrietta. "Verity said she got in from Boston this morning. Graham stayed behind at the last minute. She said she'd stay in London tonight. She thought that would be easier for me. I recommended Claridge's since I know it's one of Oliver's favorites."

"I see," was all Henrietta said. Oliver made no comment. He noticed she had only a few sips left of her Scotch. He'd approved her choice of Auchentoshan Three Wood. Of course, she didn't need or seek his approval, another of her appealing qualities.

He had a long list of things he liked about Henrietta Balfour.

The elegant hotel bar was quiet tonight, atmospheric, perfect for a meeting between an octogenarian art detective, an MI5 agent and an art thief. Oliver shook off any sense of romanticism, a bad habit, he knew, when he was trying to distance himself from unpleasant emotions. Regret, guilt, pride, embarrassment. Wendell's furrowed brow and Henrietta's serious mood—no thought of Thor movies now, clearly—confirmed to Oliver that he wasn't alone in his unease.

"Verity mentioned she suffers from terrible jet lag," Wendell added. "I tried ringing her room but she didn't answer. She could have fallen asleep. She was eager to meet when we spoke this morning—I've been debating using the key, seeing if that rouses her. I didn't ask a lot of questions. I figured we'd get to details when we met."

Oliver frowned. "Do you think she went out?"

"I have no idea. I don't like the feel of this. It's not as if I walked a couple of blocks or took a taxi for this meeting. I flew." Wendell rubbed the back of his neck with one hand, lined, bony, veins bulging. "I've never had much trouble with jet lag but a lot of people do."

"Yes," Henrietta said. "However, I can understand your concern."

"What about you, Wendell—do you have a place to stay tonight?" Oliver asked. "You're welcome to the guest room at my apartment. Henrietta has a room here herself."

"She does? I thought you two were an item."

"That's complicated and personal," she said, answering before Oliver could get in a word, her smile taking any edge off her words.

"I see. Hint taken." Wendell turned to Oliver. "I'd be pleased to bunk in your guest room. Did you leave your puppy at the farm?"

"Happily, yes. He's incorrigible without Martin, I'm afraid. Martin wants me to be the alpha dog with Alfred, but it's too late. Martin is obsessed with the idea that I need a dog. A companion. But I have Henrietta as a companion and…" Oliver stopped himself and winced. "Oh, that didn't come out right at all."

Fortunately, Henrietta burst into laughter, her eyes bright and filled with humor as she winked at Wendell. "We're still working on Oliver's people skills."

"The point is, Alfred's not at the apartment," Oliver said. "A good thing because he'd have peed on all the walls by now."

"My kind of dog," Wendell said.

Henrietta started to rise. "Shall we look in on Mrs. Blackwood?"

They took the sweeping main staircase to Verity Blackwood's second-floor room, Henrietta in the lead. If there was any trouble, Oliver would happily defer to her with any hotel staff, too. She didn't go at her usual breakneck speed, perhaps because Wendell Sharpe was in his eighties and not his thirties. He'd insisted he'd be fine, of course, and didn't look winded when they paused at the stop of the stairs. Henrietta stood back, allowing him to pass since he was the one with Verity's room number and key.

Wendell knocked on the appropriate door. "Mrs. Blackwood? It's Wendell Sharpe. I'm sorry to disturb you, but I want to be sure you're all right."

They waited in silence but there was no response.

"Hand me the key," Henrietta said. "If any of us gets in trouble, let it be me."

Wendell didn't argue and handed her the key. If the door was locked from the inside, a standard, extra measure of security, they would ask the hotel to check on her—but it wasn't, and they went in.

A single floor lamp was lit in the living area of the beautifully appointed art-deco suite. A suite was an indulgence for a solo occupant but one the Blackwoods could well afford. Oliver, hardly a pauper, would have happily settled for a more modest room to sleep off jet lag. Then again, he wouldn't have been meeting with a renowned private art detective, as had been Mrs. Blackwood's plan.

Henrietta stopped abruptly in the open doorway to the bedroom and held up a hand. "Allow me."

Oliver acquiesced without comment. He didn't want her thinking she could bark orders at him just because she was MI5, but as she tiptoed into the bedroom, he realized her status as an intelligence officer wasn't what had prompted her decisive order. She was a woman looking in on another woman. He suspected Wendell had the same thought as he, too, came to a halt. Verity Blackwood lay facedown on the bed, her yellow-blond hair tangled and matted from what Oliver guessed was sweat, spit and possibly vomit. She wore black yoga pants and a white tunic, twisted and bunched up, and her feet were bare, her toenails painted a bright coral.

Dead to the world. Had she taken a sleeping pill?

Henrietta eased toward the prone woman. "Mrs. Blackwood? My name is Henrietta Balfour. I'm here with Wendell Sharpe. We were concerned about you and—" She stopped, gasping. "Bloody hell."

Oliver sprang forward, given her shocked tone. "What is it?"

Henrietta turned to him. "We need an ambulance here at once."

"Henrietta—"

"*Now*, Oliver."

He grabbed a house phone and rang the front desk. Wendell followed Henrietta into the bedroom and switched on a bedside lamp. "Oh, dear God. Oliver…"

"I see."

Oliver saw now that Verity Blackwood appeared unconscious, and if she was breathing at all, it was dangerously shallow. Henrietta checked Verity's wrist. "She has a faint pulse but at least there is one." She pulled up one of the motionless woman's eyelids and let it close again. "Pinpoint pupils." She stood straight. "She's overdosed."

"But she's alive?" Wendell asked.

"Barely. I'm sure it's an opioid overdose. I don't know if it's too late for naloxone, but she won't make it unless help gets here fast. I'll do what I can until then."

Oliver frowned, phone in hand. "You'll do—"

"It's not my first overdose," she said, climbing onto the bed. "I need to do rescue breathing."

Verity's lips and fingernails had turned blue. Oliver shuddered, but a front desk clerk answered his call. He provided a clear, concise description of the situation. The clerk promised to phone an ambulance and send up hotel staff who could help.

Henrietta got about the job, pinching Verity's nose and then covering the dying woman's mouth with her own and breathing into it. No hesitation—Henrietta could waffle about flower borders, but Oliver was impressed with her decisive action now, with a woman's life at stake.

He looked around the bedroom and noticed an herbal medicine bottle on the bedside table. He didn't touch it. The label stated the contents were micronutrients, vitamins and minerals ideal for stress relief.

Wendell nodded to the bottle. "It might be snake oil, but it's not what caused the overdose."

A near-empty glass of red wine stood next to the bottle. Oliver was no expert, but if Verity Blackwood had ingested some sort of opioid, alcohol would exacerbate the depressant effects of the powerful drug. Had she known what she was doing? Had she hidden opioid tablets in the herb bottle and planned to get high—or had she planned to kill herself? Was this a suicide attempt?

Had she wanted Wendell Sharpe to find her body?

Wendell walked over to the open bathroom door. "I don't see a syringe. I'd guess she took pills."

"Did she sound depressed when she spoke with you?" Oliver asked.

"Not at all. She wanted to meet with me as soon as possible. She didn't want to wait. She said she'd come to Dublin if I couldn't get to London. She sounded impatient more than anything else."

Oliver glanced at the woman, still not responding to Henrietta's rescue breathing. "How did she get your number?"

Wendell hesitated a fraction of a second. "I don't know. I figured I'd ask when I saw her." He paused, staring at his would-be client. "I wonder if I should call Lucas before the cops get here."

Lucas Sharpe was Wendell's grandson and the executive director of Sharpe Fine Art Recovery in Heron's Cove, Maine. Oliver didn't know him well. He was better acquainted with Wendell, the company's founder, who'd run a Dublin office since the death of his wife sixteen years ago.

"And Emma?" Oliver asked.

"She *is* the cops."

Oliver hadn't considered law enforcement would need to get involved, but he supposed they'd have to, given the circumstances. If Verity indeed had arrived that morning from Boston—if she hadn't lied—could she have secured her drugs there? How? Why? When? Those were reasonable questions, but Oliver would let Wendell and Henrietta deal with the authorities on either side of the Atlantic.

Henrietta continued to perform rescue breathing, unflappable as she did what she could to administer basic life support to the dying woman. Oliver was well aware that as little as three to five minutes without oxygen to the brain could cause permanent damage, even death. Verity Blackwood hadn't moved that he could see. He knew that opioids were a central nervous system depressant that decreased breathing.

He turned to Wendell. "Do you know how to reach Verity's husband?"

"No idea."

"But he didn't fly back to London with her?"

"That's what she said."

Wendell stared at the woman he'd flown from Dublin to meet. Oliver could see the shock of finding her in such duress was affecting his elderly friend. Fortunately, two hotel staff members arrived, quickly followed by an ambulance crew— and, not surprisingly, the police.

The paramedics took over from Henrietta. She climbed off the bed, pushing back her hair. "I'm a garden designer in the Cotswolds," she told a police officer without a twitch of disingenuousness. "Mr. York, Mr. Sharpe and I are friends. Mrs. Blackwood was late for a meeting with Mr. Sharpe, and we looked in on her."

"What was the meeting about?" the officer asked.

"Art." Again, Henrietta didn't miss a beat. "Mr. Sharpe is a specialist in art recovery."

"And Mr. York?"

"He's a mythologist."

Oliver supposed Henrietta's smooth answers and demeanor—even after administering rescue breathing—were the result of her MI5 training and experience, or perhaps simply sitting on Freddy Balfour's knee during her early childhood. She had an explanation at the ready for how she'd known what to do to help an overdose victim. Oliver didn't hear the entire bit, but it went something like, "One knows these things nowadays, doesn't one?"

The paramedics strapped Verity Blackwood to a stretcher. Her color had improved slightly, or perhaps it was the change in the angle of the light. She hadn't regained consciousness.

"How are you holding up, my friend?" Oliver asked Wendell.

The old man stared at the woman he was to have met about forgeries. "I hope she makes it."

It wasn't an answer. Oliver clapped the older man on his shoulder. "She has a chance thanks to you."

"Thanks to Henrietta. I wouldn't have known what to do."

"It's hard to believe that just a few minutes ago we were discussing opera and Thor at the bar," Oliver said.

Wendell offered the faintest of smiles. "What a pair you two are."

Oliver was grateful to offer a moment of levity as Verity Blackwood was taken from her hotel suite.

The police, of course, wanted to interview her three rescuers.

Oliver had a feeling it would be a while before he could sneak in a call to Wendell's FBI-agent granddaughter in Boston. Emma Sharpe might not need to know about a woman who'd suffered a drug overdose hours after arriving in London from Boston, but she would without question want to know that the woman had been about to meet with her elderly grandfather.

5

Colin didn't take an immediate dislike to Adalyn McDermott, but it was close. She struck him as spoiled, entitled, ungrateful and superior, making no secret tonight's dinner with her mother and her mother's friends hadn't been her idea. On the other hand, her mother *was* late, and Colin couldn't have said he'd have wanted to celebrate his twenty-first birthday with three FBI agents. Adalyn was in the bar with two friends and the Yankowskis when he and Emma arrived at the popular Back Bay restaurant on upscale Newbury Street. It was a hot Sunday evening after a Red Sox game, and everything was crowded.

Adalyn had on wrinkled wide-legged pants, a paint-stained lace top and flip-flops, her long hair pinned up haphazardly, its color a mix of mousy brown and pumpkin highlights. She was toying with the ice in her old-fashioned and griping about her mother to the two friends who'd stopped by to wish her a happy birthday but weren't staying for dinner.

With Adalyn in no mood, Lucy Yankowski took on the role of gracious hostess and got Emma and Colin seated and their drinks ordered. Beer for Colin, chardonnay for Emma. Yank—Matt Yankowski—had a glass of whiskey in front of him. He looked as if he wanted to keep the bottle. He wasn't big on social events, and he hated small talk. Lucy, however, could make anyone feel comfortable. They were in their early forties, Yank with touches of gray in his dark hair, in a light blue suit, Lucy dressed in chic but simple slim pants and a top that matched her brown eyes and pixie-cut dark hair.

She made introductions. Adalyn's two friends were Jolie Romero, Adalyn's employer, a local art conservationist in her fifties, and Rex Campbell, a client in his early thirties, if that. "We should get going," Jolie said. She had short, spiky gray hair and blue eyes, and wore a brightly embroidered knee-length vest over a black top and pants.

"Give your mom our best," Rex said, getting to his feet. He was dressed casually in expensive khakis and a navy polo shirt, his medium brown hair cut short. Hazel eyes, square jaw, fit-looking and clearly awkward.

"Are you sure you won't join us for dinner?" Lucy asked.

"No, no, but thank you." Jolie hoisted a large tote bag onto her shoulder. "Have a wonderful evening. I'm sure Tamara's just running a bit late. Boston's changed since she was in law school here. She probably mistimed things."

Adalyn looked up from her drink. "I doubt that but thanks anyway."

Jolie smiled without comment and followed Rex out of the bar. Adalyn watched them, her eyes shining with tears, but she sniffled them back. "I've called, texted and emailed. No answer, but I wouldn't put it past my mother to turn off her phone and stand me up out of spite."

Lucy looked taken aback. "Would she do something like that at your birthday dinner?"

Adalyn reddened and waved both hands as if to cancel out what she'd just said. "Sorry. I'm being unfair. I had a mimosa at brunch, and I sucked down half my old-fashioned too fast. Honestly, I have no idea what's gotten into my mother."

"Does she often run late?" Emma asked.

"Oh, yeah. All the time. She's the 'crazy-busy' prosecutor. She's always filled with apologies and excuses. Very important last-minute work, calls she couldn't put off, emails she had to answer or the world would end. She never puts it that way." Adalyn made a face. "Why don't we take our table? I promise to cheer up."

She sprang to her feet and grabbed the hostess to seat them at their table—which Tamara McDermott had reserved. Colin took a sip of his beer. "I'm suddenly wishing I stayed behind to clean the oven."

"I'd have helped," Yank said.

"Tamara didn't give any indication she would blow off dinner when I saw her earlier," Emma said. "I didn't sense she was irritated with her daughter, either. She seemed eager for us all to have dinner tonight."

Colin narrowed his gaze on her. She was steady, analytical and brilliant, and falling in love with her had been the best move of his life. Not that he'd thought about it. It'd just happened. "Are you worried?" he asked.

"Getting there."

They joined Adalyn, Yank and Lucy at a table by a window in the main restaurant. There was an extra chair if Tamara showed up after all. Their waiter brought their drinks from the bar, but Colin switched to sparkling water. Emma and Yank did, too, a sign they were concerned about their AWOL federal prosecutor.

Adalyn tried calling her mother again. "Call me, Mom, please. Next is checking the emergency rooms, y'know?" She disconnected and set her phone on the table next to her. "Sometimes you can't be subtle with my mother."

"Where's she staying?" Colin asked.

"A couple of blocks from here. She's only in town for two nights—last night and tonight—but she booked a small apartment. She could have stayed with me but I just moved into my place—it's on the top floor of Jolie's studio in Cambridge. It's still a mess. I'm only two weeks back from three months in London. She gave me an extra key to her place." Adalyn reached for her handbag, hung on the back of her chair. "In case I got too drunk to make it back to Cambridge." She opened her bag and produced the key, holding it up as if to prove she was serious. "Or in case I wanted to hang out with her and let her grill me about my life. London. What I want to do after I graduate. Mom's a planner."

Emma lifted her water glass. "When did you last speak with her?"

"This morning. We had brunch. She picked me up at my apartment. I showed her around a bit, and we headed to her rental apartment and walked to Prudential. She flew in last night and starts vacation tomorrow. She said she needs a real break. Maybe she decided to get an early start. Maybe something last minute came up at work. It's hard for her to get away. Who knows, maybe she's mad at my dad. They've been divorced for a year, but things are still a bit raw in my family."

"Where's he?" Yank asked.

"Home in Washington. He'll come up next week to celebrate my birthday. He didn't want to step on my mother's toes with her celebration. She can be so competitive. You know him, don't you?"

Yank nodded. "I met both your parents when they were starting out in Boston."

He didn't look any more thrilled with Adalyn McDermott than Colin was. He glanced at Emma. She was harder to read. He pushed back his chair. "Why don't I go knock on her door? It'll only take a few minutes."

"I'll join you," Emma said.

"Thank you, but I should go with you—" Adalyn said.

Lucy touched Adalyn's hand. "Let's talk whiskey with Matt instead."

Adalyn gave Colin the key and the address. "Tonight…" Her eyes brimmed with fresh tears. "It's not going as planned. Sorry."

"We'll get back as fast as we can," Emma said.

Adalyn sniffled. "My mom told me about you. I'm interested in art crimes. Maybe. I don't know. We can talk more when you guys get back."

Once across the street, away from the crowded, boisterous restaurant and its outdoor café, Colin turned to Emma. "What do you think?"

"Tamara intended to be at dinner when I saw her. She'd never have invited us if she'd planned to bail. That's my take."

"Something happened between then and now?"

Emma shrugged. She'd changed into a skirt, a white shirt and a lightweight jacket, its green a shade lighter than her eyes. "It could be something as simple as a dead phone and she miscalculated the time."

"You had concerns about her when she stopped at the marina."

"I felt she was holding back."

"Something to do with her daughter," Colin said.

"That would be my guess, too."

"You know Back Bay better than I do. Lead the way."

The small apartment Tamara McDermott had rented was located on the ground floor of a brownstone on Commonwealth Avenue. The living room and bedroom overlooked an alley with tandem parking for the building's tenants. Colin couldn't tell but, according to Emma, the place was furnished in inexpensive, hip IKEA everything—fixtures, rugs, furniture, lighting, pots and pans, dishes and silverware. All of it was spotless. Tamara either hadn't made a mess or had cleaned up in case her daughter stayed overnight. He walked into the galley kitchen. Gleaming.

"No luggage," Emma said, emerging from the bedroom.

"Looks as if she cleared out."

A handwritten note lay flat on the coffee table. Colin raised an eyebrow when he noticed the turquoise ink and little hand-drawn heart at the bottom. Unexpected. He and Emma read the note together:

Adalyn—

I can't believe you're twenty-one! Enjoy the apartment. I've settled the bill. All you have to do is lock up and leave your key in the mailbox at the entrance. I decided to leave tonight instead of waiting until morning, but I promise I'll make it up to you. This is more than a vacation for me. It's a "time out." I'm going dark, as they say. No screens. No calls. No work. No family, even. I love you, always,

Mom

Colin stood back. "What do you think?"

"She says 'tonight.' To me that implies she expected to be at dinner, but maybe she decided she couldn't wait and had to leave now."

"Fight with the daughter?"

"Adalyn certainly isn't in a great mood."

"There's no apology in the note," Colin said. "Wouldn't you apologize if you cut out on your daughter's birthday dinner? Wouldn't you at least call her—call the friends you invited? Not us. Lucy and Yank."

"I would. You would. We don't know if Tamara would."

"Yank might have more insight into her behavior." Colin glanced again at the note. The handwriting flowed, without any hint of excessive pressure or uneven lettering that would indicate stress. "We could get back to the restaurant and discover she finally charged her phone and got in touch with Adalyn. If she was already desperate for a real break, it's possible the notion of her daughter turning twenty-one overwhelmed her."

Emma nodded. "It's a big milestone for a mother as well as a daughter. Tamara could be depressed, reflective—she could have simply decided she didn't want to inflict herself on Adalyn and the rest of us at dinner."

"Throw in a recent divorce and I guess it's possible. Why the drama, though? Why put her daughter through such an ordeal?"

"Couldn't risk Adalyn talking her out of leaving now, or getting swept up in her problems?"

"What problems?"

"Relationships, career, money, burnout." Emma sighed, glancing out the window at the alley. "It doesn't have to be anything out of the ordinary to tip the scales for a mother already on overdrive."

"Did Tamara have a suitcase with her when you saw her?"

Emma shook her head and turned from the uninspiring view. "She must have had it stashed somewhere—a rental car, maybe. She was hot, though. I'd say she walked at least a few blocks before she stopped by."

"Think she was already debating bolting early?"

"I didn't get that impression. Let's head back to the restaurant and see if Adalyn's heard from her mother and what she thinks of the note."

By unspoken agreement, they left the note untouched on the coffee table. Colin snapped a photo of it on his phone. "I'll text Yank to put in your dinner order," he said as they locked up.

"Those Fenway hot dogs still with you, are they?"

"Mike's a bad influence. He had four hot dogs. Andy, Kevin and I had to keep up."

Emma smiled. "Any of the entrée salads would be great for me. I can share if you decide you need a few vegetables today."

When they arrived at the restaurant, Adalyn and Lucy were sharing spinach dip and laughing over photos on Adalyn's phone. Her life from birth to twenty-one, apparently, courtesy of her father. She put away the phone as entrées arrived, and Emma explained what they'd discovered at Tamara's apartment. Colin showed her the photo of the note. "Is that your mother's handwriting?"

"Yes. No question. Absolutely." Adalyn pushed aside her plate. "It's *just* like her to ruin my dinner and make herself the center of attention. I can't believe she didn't tell me she was leaving early. I don't care if her phone's dead. Borrow one from someone on the street. Stop at a gas station. Something."

Lucy wiped her fingertips on her cloth napkin. "Adalyn, do you find anything unusual about—"

"About my mother's behavior? No. I wish I did." She didn't bother hiding her frustration. "My father asked me not to be so hard on her. She's under a lot of pressure at work, more so than I can imagine, apparently, seeing how nothing ever happens in *my* life. Her job is important. High stakes. I'm just a boring archivist. I don't know, maybe that's why I told her I was interested in art crimes. Just to… It's hard to feel as if you don't matter."

Colin glanced at Yank but said nothing.

Lucy sighed, her empathy for Adalyn impossible to miss. "Having people we love in demanding jobs can be a challenge. It's easy to feel as if what we do isn't as important."

"But it's true, it isn't," Adalyn countered. "My mother puts away terrorists who want to blow up people. Your husband catches bad guys. You and I—you sell yarn and teach people how to knit, and I'm learning how to preserve documents. If you have your great-great-grandmother's old diary, I'm your person."

"Preservation archiving plays a critical role in a number of fields," Emma said.

"I can get thanked in the future after I'm dead. That's when I'll matter."

Yank sat up straight. "You and your mother will work things out."

Adalyn's mouth snapped shut and she stared at him. After a few seconds of silence, she took in a breath. "You're right. We will. I'm sorry. I should cut her some slack. I hope she has a great time. I hope this vacation is good for her. I know she loves me, but saying it isn't the same as showing it. You know? Being here." She grabbed her napkin and put it over her face, sobbing. "I'm sorry, I'm sorry."

Lucy touched Adalyn's hand. "I can take you home if you'd like."

"It's the alcohol. I'm not used to the strong stuff. I drank in England but I was careful. Tonight..." She pulled the napkin away from her face; she was red from crying. "I'm really sorry my mother ruined dinner for you, too. Please, enjoy yourselves—on me." She faked a smile. "I'll make Mom pay me back when she surfaces."

"We're not worried about dinner," Lucy said.

"I'll go back to Cambridge. Rex wants to meet me later for a celebratory drink. I'll let you know if my mother gets in touch." With a sniffle, Adalyn turned to Yank. "If something had happened to her—you'd know, right?"

"Not necessarily."

"But if she tripped on a crack in the sidewalk or got mugged and knocked out—someone would report it even if she couldn't talk. She's a prosecutor, a friend. You'd know."

Yank nodded. "Probably."

"Which means tonight's what it looks like. She left early for her vacation and didn't show up because she couldn't put her own problems aside and focus on me—on celebrating my birthday."

"Did you two argue since your mother arrived in Boston?" Emma asked. "Were you on good terms when you finished brunch this morning?"

"I thought so. We didn't argue. We hadn't seen each other since I got back from England. We had a lot to talk about just to get caught up. She said she had some things to do to get ready for her trip, so we agreed to meet at dinner and I went home." Adalyn set her napkin on the table and pushed back her chair. "Please, enjoy yourselves. I'll settle the bill on my way out. My treat, and my apologies for my mother's behavior, and for my crankiness."

She almost knocked over her chair getting up. She flounced off without another word or a glance back. Despite her anger and sense of betrayal, Colin sensed she was starting to see her mother's behavior might be more complicated, more about her own struggles, than it had first appeared, no matter how hurtful it was.

Lucy made a move to go after Adalyn but stayed in her seat. "She needs some time. She has friends." She grabbed her wineglass. "Not the evening we were expecting. Even if Tamara had turned up a bit late, I suspect there would have been a scene. I'm so sorry." She sighed heavily. "There's a lot of mother-daughter angst there. I didn't realize. I'd have gotten us out of tonight if I had."

"Have you seen Tamara since she arrived in Boston?" Colin asked.

"She called last night to invite us to dinner tonight. We

spoke for maybe five minutes. I was under the impression we'd go back to our apartment this evening for drinks and a catch-up."

"We haven't seen much of Tamara or her ex-husband in the past few years," Yank said. "I met her and Patrick when I was an undergraduate in Boston. They were in law school. We lost touch and then reconnected when I got to Washington. Lucy and I were married by then. We saw Tamara and Patrick socially a few times, but we all had busy schedules."

"I never saw their split coming," Lucy said.

"I thought they'd grow old together," Yank added. "We knew Adalyn was attending college in Boston, but tonight's the first time we've seen her since she graduated high school."

"We had no idea she'd just finished an internship in London until Tamara mentioned it last night." Lucy smoothed a fingertip on the table, as if she were looking for something to do. "Adalyn has a tendency to feel she comes a distant second to her parents' work. That's not unusual, given their intense jobs, but it never seemed to get in the way of anything truly important. As irritated as Adalyn is right now, I'd say deep down she believes her mother is a no-show tonight because she's mentally and physically exhausted, not because she doesn't care."

"Maybe," Yank said. "Tamara works hard, and no case she tackles is an easy one. She has a crack staff, and she's tough and experienced. She's a control freak and a perfectionist. She wouldn't like admitting she needs a break. Then she comes to Boston and her daughter turns up in high-maintenance mode—I don't know. Maybe it all just caught up with her, and she took off for a quiet inn and left Adalyn to sort out her life on her own now that she's twenty-one."

Colin noticed Emma's skeptical look. "You have doubts?"

She set her water glass on the table. "I'm not convinced Tamara told me everything that was on her mind when she stopped by after lunch, and I'm not convinced Adalyn told us everything just now."

A curt nod from Yank. "I'm not, either. Lucy?"

Colin wanted her take, too. As a psychologist and the only non–FBI agent at the table, Lucy Yankowski would have a different perspective on the situation. "Adalyn and I arrived at the restaurant about the same time, just before her friends. We sat in the bar. She was already agitated. Her mother was only a few minutes late at that point. She tried to put it aside when Jolie and Rex got here. It was a birthday celebration—everyone wanted to have a good time—but Adalyn clearly had other things on her mind."

"What did you do to celebrate your twenty-first birthday?" Yank asked her.

She frowned at him, his question obviously taking her by surprise. "What?"

"You don't remember what you did?"

"Wasn't I with you for my twenty-first birthday?"

"That was later."

She smiled. Clearly she'd known that. "I have an October birthday. I was studying for an exam."

"Right." Yank turned to Colin. "And you were out pulling lobster traps when you turned twenty-one?"

"Could have been. I don't remember." It was the truth. Colin smiled. "I just remember my folks breathing a big sigh of relief that another of us boys had turned twenty-one. My mother had a rolling bail fund that she started with Mike. None of us ever got into the kind of trouble she expected we would. She ended up buying a new couch with the money."

"Good for her," Lucy said. "What about you, Emma?"

"You were Sister Brigid then," Yank said. "Do nuns celebrate birthdays?"

Indeed, Emma had been a novice with the Sisters of the Joyful

Heart on her twenty-first birthday. "We had Victoria sponge cake in one of the convent gardens. I celebrated with my parents and brother, too. My grandfather was already living in Dublin then."

"And you, Matt?" his wife asked. "I don't think I've ever known how you celebrated your twenty-first birthday. Do I want to know?"

"I wish I had a juicy story, but I worked a double shift at an ice cream shop here in Boston. I had peppermint ice cream for the first time."

"Living large," Colin said with a grin.

"Yeah. I decided I didn't like it and haven't had it since. I was in back cleaning up after closing when four kids broke in and made off with cash out of the register. I chased them until the police arrived. They caught them and lectured me about taking my life into my hands. The kids had one baseball bat between them, but the cops pointed out they could have had concealed weapons. All in all, a pretty good first day of being twenty-one. Can't say the same for Adalyn. Her mother should be here. I don't understand why she isn't." Yank paused, eyeing his drink. "I need to understand."

They cut dinner short. The Yankowskis had their leftovers boxed up, but Emma didn't bother with hers. Colin could see she was processing today's events. They all headed outside, no noticeable reduction in the heat even now that it was approaching dusk. "I'll touch base with Patrick McDermott," Yank said. "See if he knows anything about Tamara's plans."

He and Lucy started across Newbury Street, toward their own Back Bay apartment. Emma was watching them, but Colin could tell her mind was elsewhere. He put an arm around her. "Let's get a cab."

The marina was crowded with pleasure boats and their owners and guests when Colin exited the cab two seconds after Emma. She'd said little on the short ride from Back Bay. She didn't seem to notice the summer fun around them as she unlocked their apartment door and went in. The place smelled faintly of her cleaning extravaganza. He'd done a similar deep-clean at their house in Rock Point after they'd returned from their honeymoon. He hadn't finished. She'd come home after spending the day with her parents in Heron's Cove. He'd been cleaning the upstairs bathroom, and that was that. Somehow they'd found themselves in the tub together.

She paused in the middle of their tiny Boston living room. "I wonder if Tamara stopped at our offices before she stopped at our place. She looked as if she'd been walking at least a few blocks. Sam was working today, wasn't he?"

Colin got out his phone and called Sam Padgett, another HIT agent, and explained the situation. Emma's instincts paid off. "Yeah, she came by at noon, unannounced but with proper credentials," Sam said. "I showed her around. She thanked me and left. She didn't say she planned to stop at your place next. She did mention she had a daughter in town who'd just turned twenty-one. Nothing about dinner. Maybe she didn't want to hurt my feelings because I wasn't invited."

Colin knew Sam's feelings wouldn't have been hurt. "She ask any questions?"

"Usual small talk. She struck me as your basic driven prosecutor. She said she and the Yankowskis were friends, she wasn't in town for long and wanted to seize the moment to see the HIT offices. She supports the idea of HIT. That's it. I thought she might be up to something and figured I'd mention it to Yank in the morning. Should I not have waited?"

"Doubt it would have made a difference if you hadn't."

"She was definitely uptight. I could see her starting vacation early and blowing off her daughter's birthday dinner. I could also see her trying to manage a rough situation on her own, without asking for help, and getting herself in deeper."

"Did her visit seem like a spur-of-the-moment thing?"

"She said it was. I wondered why she didn't have Yank meet her, but I didn't ask. Why don't I check with BPD, see if they have anything? I'll call you back."

He was gone before Colin could respond. Sam had joined HIT last fall from his native Texas. He was an expert in numbers and had strong field experience. Except for its long winters, he said Boston was growing on him. He liked the current heat wave. Argued that it didn't classify as a proper heat wave in his world since the temperature hadn't hit triple digits.

Colin sat next to Emma on the couch and relayed what Sam had told him. Two minutes later, Sam called back. "Zip. No Jane Doe in the hospital, no lost phone, no witnesses reporting anything unusual involving a woman fitting our prosecutor's description. They'll keep an eye out."

"Thanks, Sam."

"No problem. I'll type up notes on my meeting with her. Make sure I didn't forget something."

But he hadn't. Colin knew that without seeing the notes. Sam Padgett was a dogged, thorough law enforcement officer—but he hated being called dogged, so Colin thanked him again and said good-night.

He got up and splashed whiskey into two glasses. Redbreast 21, an Irish pot-still purchased on their honeymoon. He returned to the couch. "Yank's threatening to give me my own office," he said, handing Emma a glass.

"Uh-oh. An office means you'll be a full-fledged member of HIT." She angled a look at him as she held her glass. "Do I hear a *but* in your tone?"

"I might have to go to Washington soon."

It was his way of saying another undercover assignment was

in the works, with or without HIT's involvement. Regardless, it would be on a "need-to-know" basis. It could last months. Emma knew that. She clicked her glass against his. *"Sláinte."*

"Sláinte."

They sipped the expensive, rich whiskey, definitely one to savor. She edged closer to him, their thighs touching. "I doubt Washington's any hotter than Boston right now."

"I'm not going to stay in undercover work forever." He drank more of his whiskey. "I can clean the oven while you take a bath. There's not much to it. Switch it to the cleaning setting and let it do its thing. Then I can come sit on the edge of the tub and read poetry to you while you relax under lavender-scented bubbles."

Emma sputtered into laughter. "I should call that bluff. I have poetry books on my bedside table, you know. William Butler Yeats, Oscar Wilde, Emily Dickinson—"

"Do you have lavender-scented bubble bath?"

"Lavender-scented bath salts. No bubbles."

"Then I can see through the water? No suds in the way? Even better."

"Colin..."

He knew this woman, could see the worry etched into her brow. "I know, Emma. We need to find Tamara McDermott. We will. Why don't I draw your bath while you get out poems and bath salts?"

"What about the oven?"

"It can wait. I have you in warm water and bath salts on my mind."

"That works for me. We can save the poems for another night, though. I'm not sure I could concentrate on poetry with you sitting on the edge of the tub."

He set his glass on the side table. "I was hoping you'd say that."

6

Adalyn's heart wasn't in a drink with Rex. She thought he noticed, because he eased to his feet and claimed he was tired and wanted to get home. They'd met on the front porch of Jolie's studio. She lived on the second floor but had declined to join them. Adalyn suspected her new boss and landlady might have ideas about her and Rex, but they were all wrong.

"You could have stayed at your mother's apartment," he said. "No worries then about Jolie seeing you tipsy."

"I didn't bring an overnight bag or anything to dinner. No—staying was my mother's idea, not mine."

He smiled softly, the porch light catching his eyes. "I miss my mother giving me orders disguised as suggestions."

"Sorry, Rex. I'm being a brat."

"You're worried." He leaned toward her. "Underneath that aggrieved, spoiled-brat shell of yours is a smart, devoted daughter."

"Yeah, right. Safe travels back to your place."

"If I'd gotten drunk, would you have let me sleep on your couch?"

"I wouldn't have to. Jolie would. But of course I would."

"Happy birthday, Adalyn."

He and Jolie had turned down Adalyn's invitation to join her and her mother for brunch that morning. Jolie had subtly expressed the need to keep a proper boundary between them now that Adalyn was an employee and tenant. They'd met a few weeks ago in England and didn't know each other well, but they weren't going to have a pseudo mother-daughter relationship. They hadn't come right out and set those terms—they'd used code words that were crystal clear to Adalyn.

She was less certain about her role with Rex. It struck her as squishier. He was a client of Jolie's through his parents, both famous artists. Rex, who wasn't an artist, managed their business affairs. His mother died in April and his father had Alzheimer's. Rex lived at the old farmhouse the family owned in southeast New Hampshire, about an hour north of Boston, but he and Adalyn had met three weeks ago in Oxford, where his parents had a cottage. He'd already hired Jolie by then to salvage paintings after a fire at his father's painting studio on the farm—a fire he'd inadvertently set, prompting Rex to insist on round-the-clock care for him.

Adalyn thanked him and stood at the stop of the stairs as he descended to his car. He turned as he pulled open the driver's door. She waved. He waved back.

What a night, she thought, heading upstairs. Jolie's work studio occupied the entire first floor of the former single-family house. The house was old but not *that* old—1930s, maybe? Adalyn didn't know its history and wasn't particularly curious. Finding an affordable apartment she wouldn't have to share had been a feat, not that her parents would ever give her credit.

There was no elevator, but walking up and down two flights of stairs multiple times a day was good exercise. Tonight she trudged up. She didn't care about burning off the alcohol she'd consumed or getting her heart rate going or anything. It'd been a lousy night.

She *never* should have mentioned Stefan's death to her mother.

That had to be what had driven her off tonight. The last

straw. She'd gone into fight-or-flight mode and had decided
to flee. Clear out, skip dinner, let her daughter and friends
figure it out. She was done.

Adalyn unlocked the door to her attic-like apartment and
went inside. A combo kitchen and living room, a bathroom,
a bedroom. What more did she need? She'd looked forward
to showing it to her mother. She'd been unimpressed with
her last apartment in Allston. *What, Adalyn? Are Boston rents
so high this is the best you can do with the money your father and I
send you, or are you pocketing the difference and buying drugs, playing the horses—what?*

Her mother hadn't been serious about drugs and horses.

Jolie had given Adalyn a break on rent on this place, saying she liked having a tenant she knew. She'd had some duds,
apparently.

Adalyn dropped onto the couch. She'd bought it for a pit-
tance on Craigslist. She'd never tell her mother. She'd go on
about bedbugs or something. She knew it would be easier on
both her parents if she attended a tidy, isolated college with
a picturesque campus in a pretty New England village, but
it wasn't as if Boston was new to them. It was a great student
town but it was urban. Adalyn liked that about it. She was
starting her last year in school. She'd have her master's in archiving and be on her own soon. She sometimes thought her
parents secretly wanted her to go to law school, despite their
constant assurances they wanted her to live her own life, follow her own path. She had as much desire to be a lawyer as
they did to preserve musty old books and documents.

She heard cars driving by down on the street. She'd lived
here for only two weeks and was still getting used to the
sounds.

She got her phone out and stared at the dark screen. "Call

Dad," she said finally. In a few seconds, he answered. "You haven't heard from Mom, have you?" she asked.

"I just talked to Matt Yankowski. No, I haven't heard from her. I'll let you know if I do."

"Are you worried?"

"I've never worried about your mother except for the night you were born and her blood pressure spiked. But it all worked out. She knows how to take care of herself. I'm glad she's taking this time if she needs it."

"It was selfish and inconsiderate not to tell me she was leaving early."

"Maybe right now she needs to be selfish, Adalyn."

"Her work is the most important thing to her. I know that. She's making a huge contribution as a federal prosecutor. She jumps on the nasty cases. I think the only reason she wanted a daughter is because she liked the idea of giving me a cool name."

"Adalyn is a cool name, don't you think?"

He'd never bad-mouth his ex-wife in front of their only daughter. Adalyn supposed that was a good thing. "Did you have any say in my name?"

"I could have vetoed it if I'd hated it."

"Mom would have argued you out of your veto." Adalyn felt an unexpected rush of affection for her mother. "You know her, Dad. She never gives up without a fight."

He laughed. "She never gives up, period."

"I love and admire her, but I won't lie and say I never wished she'd been a homemaker."

"She does her best by you every day, Adalyn. Never doubt that."

"I don't doubt it," she said. "I just wish she'd been there tonight."

"And you're mad at me for walking out on our marriage," her father said quietly.

Tears sprang to her eyes. At least he wasn't here with her to see them. "I was mad. I'm not anymore. I had no part in what happened." The affair with a paralegal now no longer in his life was not her responsibility. "It's between you and Mom."

"I'll see you soon, okay? How are you settling in?"

"Fine. I'm on the third floor. No rats."

"That's something, anyway. Call me anytime. If I can't answer, I'll get back to you as soon as I can."

Adalyn thanked him, but she didn't feel any relief or reassurance when she set her phone next to her on the couch. She'd learned at a young age she was expected to make her parents look good to their colleagues in law enforcement. To anyone, really. She'd failed tonight.

Of course, her parents had always denied placing such pressure on her. *Really, Adalyn, that's all in your head. We want you to be you.*

Provided "you" was interesting, respectable, successful and a source of pride.

She checked her messages again. Nothing from her mother.

Adalyn wished she'd never agreed to tonight's dinner. Her mother had blown into Boston and would blow out again, and it was obvious she was rushed, stressed and caught up in finally taking this vacation by herself. She had a high-powered job. She deserved a break. Adalyn had her own life, and while it wasn't insanely busy at the moment, it soon would be with the start of school and her job ramping up. Jolie had promised her more hours. Adalyn wanted the rest of the summer to make a little money, hang out with friends, network with people in her field and have a good time.

It's one night, she'd told herself about the dinner.

Then her mother hadn't shown up.

Adalyn stifled a surge of worry. Three FBI agents had been at dinner. If her mother was in some kind of trouble, they'd jump on it.

She glanced around her apartment. It had potential. She'd add eclectic fabrics, plants—make it her space. If her parents wanted to check for rats, fleas and bedbugs, let them.

Ever since her father's affair and the shock of her parents' divorce, she'd gone back and forth between hating and loving them, but she was confident—at least for the moment—that love would win out. Eventually. Seeing them as real people, with virtues and flaws, was part of the process of truly becoming an adult.

She laughed to herself. "Welcome to being a full-fledged adult."

Adalyn took a shower, hoping it would settle her mind and help her sleep. She'd been looking forward to having a proper, legal drink with family and friends, and her mother had gone and ruined the evening. She knew she had to get off that subject. Her mother's behavior wasn't her fault or her responsibility. Adalyn didn't want to stay worked up, and was sorry she'd let it happen. She didn't want to give her mother that power over her.

"I have my own life to live now."

She sniffled back tears and let the hot, soothing water course down her back and front. She didn't wash her hair, but the ends got wet anyway. She'd found a circular shower curtain since there was a window above the tub, the showerhead a late addition to the bathroom. She'd put special film on the panes so no one could see in through the window, but she didn't trust it. The shower curtain was new, a bright, tropical theme complete with parrots. It was inexpensive, but perfect for cheering up the small bathroom and its old fixtures.

When she stepped out of the shower, she wobbled slightly—from unfamiliarity with her new space, not unsteadiness and her raw emotions. She wrapped up in a fuchsia towel—it went well with the parrots—and returned to her bedroom.

She smiled when she saw she had a text from Rex. He was such a pal. Home on the farm. Quiet here on my own. I hope you're not passed out on your kitchen floor.

She laughed as she typed her answer. I didn't drink as much as everyone thinks.

I wouldn't blame you if you were dipping into a fifth of Scotch after tonight. You're okay?

I'm fine. Thanks for checking in.

I'll be at the studio tomorrow. See you then.

G'night.

She had a comfortable feeling when she placed her phone on her bedside table and sat cross-legged on her bed, the towel still mostly around her. She had no siblings, and Rex felt like an older brother to her, their ten-year age difference enough for him to have solid life experience but not so much they had nothing in common. She could talk to him. He understood her. She was glad he didn't want more from her. That would ruin their friendship. If only her father had realized that sex wasn't everything. He wouldn't have destroyed his family over a tawdry affair.

"Skank," Adalyn muttered, picturing his ex-girlfriend—younger than her mother, of course, and not nearly as accomplished.

She'd met Rex and Jolie at a dinner party in Oxford hosted

by mutual friends, Verity and Graham Blackwood. It had been Adalyn's first visit to Oxford. She'd taken an early train from London and spent the day soaking up the historic city's atmosphere and checking out some of its well-known sites. She could have wandered around for days but had only hours before arriving at the Blackwood home. She and Verity had run into each other and become instant friends at an exhibit at the National Gallery, where Verity used to work and where Adalyn had an internship. They'd have coffee or lunch whenever Verity was in London. It wasn't often, but Adalyn got the impression Verity missed her life there. She and Graham had been married only a year and a half. He'd joined her in London twice after she and Adalyn met, but he'd had other things to do when it came to coffee or lunch with his wife's young American friend. Adalyn didn't mind. He was her parents' age, and her three months in London had been a time to get away from them. Still, when Verity had extended the invitation to Oxford, Adalyn had accepted without a second thought.

She'd met Stefan Petrescu that night at the Blackwoods' home, too. Such a kind, interesting man. To think he'd been murdered...

Adalyn dried off, cast her towel onto the floor and grabbed an oversize T-shirt off another pile on the floor. She put it on. She had a feeling tonight's outfit hadn't worked well. She'd wanted to come off as artistic and bohemian but probably had looked like a slob.

She could see Stefan that evening in Oxford, a short, plump Romanian linguist who lectured at Oxford and did occasional work for Graham's think tank. Translations, mostly, Adalyn assumed, since the think tank focused on foreign policy analysis. Such a different world from the one she knew as a student in Boston and with her lawyer parents in Washington, DC.

At least at first. Stefan had been killed a week later—shot two days before she'd returned to Boston. Horrible. Unimaginable. Who would want to kill such a quiet, charming man?

Verity insisted Stefan hadn't been targeted. Just a random shooting...

But that was an opinion not a fact, as Adalyn knew her parents would say. Graham and Verity hadn't wanted to talk about Stefan and his death on their visit last week. They were there to put the tragedy out of their minds, at least for a few days.

Telling her mother about Stefan's death had definitely been a mistake. That was crystal clear to Adalyn now, but it had nothing to do with her or her new friends. The police hadn't questioned her. Given what they saw every day, her parents had a jaded view of the world and tended to fret about her—not that they ever went out of their way to be a real part of her life, especially since their divorce. They'd lectured her about safety measures when she'd left for London but hadn't come to visit her.

No, there'd been no reason to tell them about Stefan, a tragedy that had occurred an ocean away from Boston—but she'd blabbed to her mother, anyway.

At least she hadn't made the same mistake with the FBI agents.

Shower, alcohol and the emotions of the day had taken their toll, and Adalyn couldn't keep her eyes open. The ends of her hair were still damp. If she woke up with serious bed head, so be it. She kicked off her covers. There was no air-conditioning in her apartment. It was a shortcoming her mother had, of course, noticed first thing. Her father?

"Yeah, he'll notice, too."

She'd text or email Verity in the morning and see how she was doing now that she was home. If she could get a job in London when she graduated, she'd take it in a heartbeat. She loved Boston, but right now, it felt too close to Washington, where her parents were.

Just getting adjusted to her new job and apartment after three months away, maybe, and to being twenty-one. It wasn't as if a gong had gone off at the stroke of midnight and she'd suddenly had her act together. She was still figuring things out, still wishing her family hadn't dissolved...still upset that her time in England had been marred by murder and her mother had seen fit to skip out on her daughter's twenty-first birthday dinner.

"Wherever you are, Mom, I hope you're having a good time."

Did she mean it?

"Yes."

Adalyn flipped onto her back and stared at the ceiling.

"No, I hope she's racked with guilt and can't sleep a wink."

She didn't like the anger and resentment in her voice, but maybe being honest with herself would help her get to sleep.

"I'm worried, too," she whispered, flipping onto her side. "Be okay, Mom. Please be okay."

7

London, England

Despite a late bedtime after discovering a woman near death and enduring a chat with two London detectives, Wendell Sharpe managed to beat Oliver to the kitchen. His elderly friend was groomed and fully dressed, drinking coffee at the table, the coffee press empty but for the grounds. "I'd have saved you some, Oliver, but it'd be cold by now. You're a tea drinker, anyway, aren't you? I have tea more often since I moved to Dublin, but I need coffee this morning."

"Yes, tea for me."

Oliver had collected Wendell's suitcase—such as it was—from the porter at Claridge's and got him settled into the guest room. He looked tired but not too worse for the wear, given the shock of last night. Oliver filled the kettle with fresh water and put it on to boil. It was a large kitchen with white cabinets, updated since his parents' day but along the same basics lines. He'd found he liked keeping things much the same here. A comfort, he supposed, but he could have chucked everything and started over, cleansed the apartment of every reminder of his parents and their untimely, inexplicable deaths, and that would have made sense, too.

"Shall I prepare poached eggs for us?" he asked his guest.

Wendell's eyebrows went up. "You know how to cook?"

"For myself. I can't say I've ever cooked for a guest."

At the farm, Ruthie Burns, his longtime housekeeper, would handle tea and bring fresh scones or whip up whatever struck her fancy. Martin Hambly, Oliver's friend and personal assistant, often joined him in London and would take care of breakfast, but he was at the farm. Oliver's wire-fox terrier puppy was still in training and wasn't particularly suited to city life. Best Alfred and Martin roam the Cotswolds country-side together rather than try to manage in London. Oliver didn't mind being on his own, and he knew how to make tea and toast and, in a pinch, he could manage to poach an egg.

Wendell suggested Oliver have tea first, before tackling eggs. Oliver joined him at the table. The kitchen opened onto a balcony that looked out on St. James's Park, but it was a chilly, gloomy morning.

"Any update on Verity Blackwood?" Wendell asked.

"Not yet."

"Henrietta told you to leave poor Verity to her?"

"She did, and I always do what Henrietta says."

"Smart man," Wendell said.

Oliver poured his tea from a simple white pot, but he couldn't sit still. Normally he started his day with tai chi—sometimes in the park—but he'd rolled out of bed, showered, got dressed and come straight to the kitchen. He took his tea to the Aga and got busy with the eggs.

The eggs were brilliant, if he did say so himself. The toast was less of a success, meaning there wasn't any. He hadn't bought bread, and there was none in the freezer. Wendell didn't complain, but he looked very pleased, indeed, when Henrietta breezed in with fresh croissants. "They're spectacular." She set the bag on the table. "I got them at the hotel. I've already had two, but I went for a run first thing to clear my head."

The run was the MI5 officer Henrietta, the croissants the

garden designer Henrietta. In her own way, she was as big a mess as Oliver was, both of them trying to integrate warring parts of themselves. At least being a garden designer wasn't illegal. If she'd ventured into legal gray areas with her intelligence work, she'd never tell him. Not that Oliver had asked or wanted to know.

No. He wanted to know.

She set out three small plates and placed a croissant on each. "I'll just stare at mine. Three's a bit much even with a run, but if I leave it in the bag, I'll eat it for sure."

"That makes no sense," Oliver said.

"It does to me." She dropped into a chair across from Wendell, eyeing her croissant as she poured herself tea. "I have information on Verity Blackwood."

"Great," Wendell said. "Spill."

"Spill? That suggests I'm divulging classified information."

"It's just an old-fashioned expression."

Oliver knew this mood of hers. There'd be no talk of Thor movies and opera. She was MI5 now, down to her skirted suit, simple blue shirt, flats and tidy hair. As a garden designer, she never had tidy hair. "Tell us what you can, then," he said softly.

"Verity is stable but intubated and unable to speak. There are many variables in her recovery, including whether she's suffered any permanent damage, given her overdose. She will stay in hospital at least overnight, and more likely several days. Longer, obviously, if there was damage or there are complications with her recovery."

"What about family?" Wendell asked. "Is someone with her?"

"Police have yet to contact her husband. He was scheduled to fly home with her, but canceled his reservation two hours before their flight. He hasn't rescheduled. Verity has a sister in Edinburgh. She's arriving in London this morning to be with her." Henrietta produced her phone and swiped to a photograph. "This is Verity when she isn't in the midst of an opiate overdose."

Oliver took the phone, Wendell peering at the photo with him. Verity Blackwood was smiling, pale blue eyes crinkling as she stood in front of a hanging basket of flowers and a trellis of more flowers. "Where's this, do you know?" Oliver asked.

"The Blackwood home in Oxford."

He pointed at the trellis. "Clematis?"

Henrietta beamed at him. "Yes, very good." She took her phone. "Here's Graham." She flipped to another photo and handed her phone back to Oliver. "Best I could come up with in a pinch."

A balding man in fly-fishing gear grinned from a riverbank. "Do you suppose Graham stayed in the US to go fishing?" Wendell asked.

"Put the wife on a plane, turn off the phone and head to the wilds of New England to catch fish and shut out the world?" Henrietta shuddered. "Not my cup of tea."

"Mine, either," Wendell said, handing her the phone. "I'd rather have a root canal myself."

Oliver decided not to admit he rather enjoyed fly-fishing.

Henrietta sighed. "Verity's more urban than her husband, at least from what I can see so far. I can imagine a younger wife with a passion for art not caring to stick around for a last-minute fishing expedition." She glanced at Oliver. "My grandfather was a keen fly-fisherman, did I tell you?"

Oliver hadn't known that. "Freddy?"

"No, my mother's father. The only time he appreciated country life was when he was fishing or tucked by the fire with a good Scotch. But, moving along. Graham and Verity met two years ago at a London cocktail party and were married six months later. They had a church wedding in Oxford. He's fifty-one, she's thirty-six—not as great an age difference as I'd thought. He looks older in his fishing photo. They have no children together or separately. Verity appears to have quit her job at the National Gallery just before she and Graham married. He's wealthy, and she supports causes dear to her, such as art conservation, preservation and restoration." Henrietta raised her gaze to Wendell. "I gather there's a difference."

"There is," he said.

"Just confirming."

Oliver smiled. "That means she doesn't want a lecture in the subject."

"Another time," she said. "Graham has never needed to work to keep a roof over his head, but he's not super-rich, just quite well-off, and he tends to live beneath his means. He served as a respected diplomat for twenty years, but he was never high profile. He never sought the limelight, but he positioned that as an asset, apparently, rather than a drawback now that he has his own think tank. It's a small and low-profile think tank but respectable."

"Had you heard of it?" Wendell asked Henrietta.

She shook her head. "Not until Oliver mentioned it last night. I'll look into it further should events warrant. At this point, there's no indication Verity Blackwood was taking opioids on prescription to treat pain or another medical condition, either currently or recently, or has a history of drug abuse of any kind. Her overdose could be an accident—a simple mixup that had her thinking she was taking herbs—or it could be drug abuse or an attempt to kill herself."

"Or someone to kill her," Oliver said.

"Yes, there's that."

Wendell broke off a piece of croissant. "If Verity was suicidal, why go to the trouble of meeting me?"

"So you'd find her?" Henrietta shrugged. "Impossible to say, really. I wonder if she forgot she had slipped the pills into an herb bottle and she took them by mistake when she was half asleep and a bit disoriented from jet lag. Some people suffer terribly switching time zones, particularly when flying east."

Oliver picked at his croissant, not sure he wanted any. Henrietta wouldn't be offended if he saved it for later or chucked it altogether. She muttered under her breath and then dove into hers. "I see you're not resisting," he said.

"I did resist. I just gave in after...how many minutes?"

"Not many," Wendell said. "Have at it, kid. Life is short. Do you have any idea why Mrs. Blackwood wanted to talk to me about forgeries?"

"None, I'm afraid," Henrietta said.

"I wish I'd pressed her for more information. Given her background, I would think she'd know a fair amount about forgeries."

"Historical forgeries, maybe," Oliver said. "Not the kind she wanted to ask you about."

Wendell nodded thoughtfully. "Good point. She didn't waste any time calling me once she landed, but I'd just be speculating about what she was thinking. Figured we'd get into details when we met." He sighed, scooping up a few last croissant crumbs. "Drugs. Hell of a thing. My son became dependent on opioids. He worked up a tolerance—needed to take more to get the same effects. It wasn't an addiction, technically, but it was tough to get off them. He never overdosed."

"Depressed breathing is usually what leads to death in an opioid overdose," Henrietta said. "Verity probably thought she was falling sleep. She would have stopped breathing altogether and died if we hadn't come upon her when we did."

Wendell tossed the crumbs on his napkin. "An unpleasant business. Anything else you can tell us?"

"I've told you everything I've learned." She frowned at her plate. "Oh, dear. Look, I've eaten half the bloody croissant."

"You need to practice mindful eating," Oliver said. "If you're going to have a croissant, enjoy it. Don't wolf it down without paying any attention—"

"Thank you, Oliver, I did mindfully enjoy every bite of my first two croissants."

He grinned. "You don't need my advice?"

"I might but certainly not on eating croissants."

"Going to finish it, aren't you?"

"Every crumb." She turned to Wendell. "You should feel free to carry on with your other business in London. The police know how to reach you if they have further questions, and Oliver and I will keep you updated on any new developments."

"I don't need to be a fifth wheel," Wendell said. "I'll clear out, head back to Ireland. I'll see my friends another time, and I can do any business from Dublin. If Verity Blackwood wants to talk to me once she's recovered, she can get in touch. I'm glad she's hanging in there, and I hope she makes a full recovery."

Henrietta shifted from her croissant to her tea. "I suspect our Verity is a novice opiate taker. A habitual user or an addict would more easily tolerate the amount she apparently ingested. As you mentioned, Wendell, people build up a tolerance and often need more and more for it to have the desired effect."

Oliver added more tea to Henrietta's cup. "There was an empty glass of wine on the bedside table. Alcohol enhances the effects of opioids."

"Damnable stuff," Wendell muttered.

"It can be, for sure." Henrietta stared at her tea. "I don't know if or for how long her brain was deprived of oxygen. Brain injury can occur after just a few minutes. Memory loss, difficulty concentrating, impaired coordination, impaired hearing and vision—they're all possibilities. Her ability to read and write could be affected. Doctors won't know for a bit. Maybe she can tell us what happened when she's through the worst. How she got the drugs. Why she took them."

Wendell nodded. "I want to know where her husband is."

"But you're going to leave the investigation to the authorities, aren't you, Wendell?" Henrietta's tone was cheerful but with a dictatorial undertone. "Mrs. Blackwood is receiving treatment. There's little we can do right now, anyway."

Wendell angled a skeptical look at Oliver. "And I suppose you two are going to have tea and crumpets and talk about puppies, or do a bit of shopping, maybe? Take a walk in the park? Pop in on the queen?"

"Sarcasm doesn't become you, my friend," Oliver said. "I suspect Henrietta and I will drive out to the Cotswolds today."

"Through Oxford," Wendell added knowingly. "If you need me to analyze anything you learn at the Blackwoods' residence, you know how to reach me."

Oliver ignored him. "Have you spoken with your grandchildren?"

"Emma and Lucas? No. It's the dead of night in New England."

"Do you plan to ring them?" Henrietta asked.

"I probably should before the police do. If Graham Blackwood's fishing and Verity Blackwood got her drugs in Boston…" Wendell didn't finish. "I'll wait until the sun's up there, or you two can call them."

Oliver collected the breakfast dishes and took them to the sink while Henrietta finished the rest of her croissant. She was eyeing his when he grabbed it and took a huge bite. She scowled. "Not going to offer me a bite, are you?"

"It's delicious. I'm saving you from yourself. Even one bite of a fourth croissant would ruin you on them."

"I sincerely doubt it."

He glanced at the clock on the wall, a wedding present to his parents from a friend. It was a few minutes after nine. That meant it was only 4:00 a.m. in Boston. Yes, too early to ring Emma Sharpe. Last night had been a terrible shock for her grandfather. As experienced as he was in the ways of the world, a young woman near death from a drug overdose wasn't remotely what he was accustomed to encountering in a day's work.

"Would I was here chasing a cheeky art thief," Wendell said, as if he'd read Oliver's mind.

"Would you were, too, my friend."

"Just don't go stealing a painting for old times' sake. You'll be in touch if you need me?"

"Of course," Oliver said. "Without hesitation. Stay here as long as you'd like."

"I'll book my flight. You'll call Emma, won't you?"

"She'll worry—"

"Tell her I'll call her when I get back home."

Oliver didn't argue. He offered the rest of his croissant to Henrietta, but she was well and truly done now and instead helped him clean up. He could see that she was as concerned about their octogenarian friend as he was. Good he was returning home to Ireland.

Oliver drove. He often took the train, avoiding clogged roadways, but when he'd left the farm for what he'd anticipated would be a quiet few days in London, he'd packed his Rolls-Royce. It wasn't new, but it was luxurious and a dream to drive, whether on a lane winding through the rolling Cotswolds countryside or on a crowded motorway. He suspected Henrietta could be in a rusted heap for all she would have noticed or cared. She often took the train to London—or so she claimed. He'd ridden with her once in her mud-encrusted Mini. She'd been a mad driver in her teens, but now, with her MI5 training, she could turn a simple drive to Stow-on-the-Wold for tea into a white-knuckle adventure.

When they came to Oxford, Henrietta tapped the Blackwood address into her phone and produced turn-by-turn directions. She didn't switch on the voice commands. She pointed, phone in hand. "Bear left."

"I know the way."

Oliver hated using GPS. He kept stacks of maps in the car. Real maps. Printed on paper. He didn't tell her he'd looked up the address on his Oxford map while she'd checked out of Claridge's. He'd memorized the route. Better for the brain than relying upon a device, and he was familiar with Oxford.

"Have you spent much time in Oxford?" he asked her.

"I kayaked on the river with an old boyfriend. I don't mean old as in former, either. He was thirty years my senior. I don't know what I was thinking."

"When was this?"

"Eons ago."

"You're only thirty-six, Henrietta."

"I did quite enjoy the river," she said vaguely. "What about you? Have you been back here much since you flunked out of Oxford?"

"I didn't flunk out. I withdrew."

"Mmm."

"My grandparents had died, and I realized I wasn't one for a formal education. Martin urged me to give it more time. He told me I'd only get into mischief if I left prematurely."

"Truer words never spoken."

Oliver didn't indulge her with a response. He hadn't begun thieving until a decade later. He'd studied on his own, reading everything he could find on myths, legends and folklore, particularly Celtic, and prowling through museums, libraries, churches, graveyards and ruins. He now understood he'd been trying to make sense of what he'd witnessed at eight, kidnapped and held in a Scottish ruin by his parents' killers, escaping on his own, picked up by a priest out for a walk...

"It's not as grand a house as I'd imagined, but it's nice," Henrietta said, yanking him out of his meandering thoughts. She pointed. "We're here, Oliver."

"Oh, right. Yes."

He pulled up in front of a handsome detached brick home on a quiet, shaded residential street. "Shall we see if anyone's home?"

Henrietta unsnapped her seat belt. "Who would be home with Verity in hospital and Graham in New England?"

A good question. Oliver stayed behind Henrietta and let her ring the doorbell. Not surprisingly, no one answered. She sighed. "Well, it's good to get a look at the place."

"Let me see if anyone's in back. You can wait here."

She narrowed her turquoise eyes on him. "If you set off an alarm, Oliver, I'm fleeing the scene. You're on your own."

He'd never triggered an alarm, but he kept that tidbit to himself and set off along a stone walk leading past a flower border and fence between the Blackwood house and its neighbor. He ended up on a stone terrace—table, chairs and barbecue left out as if the residents would be arriving for lunch any moment.

He found a key tucked on a gutter and let himself in. He didn't linger, but went straight through the kitchen to the entry and opened the front door for Henrietta. "I was beginning to sweat," she said.

"Somehow you managed to apply fresh lipstick in the five minutes I was gone."

"For the police. I want to look good in my mug shot."

He pointed behind him. "I smelled gas. I was afraid there might be a leak and let myself in."

"Did you ever use that line in your thieving days?"

He'd never had to, but he didn't answer.

"I don't suppose the Blackwoods would mind if I used the loo now we're here," Henrietta said, stepping past Oliver into a traditional sitting room decorated in robin's-egg blue with accents of raspberry. "Nothing's new. I'd say Verity has yet to put her mark on the place."

"She might like it the way it is."

"Even the books look as if they've been here for years." She peered at a shelf. "No art books. If you'd worked as an art exhibitor, wouldn't you have art books?"

"Turning over a new leaf. Maybe Verity's taken up gardening."

Oliver was playing devil's advocate. Henrietta didn't seem to mind. He examined the art in the attractive, if rather uninspired, room. A display of carved wooden ducks and geese appeared to be original, as did the three paintings—two small oil paintings, one a portrait of an early nineteenth-century gentleman, the other depicting a late-Victorian fox hunt, and a large acrylic painting above the mantel of kayakers on the River Cherwell.

"I didn't realize Fletcher Campbell painted English scenes," Oliver said, noting the signature in the corner.

Henrietta frowned. "Who?"

"An American painter in the tradition of Andrew Wyeth."

"Ah. That's the simple explanation, I imagine." She stood next to Oliver. "Nice."

"Did you and your elder fellow kayak here?"

"I don't remember. I was focused on not tipping over and how to get rid of him before dinner."

"Did you?"

"I didn't tip over." She pointed toward the back of the house. "I'll find that loo now."

He followed her into the kitchen, also traditional, with creamy white cabinetry, an older Aga, tiles and a sturdy wood table with an empty glass bowl in the middle. "Cleared out the fruit bowl before they left, at least," he said.

Henrietta was reading something on the worktop. "It's from a local funeral. Stefan Petrescu, dead at forty-eight. Why do I know that name, Oliver?"

He read the simple sheet over her shoulder. It included a short biography—an obituary, he supposed. The dead man was born in Bucharest, attended the University of Bucharest and moved to Oxford eight years ago, where he'd lectured in linguistics and worked as a consultant. He'd never married, and left behind his mother and two brothers in Romania.

"A friend, I gather," Oliver said.

"It doesn't say how he died." Henrietta was typing on her phone. In a moment, she sighed heavily. "He was murdered two weeks ago. No wonder his name seemed familiar."

"How—"

"He was shot on his way back to Oxford from London. He pulled over in a wooded area, apparently for a comfort break. It was at night—about 11:00 p.m. Police haven't released many investigative details, but there hasn't been an arrest."

"Can you find out more?"

"Honestly, garden design looks better and better." She put

away her phone. "I'll do what I can. Now, if you'll excuse me, I wasn't joking about the loo…"

Oliver returned to the sitting room. Verity Blackwood had flown from Boston. Graham Blackwood had stayed behind. Wasn't Fletcher Campbell from Boston—near Boston? Oliver thought so but wasn't positive. He took a closer look at the painting. Did it have anything to do with what had prompted Verity to contact Wendell Sharpe? Oliver knew little about forgeries. The Sharpes would know more.

Henrietta returned. She put out her hand. "I'll drive while you phone Emma."

"I can phone her now—"

"We need to leave, Oliver. There's no gas leak. We've checked."

"Point taken." He handed over the key. "If you crash my car, you're paying for repairs."

She grinned at him, folding the key into her palm. "I've never driven a Rolls. Shall we?"

Oliver waited until they were on the A40, almost to Burford, before he rang Emma Sharpe. He didn't relish speaking with her with Henrietta next to him. He'd never been a passenger in the Rolls-Royce, this was her first go at driving it *and* she was MI5. But he had no choice. All in all, Emma took what he had to tell her well, despite the early hour and the call being from an art thief she and her family had chased for a decade. Her husband of a few weeks took it less well. "Is that Agent Donovan I hear grumbling in the background?" Oliver asked.

"He thinks you should have called me last night."

"Of course he does."

"Where is my grandfather now?"

"I believe he's at Heathrow for his flight back to Ireland.

He's seen quite a lot in his day. He'll have a pint with his mates and put last night behind him." Oliver thought it might take more than one pint, but kept that to himself. He'd focused on informing Emma of the facts of the situation, whether because of Henrietta's glances or his own instincts he wasn't sure. "The police will want to speak with Graham Blackwood. They'll want to know what he and his wife did—"

"Of course. Thanks for the call, Oliver. My best to Henrietta."

He disconnected and sighed. Emma had gone FBI on him, hadn't she? Well. *He* considered her a friend. Colin, too. "Agent Donovan and I have a ways to go before he'll acknowledge me as a friend," Oliver said, more to himself than to Henrietta.

"He's a tough one," she said. "Did they have anything for you?"

"The FBI isn't in the habit of sharing information with me."

"There is that, I suppose. Did they seem surprised by your call?"

He considered the question. Henrietta's driving wasn't as wild as he'd anticipated. Fast, smooth, sure. That was Henrietta Balfour in a nutshell, wasn't it? He turned from the bucolic view, watching her as he answered. "I only spoke with Emma. Thankfully."

"Wendell hadn't been in touch with her?"

Oliver shook his head. "No."

"Interesting. We'll be at the farm soon. I'll see what I can find out while you walk Alfred and get lunch sorted. I'm in favor of protein and vegetables. I swear I'm blurry-eyed from the croissants."

"Not something I want to hear with you cruising along at a hundred kilometers."

"Only a hundred?" She grinned at him. "I can do better than that."

8

Tamara licked her lips, dry and chapped, cut in places from biting them and spitting out bile and bits of the blanket her attacker had tossed over her. She'd wrestled it into a heap next to her. She'd vomited on it. The place reeked.

She was in...*what?*

Milky sunlight slanted through a small, fixed window above her. Thick, filthy plastic covered the glass. She wasn't steady enough to find a light switch, but she could make out a rusted, brown-ringed toilet and a stained pedestal sink.

A bathroom.

She'd been dumped in a filthy little bathroom.

Where?

Maine? Boston?

She had no idea. She didn't know what time it was. Didn't remember anything between the hood coming over her head and now...

Puking. She remembered puking in the dark. Here? In the car?

She sat up, groggy, sick to her stomach but not vomiting. She was on a mat—a smelly yoga mat. She licked her lips again. She was thirsty. She couldn't remember ever being this thirsty.

The air was relatively cool. Dank. The bathroom had a concrete floor, and the wall with the window and wall opposite the sink and toilet were constructed of cinder blocks.

A cellar.

She fought back a wave of nausea. Had her attacker carried her down here? Dragged her? Coaxed her? Threatened her with a weapon? She couldn't remember. She checked herself—head, arms, legs—and noted bruises here and there but nothing major or out of the ordinary after, say, getting shoved onto the floor of her car.

Why couldn't she remember any details?

"Drugged."

Her voice was little more than a croak. Anger surged through her.

Bastard. Bitch. Whoever you are...

Tamara shut her eyes and forced herself to take a calming breath. She had to keep her wits about her, rely on her self-control, her training in basic survival techniques and her sheer determination to get out of here. Even if she could find a way to get the plastic off the window, the opening was too small for her to crawl through. Maybe she could alert someone. She didn't hear any cars or voices—no birds, ocean or anything else for that matter. Not even any cellar noises or mice scurrying in the walls.

It's like being dead.

She stopped that line of thinking in its tracks. As she shifted position, her hand struck a plastic plate. Food. Protein bars, apples.

Well, how nice. She hadn't been left to starve.

She felt around and knocked over a plastic water bottle. Her heart raced in panic, but the bottle wasn't open and didn't spill out its precious contents. Her stomach wasn't ready for food yet, but she knew she needed to stay hydrated. Open the bottle now? Take a few sips and see if she kept them down?

You have a sink.

What if it didn't work?

Slowly, bracing herself on the wall and sink, Tamara struggled to her feet. She was dizzy and her stomach lurched, but she didn't pass out or barf.

All good.

She turned the rusted faucet. It creaked and groaned, but a trickle of water came out—and then more, a normal stream. She cupped some in her hand and took a few sips, and splashed the rest on her face. She wouldn't die of dehydration. That was something to hold on to. A ray of...what? Hope? Sure. Hope. Why not?

She sank back onto the mat. It smelled like stale sweat. Hers? Its owner's? Had it been used with another captive? What if she wasn't the first woman to be held down here?

Should I yell and scream? Is anyone out there who can help me?

Adalyn...

She's safe. She has to be.

I missed her birthday.

Tamara heard a small cry and realized it had come from her. She smacked her mouth shut, biting her lips again, tightening her jaw to keep herself quiet. If she cried out, she wanted it to be on her terms.

She'd made her abduction easy, hadn't she? Preoccupied. Meeting a man she didn't know in an unfamiliar place that had turned out to be isolated. She hadn't checked in advance. She'd just blasted her way to Maine.

Phone dead.

Hot, sweaty and out of shape.

She'd cut corners. No question, no excuses. She'd been desperate for a break, time on her own. She'd wanted to get this Blackwood business settled in her mind so that she could head to Nova Scotia in peace. As a result, she'd made herself easy to snatch and harder for anyone to realize she was in distress.

They'll think I left on vacation early.

That *had* been her plan, but not until after Adalyn's birthday dinner.

"The note. Oh, hell."

She'd written it in case she did decide to leave early. She'd taken her suitcase with her after brunch. Adalyn had gone back to Cambridge on the subway. When she found the note, she'd be irritated.

No one will miss me until I don't show up in Portland for the ferry.

And even then, who would care? She'd *deliberately* kept her itinerary to herself. Spite, Adalyn would call it. Probably right, but it was navigating this new world she was in as a single woman. She'd been with Patrick since their first year in law school. They'd always done up vacation itineraries together and sent them off to his folks, her folks, their offices—and Adalyn, of course, when she was away at school.

I've never gone on vacation alone until now. Why would I have?

Tamara squeezed her eyes shut. She had to get out of here. She couldn't let Adalyn think any of what happened was her fault. Emma Sharpe, Colin Donovan and Matt Yankowski were three top-notch law enforcement officers. If they saw the note she'd left for Adalyn, would they question it—suspect she might have been forced to write it? If they got so much as an inkling something was off about her not showing up for dinner, they'd pounce. They'd get the bit in their teeth and wouldn't let go, no matter where it led. Right now, Tamara had no idea where it *would* lead. Who had her. Why.

The man she'd been meeting… Graham Blackwood…

She opened her eyes, willing herself to remember any details of her kidnapping. Adalyn liked the Blackwoods. She'd been in a prickly mood at brunch, bringing up her disappointment that her mother hadn't come to see her in London. This two weeks *after* she was already home. Why hadn't she said something while she was still in England, when Tamara could have done something about it? She hadn't realized Adalyn wanted her to visit. London was her chance to be on her own for three months before her intense final year in school. Tamara had been socked in with work, but she'd have carved out a long weekend or something if she'd known Adalyn had wanted to show off her life in London. What could she do about it after the fact?

Then had come that bit about the murdered linguist.

And this was *after* Verity Blackwood wanted to meet her at the airport. Tamara had assumed it was about a birthday surprise in the works for Adalyn. Then Graham Blackwood had shown up instead.

Tamara couldn't hold on to the image of him, the memory of their brief exchange. She was so tired. She hadn't felt such bone-deep fatigue since giving birth to Adalyn...*my baby girl...*

She curled into a fetal position on the smelly mat. What if that memory of Graham Blackwood wasn't real? What if it was the drugs messing with her mind?

Maybe she didn't want the FBI to find her. Maybe Adalyn was in trouble and needed her. Maybe she should figure out how to escape and then pretend nothing had happened to her.

Escape? How would she escape?

She could hear water dripping. She hadn't turned off the faucet all the way.

She lay still. She needed to sleep.

Just sleep.

Then she'd find a way out of here.

9

Verity Blackwood's overdose, her scheduled meeting with
Emma's grandfather in London, her husband's last-minute
flight cancellation, a recent murder and the Blackwoods' connection to Adalyn McDermott's new friends had changed everything. Emma could see it in Matt Yankowski's face when
she sat opposite him in his office. Behind him, Boston Harbor
glistened under a hazy sky. "What if we're not dealing with a
mother-daughter fight and we have a missing prosecutor on
our hands?" He didn't wait for an answer, clearly didn't expect
one. "Where are Oliver York and Henrietta Balfour now?"

"Oliver's farm," Emma said.

"Your grandfather?"

"On his way to Ireland."

"He tell you that?"

She shook her head. "Oliver did. I left Granddad a voice
mail asking him to call me."

"What do we know about this Stefan Petrescu?"

"I only know what Oliver told me." Emma paused. She'd
learned to be as concise and precise as possible with Yank
when he was trying to get a read on a situation. He'd go for
details later. "I hadn't heard of Mr. Petrescu until Oliver's
call. His murder wasn't on my radar."

"A Romanian linguist. What kind of enemies would a

linguist have?" Yank sighed, glanced behind him. The HIT offices were discreet, but their harbor view was impressive. "Heat's supposed to break today. Lucy doesn't mind it. Reminds her of Northern Virginia." He swiveled back to face Emma. "Were Graham and Verity Blackwood on your radar before you got word of her overdose this morning?"

"No." But she knew what Yank was asking. "My grandfather didn't tell me he was meeting Verity in London—or that he was going to London, for that matter."

"Not unusual for him," Yank said.

It wasn't a question but Emma responded. "He's accustomed to doing what he wants, when he wants, without letting anyone else know unless it suits him."

A grudging smile from her boss. "Old codger. I'm going to be like that when I'm in my eighties. Or is he in his nineties now?"

"Eighties and fit in mind and body, according to him. I speak with him at least once a week."

"Flying to London at the last minute..."

"He would remind us that Ireland is an island. Flying isn't unusual."

"I guess it's better than having him behind the wheel." Yank drummed his desk with two fingers. "The American artists Henrietta and Oliver mentioned—what's the story with them?"

"Fletcher and Ophelia Campbell. We met their son, Rex, last night. Their primary residence is in southeast New Hampshire, about an hour north of Boston. Ophelia died of cancer there in April. Two weeks later Fletcher set fire to his studio in an old barn on the property."

"Accident?"

"He has Alzheimer's," Emma said. "He's more well-known than his wife, but he's too ill to paint anymore. I did a quick check of news accounts of the fire after Oliver called. Apparently, Fletcher was stirring the fire in the woodstove in his studio and hot coals fell out. The barn's two hundred years old. It wouldn't take much for a fire to spread."

"Was he hurt?" Yank asked.

"Minor smoke inhalation. Rex was at the house and called the fire department. The studio didn't burn down completely, but a number of the Campbells' works and paintings in their personal art collection were badly damaged or destroyed."

"Fletcher in a home now?"

"I don't know. I don't know if Sharpe Fine Art Recovery has ever worked with the Campbells. I don't know why Verity Blackwood would specifically contact my grandfather." Emma glanced past Yank at the hazy sky. A cold front was supposed to move through later that afternoon, bringing with it cooler, drier air. She shifted her focus back to Yank, still with his dark eyes narrowed on her. "I'll find out."

"Did Oliver offer any thoughts on where we might find Graham Blackwood?"

"He speculated Graham might have stayed to go fishing on his own, but that was based purely on a photograph of him in fishing clothes. I suspect Henrietta will follow up with MI5 on Stefan Petrescu. I didn't speak with her but I'm not sure what she would say with Oliver there."

"Those two." Yank left it at that. "Do you know this art conservationist Adalyn McDermott is working for—Jolie Romero? I didn't get a good fix on her last night at dinner. Rex, either."

"I don't know much about her."

"Good reputation?"

"Yes. Tamara asked about her yesterday."

"Checking out the daughter's new job, new friends?"

"She also mentioned the convent and their work in art conservation, and my family."

Yank got to his feet and came around his desk. His utilitarian office suited his pragmatic approach to his work. His one personal item was a framed photograph from last fall of Lucy in Ardmore, a historic village on the south Irish coast. She'd gone to Ireland alone, trying to figure out herself—her marriage. Yank's move to Boston—the way he'd handled it with his wife—had nearly destroyed fifteen years of marriage.

"Sam checked with Tamara's office in Washington," Yank said. "She pushed hard to clear the decks so she could take off for three weeks without interruptions."

"Can her office reach her in an emergency?" Emma asked.

"By phone, assuming she turns it on. She delegated another prosecutor to handle emergencies in her absence. No one's expecting any problems while she's away. She didn't leave an itinerary with her assistant. She said she didn't have one beyond hitting the road and heading 'down east' and going from there."

"Down east. Maine, then."

"It's a popular spot in summer." Yank started for his open office door. "I want to know if there's a connection between Tamara McDermott not showing up for dinner last night and this situation with the Blackwoods. I want to know where Graham Blackwood is. I want to know he's safe. I want to know why he didn't get on that flight with his wife at the last minute, what he knows about her overdose and the details of their relationship with the Campbells, Jolie Romero and Adalyn McDermott."

Emma eased to her feet. "I'd like to go over to Jolie Romero's studio in Porter Square."

Yank nodded. "Take Colin." He paused, inhaling deeply, his concern evident. "We don't know that whatever is going on with this British couple and your grandfather has anything to do with Tamara and Adalyn. I'm good with Tamara leaving early on vacation because she had a fight with her daughter."

"That'd be a positive outcome," Emma said.

"I want us to find Tamara having popovers at Jordan Pond."

Yank shut his door after Emma left his office. She found Sam Padgett at a table in the open-layout area in the center of the main floor of HIT's dedicated waterfront offices. He was alone, the rest of the team in their offices, the conference room or on the road. Despite his no-nonsense approach to his work, Sam was a man with a keen sense of humor. He was dark, tall and ultra-fit, the sleeves of his white shirt rolled up, suit jacket laid neatly on the table next to him. He was in his element with the Boston heat wave. "Tamara's rental apartment is getting cleaned for a new tenant as we speak," he said. "Adalyn stopped by to make sure everything was set and her mother didn't leave anything behind—except the note, which she grabbed. Colin sent me his photo of it. Tamara's state of mind when she wrote it isn't obvious to me. I have the contact info of the owner of the apartment. I'll talk to him and see what he has to tell us."

"That sounds good," Emma said. "I'll let you know what we find out at Jolie Romero's studio. Yank's picturing Tamara having popovers at Acadia. I like that image."

"Popovers? Acadia? Do I want to know?"

"Acadia National Park. It's in Maine. You can have warm popovers and tea at tables on a lawn overlooking Jordan Pond."

"Got it," Sam said. "I've never had a popover."

Emma left him to his work and whatever he wanted to learn about Acadia, Jordan Pond and popovers. She collected Colin from her small office. He wore a light gray suit, white shirt and a blue tie, with thick-soled shoes that wouldn't slow him down in a chase on foot. They'd walk the short distance to their apartment and take her car to Cambridge. She asked him to drive. She wanted time to think.

She checked her messages, but she had nothing else from Henrietta and Oliver, and nothing yet from her grandfather.

Colin glanced at her. "Your granddad's still AWOL?"

"I assume he'll get in touch once he lands in Dublin. And no," Emma added, "I didn't confirm he's actually on his flight."

Emma was familiar with Porter Square and Jolie Romero's work in art restoration, conservation and preservation, but she'd never been to her studio, located on the first floor of her 1930s house on a residential street. "Please, have a look around, ask any questions you'd like," Jolie said, gesturing broadly with one hand. "I store a few things in my apartment on the second floor when I run out of room down here. I rent out the top-floor apartment. Adalyn has it now. She's still getting settled. We do most of our work here in the front room. The lab's in back for the fussy work. It has the appropriate climate controls. I hate air-conditioning and only use it when the heat's unbearable—as it will be by noon, I'm sure."

"It's a great space," Emma said. Given her own background in art conservation, she recognized supplies and equipment for cleaning, repairing, protecting and preserving works of art—brushes, gloves, specialized cloths, backing materials, microscopes, photographic equipment, chemicals, technical lamps, easels.

Jolie smiled, but she was visibly tense with two FBI agents in her workspace. "Thanks, it suits me and my work. I keep things more casual here than Sister Joan did with her conservation work."

"You two knew each other?" Emma asked.

"We ran into each other a number of times over the years.

She was a perfectionist, but that's why she was so extra-ordinary at her work. I saw her last August. We were at a conference together in Boston. Then a few weeks later she was gone…murdered…" Jolie brushed her fingertips across a scratched metal worktable. "She's missed."

"Very much so."

Sister Joan Mary Fabriani had been Emma's mentor and friend, an exacting art conservationist and a dedicated, kind member of the Sisters of the Joyful Heart. Eleven months ago, Emma had discovered Sister Joan minutes after she'd been knifed to death at her convent on the southern Maine coast. She glanced at Colin, standing by the front door. They'd met in the days after Sister Joan's murder.

"Sister Joan could handle a Picasso with ease," Jolie said. "She'd relish it. I probably could, too, but I wouldn't relish it—I wouldn't want to touch it, not anymore. In my brash younger days, I suppose. But you're not here about Sister Joan. I heard about last night. Adalyn's embarrassed by her mother's behavior, but there's no cause for alarm, is there? I gather she got herself into a snit and took off early. Nothing more to it."

"Have you heard from her?" Emma asked.

"No, but I wouldn't. Adalyn was down here a little while ago and hadn't heard from her, either. She showed me the note her mother left. At least it's something. She'll be down in a minute. She's a godsend. She's a quick learner, and her expertise with archival evidence and research is helping with a client—Rex Campbell, as a matter of fact. I don't know if you heard about the fire at his father's studio. All I can say is it's a hell of a mess to sort through." Jolie eased onto a high task chair. "How can I help?"

Colin checked out a seating area by the front windows, with two club chairs and a small round table stacked haphazardly with art magazines. "Who else works here?"

"No one at the moment," Jolie said. "I hire freelancers when I need to, and I'll take on a couple of interns in the fall. August is quiet. I have the Campbell paintings salvaged from the fire, but not much else. I was in England for a few weeks—part of the work I'm doing for Rex." She paused, adjusting her position. She had on a black tunic and leggings, not as dramatic an outfit as last night. "And I live alone," she added. "I've never married and I'm not in a relationship." She smiled, a touch of color in her cheeks. "There. Got that out of the way."

"You've had your studio here for a while," Emma said.

"Twenty years. I started my career at a museum in New York, but I grew up in Arlington and couldn't wait to come back to the Boston area. I wanted to be closer to my mother. She was widowed—she's gone now. She was something of a painter herself. That's one of her works there." Jolie nodded to an oil still life, a classic scene of apples in a wooden bowl. "Lovely, isn't it?"

Emma took a closer look. "It is." She smiled. "I love apples."

"Mom picked them herself. She inspired me to get into this work. I handle a wide range of art, but I have a soft spot for works by accomplished amateurs like my mother. Their monetary value is generally of less importance than their sentimental value."

"Where do the Campbells fit in?" Emma asked.

"Fletcher's paintings in particular are in high demand, and have been for a good long time. Now that he's unable to paint and Ophelia is gone, Rex thinks of himself as a caretaker of any works they left behind—or owned, for that matter. That's the approach I take here. I do my best to protect art for future generations. I'm always mindful that anything I work on will outlast me. Sister Joan shared that attitude."

Emma moved back from the still life. "Did you work with the Campbells before the fire?"

"I've known them for years, but they never were a client until the fire. I'm still sorting through the paintings that survived and assessing the damage and what I can reasonably do. I don't want to make any precipitous moves. It's quite an undertaking." Jolie shuddered. "It's like running a burn unit for paintings."

Emma pointed at a watercolor on an easel by a window, its image—a simple farmhouse table—barely visible under a film of grime and soot from the fire. "Is that one of the damaged paintings from Fletcher Campbell's studio?"

Jolie nodded. "It's one of Ophelia's last works. It's filthy, obviously, but it's mostly on the surface. There's no damage from the heat and the flames. It shouldn't be too difficult to restore it to what it looked like before the fire."

"Did she paint at the studio?" Emma asked.

"No, mostly at a cottage on the property. Rex brought this painting into the studio because it seemed to help settle his father after her death. She knew Fletcher's mind was failing and didn't want to leave him, but she knew she was terminal. All I can say is thank God for Rex." Jolie waved a hand, as if dismissing the sad topic from her mind. "I think of myself as an art doctor. My first priority is to do no harm. You must understand that, Special Agent Sharpe."

"I do. It's painstaking work."

"The rewards are often only ones I can see. I can't restore the rescued Campbell paintings to their original condition, but I don't want to do extensive retouching—we want what's there to be the artist's work not mine. It's a shame, really. Ophelia and Fletcher were careless with storing their art. I warned them, but they were always on the go. Then the fire..." Jolie turned from the watercolor, shaking her head.

"I keep reminding myself no one was hurt and the house and guest cottage didn't catch fire, and for that we can be grateful."

"What were you doing in England?" Colin asked.

His abrupt question clearly caught Jolie off guard. "The Campbells have a cottage in Oxford. That's how Rex and I met Adalyn, as a matter of fact. We were all at a dinner hosted by mutual friends. Rex was in Oxford to start the process to close up the cottage, and I flew out to help him sort through canvases. I thought I might find something that would help me with my salvage work here, but most of the paintings were half-finished or junk from friends Fletcher and Ophelia indulged. Fletcher didn't have a huge inventory of his own work. His paintings tended to sell fast once he put one on the market."

Emma touched a boar-bristle brush. "How long were you in England?"

"Almost three weeks. I started in London and then stayed in Oxford for a few days. I flew back here the day after Adalyn two weeks ago. Anyway—Adalyn and I got on well at the dinner, and her skills and needs dovetailed with my needs and what I could offer. I got her card, met with her in London and here we are."

"An apartment and a job," Emma said. "This dinner—where was it?"

"What does it matter? Never mind. Sorry. The Blackwood home," Jolie added quickly. "Verity and Graham Blackwood."

Emma heard rapid footsteps on the stairs in the front entry, and in a moment, Adalyn McDermott burst into the studio. She was flushed, breathing hard. "Agent Sharpe, Agent Donovan—nothing's happened—"

"We don't have any news on your mother," Emma said.

Adalyn exhaled in obvious relief and smiled awkwardly at Jolie. "I'm sorry. I warned you something like this could happen when you hired me. It's the price one pays for hiring the daughter of a federal prosecutor. The price I pay for *being* one."

"It's okay, Adalyn," Jolie said. "It keeps things interesting."

"Thanks, that's decent of you. Last night was awkward when my mother stood us up, but her note says it all, doesn't it? I'm past it. She just left twelve hours or whatever earlier than her original plan. I hope the break's good for her."

Colin picked up an art magazine. Emma knew he wasn't distracted. "We were just talking about how you met Rex and Jolie."

"Dinner with the Blackwoods. I overheard the tail end. Hard to believe how much has happened since then. I loved England, but Porter Square is great and the work here is fascinating. Jolie says summer is quiet." Adalyn turned to Emma. "This all must be familiar to you, Agent Sharpe, given your background."

"Some. I'm a little rusty."

Adalyn sat tenuously on another task chair. She was dressed with the same apparent disregard for wrinkles, mending, stains and what went with what as last night, but her look suited her—and she had other things on her mind, clearly. "I've learned so much in the short time I've been here. The idea isn't to restore a work of art to how it looked the day it was painted. That sort of meddling is often too intrusive and unrealistic. That's the standard in art conservation nowadays." She smiled brightly at Emma. "But you know that."

Emma stood next to floor-to-ceiling shelves jammed with supplies. "How well do you know Graham and Verity Blackwood?"

Adalyn's face drained of color. "They're friends—Verity especially. We met when I first arrived in London and hit it off. She and Graham were here last week. Why?"

"I'm sorry to tell you that Mrs. Blackwood is in a London hospital," Emma said. "She was found unresponsive last night.

She's recovering from what appears to be an opioid overdose. When did you see her last?"

"Before she left on Saturday," Adalyn blurted. "At Logan. My God—will she be all right?"

"We don't have any details on her condition." Emma decided to come back to Adalyn and shifted to Jolie. "What about you? When did you last see Verity Blackwood?"

"Tuesday." Jolie didn't hesitate. "We drove up to see Fletcher. He's in a small, private home but Rex had him to the farm. Graham and Verity wanted to see Fletcher while he might still recognize them. He seemed to, or he did a good job faking it. We didn't stay long. We came back here and had dinner together—the Blackwoods, Rex, Adalyn and me."

Adalyn jumped to her feet. "I can't believe this. I hugged Verity and Graham goodbye at the airport. We met at check-in and promised to see each other again soon."

"Where was your mother then?" Colin asked.

Adalyn reddened at his question and raked a hand through her hair, flustered. "She'd just landed from Washington. I met her at baggage claim. Verity—actually, Verity wanted to talk to her. She said she'd wait at check-in, and I could just text her if Mom couldn't make it."

Emma leaned against a counter-height table. "Did they connect?"

"I stayed at baggage claim to wait for my mother's suitcase while she headed to find Verity. She got back after a few minutes and said she only saw Graham. I didn't think twice about it, honestly. Mom was beat. We collected her rental car, and she dropped me off here and went on to her apartment. She could have stayed with me. She didn't want to. Said she knew I was still getting settled." Adalyn attempted a faltering smile. "Too much like camping for her, I guess."

"Why didn't Verity meet your mother, do you know?" Colin asked.

"I think she got jittery about being late for her flight. She's not as experienced a traveler as Graham is. I don't know if my mother said that or I just thought it. I can't..." Adalyn sniffled, brushed a knuckle at some tears. "I don't know how Verity could have overdosed. She's not an addict. She hasn't had any recent surgery."

Emma glanced at Jolie, saw that she, too, had stood up from her task chair. "What about you, Jolie? How did Mrs. Blackwood appear to you when you were together?"

"She absolutely was not on drugs." Jolie shook her head as if for added emphasis. "I know it can be difficult to tell if a person is addicted to drugs, but Verity wasn't—isn't. Graham isn't, either. I'm sure of it. They don't smoke, and they have one drink each and that's it."

Colin uncrossed his arms. "Tell us about Stefan Petrescu."

Not the question either Jolie or Adalyn was expecting. Jolie rubbed the back of her neck with both hands and let out a breath. "That was awful. Just awful. His death, I mean. I assume that's what you're getting at. I was staying at a bed-and-breakfast in Oxford. It's within walking distance of the Blackwood home and Fletcher and Ophelia's cottage. I ran into Graham while he was out walking, and he told me about Stefan. He said he and Verity were devastated. I didn't know Stefan. I'd only met him at the dinner the week before, when I met Adalyn."

"That was the only time I met him, too," Adalyn said, more subdued. "I was in London—Verity texted me about his death. She couldn't believe it. I almost postponed my flight home, but it would have cost a fortune to reschedule."

A window air conditioner creaked to a start. Jolie jumped, then tried to laugh it off. "I hate that damn thing, but I know

I should be grateful for it on a hot day like today. Look, I know you're FBI agents and this poor man's death must set you off, but he was Verity and Graham's friend. Part of the reason they visited last week was to get away for a bit. They arrived on Monday afternoon and left Saturday. They stayed two nights at the Four Seasons in Boston. We saw them on Tuesday. Then they rented a house in Maine for a couple of days and drove up there early Wednesday."

Adalyn sat on one of the club chairs next to Colin. "They wanted to get out of the city for a few days."

Jolie picked a thick brush from a jar and touched the bristles to her palm. "Verity wanted to see Heron's Cove. She knows about the Sisters of the Joyful Heart and their work in art conservation, and, of course, about your family, Agent Sharpe. Heron's Cove was a natural choice for them."

Colin steadied his gaze on her. "Did you discuss Sharpe Fine Art Recovery with the Blackwoods?"

"I didn't, no," Jolie said.

He shifted to Adalyn. "Did you?"

"Not really. They know I'm interested in art crimes." Adalyn grabbed Colin's abandoned magazine. Nervous energy, clearly. She smacked it back on the table. "It's insane to think Verity overdosed. If she did, it was an accident. How's Graham taking it?"

Colin sat on a matching chair next to her. "Have you spoken with him or Verity since Saturday?"

Adalyn frowned at him. "No, why?"

"I haven't spoken with them, either," Jolie said. "Graham's with Verity, isn't he?"

"He didn't return to London with her," Colin said.

Adalyn nearly jumped out of her chair. "You mean he went back to Maine? He's still *here*? Why didn't he go to London with her? My mother didn't say anything to me about him not going back. When did he decide?"

"He canceled his flight around the time they met at Logan," Emma said.

Jolie was shaking her head. "I'm surprised he stayed. Shocked, even. I didn't notice any problems in his and Verity's relationship, if that's your next question."

Emma kept her attention on Adalyn. "You had brunch with your mother yesterday. Did you discuss the Blackwoods, Heron's Cove or Stefan Petrescu—anything that might help us understand what's going on?"

"What do you mean? She's on vacation. That's all that's going on. She's not—" Adalyn stopped herself. "Oh. You mean because Verity wanted to speak with her at the airport and now she's overdosed and Graham…" She sucked in a breath. "It's a lot to absorb. As you can imagine, my mother didn't take it well when I told her about Stefan, but I expected that. She's a prosecutor. She's seen it all. She thinks the worst. She worries I'm naive. I don't remember if I told her Graham and Verity rented a house in Heron's Cove. Probably. It wasn't a secret."

"What did your mother think of your friendship with the Blackwoods?" Colin asked.

Adalyn clasped both arms of the chair. "She didn't offer an opinion. She could have met them in England if she'd come to see me, but she didn't. Too busy. Wanted to dig out so she could take this break. Verity will be okay, won't she? We want to stay in touch. I'm considering taking a job in England after I graduate."

"I have one more question for both of you," Emma said. "Did Verity or Graham mention forgeries to you?"

Adalyn shook her head, her cheeks red, tears in her eyes.

Jolie said nothing.

"Do you have any experience with forgeries?" Emma asked her.

"Some. Not much, thankfully. Clients rarely ask me to authenticate a work, but if I noticed something obvious I'd speak up—acrylic paint on a work supposedly done in the seventeenth century, for example. Of course that wouldn't automatically make it a forgery. People imitate and copy paintings all the time. It's when you try to pass it off as a genuine Rembrandt or whatever you get in trouble." Jolie dropped onto a chair at a tidy desk and raised her gaze to Emma. "I'm not telling you anything you don't know."

There was an edge to her voice. Emma understood. She and Colin had come at them with a lot, including the near-death of a friend. She thanked them for their time and placed her card on Jolie's desk. "If you hear from Graham Blackwood or Tamara McDermott or think of anything else, I'd appreciate if you'd get in touch."

Jolie nodded, glancing at the card. "Of course."

Adalyn used the chair's arms for support as she got to her feet. She swayed as if she was about to pass out but recovered. "Are you worried about my mother?"

"We want to locate her," Colin said.

"Okay. Um—is Agent Yankowski concerned? He and my parents have been friends for a long time. He knows what my mother's like."

"I'm sure he'd appreciate hearing from you," Emma said.

"A diplomatic response. It means you're not going to tell me if he's worried."

Colin shifted to Jolie. "We'd like to speak with Rex, too."

"He'll be upset about Verity. He's known Graham longer, but Ophelia in particular was so happy when he and Verity found each other. I doubt Rex knows Verity overdosed and Graham didn't go back with her on Saturday. He'd have said something." Jolie rose, smoothing her tunic. "Not the way I expected today to go, that's for sure, but I'm sure everything will work out. Verity will recover, you'll find Graham and

Adalyn's mom will have a wonderful vacation." She waved a hand. "You can see yourselves out?"

"No problem," Emma said. "Thank you again for your time."

Jolie and Adalyn mumbled a goodbye. Emma followed Colin out to the porch. The hanging baskets of petunias and wicker furniture were more traditional than she'd have expected of Jolie Romero. "Adalyn's worried about her mother," she said as they descended to the street.

"She should be." Colin turned to her when they reached the car. "On to Maine?"

"You drive. I'll call Yank and fill him in."

10

"I wish we'd recommended Cape Cod to the Blackwoods," Jolie said after the FBI agents left. "Emma Sharpe did *not* look happy about Heron's Cove. I guess I don't blame her."

Adalyn said nothing as she returned to the worktable. Jolie had her sorting through documents Rex had salvaged from his father's burned studio. Smoke, soot, flames and water had done varying levels of damage to the papers. It was tedious but not difficult work, which Adalyn appreciated, given the distractions of the day. She worked only part-time and didn't have set hours yet.

Jolie grabbed the bright vest she'd worn last night from a hook by her desk. "If it gets too chilly in here, let me know. I was starting to sweat and turned up the AC, but it could have just been having the FBI here." She slipped into the vest. "I can't wrap my head around what happened to Verity. You know her better than I do. Did she seem despondent at all to you? Did you get any hint she was on drugs?"

"No and no," Adalyn said without hesitation. "She seemed herself. Sad about Stefan's death, but Graham was closer to him than she was. He was sad, too."

"Sad and horrified." Jolie returned to her desk. "They hoped a few days here would help them wrap their heads around what happened. I've never lost a friend or loved one to murder. It has to be awful."

Adalyn opened an archive-quality folder. "I hope I didn't miss anything that could have helped her."

"Don't go there, Adalyn. I might never have dealt with murder, but I've dealt with enough tragedies in my life to know second-guessing gets you nowhere. Let's just focus on our work, shall we?"

"Makes sense."

Sixty seconds later, Rex burst into the studio, pulling the door shut hard behind him. Jolie typically left it unlocked during work hours—a habit she'd promised Adalyn she'd break. Adalyn hoped she would follow through. It was a safe neighborhood, but still.

The prosecutor's daughter, she thought, smiling to herself.

Rex laughed in disbelief. "I just got grilled by the FBI. I'm sitting in a coffee shop on Mass. Ave., enjoying a double espresso, when in come your agents Sharpe and Donovan. They saw me going in. Scared the hell out of me. They told me they'd stopped here first and spoke to you two. They told me about Verity…" He shook his head. "Can you believe it? An overdose. I never saw that coming. Have you had any updates on her condition?"

"I texted a mutual friend in London," Adalyn said. "I haven't heard back."

"And your mom? Still nothing?"

Adalyn bit down on her lower lip, trying to control a flood of unruly emotions. "No, nothing. It's bad timing, her taking off on her FBI-agent friends and Verity overdosing on opioids."

"No kidding," Rex said. "Graham staying behind at the last minute doesn't help. He didn't clue me in. Maybe he needed a few days on his own. He and Stefan Petrescu had been friends for a long time."

Adalyn pictured her mother's face when she'd realized one

of her daughter's acquaintances in England had been shot to death. Irritation. As if *Adalyn* had done something wrong. The wrongdoing had been on the part of the shooter, but in her mother's world, Adalyn should have been in London, watching a baking show with friends her own age.

Rex laughed, interrupting her irritable thoughts. Jolie had repeated her crack about Cape Cod to him. He and his parents had never had direct dealings with the Sisters of the Joyful Heart or Sharpe Fine Art Recovery, but probably knew people who had. Jolie, for one, at least with the sisters.

"I have a few errands to run," Rex said, clearly restless after his chat with the FBI. "I was going to do them after my coffee, but I wanted to check with you two first once those two agents barged in. I'm still not over it. It'll take a while for my blood pressure to return to normal." He grinned suddenly. "Now I sound like my dad, before his mind started to slip. I've spent so much time with him lately I have to remember I'm only thirty-one. I'll be back later. Glad you two aren't in cuffs."

After he left, Jolie chose a fat boar-bristle brush from a jar of brushes. "You could do worse than Rex, you know," she said.

Adalyn smiled. "I could and I have."

Jolie's eyes widened, and she sputtered into laughter. "I hope you didn't tell your parents that. Have mercy on them, Adalyn. They're getting used to having their only daughter turn twenty-one. One shocker at a time."

Adalyn was grateful she'd managed to lighten the mood, but then she got a text message. Not from her mother, of course. Her friend in London—another archivist—had responded.

Everyone's shocked about Verity. I heard she could have suffered permanent brain damage due to lack of O2. I hope not.

Adalyn typed a quick text. Thanks. Keep me posted and I'll do the same.

Will do. xoxo

"I need some air," Adalyn said after reading the text to Jolie. She closed the folder with the documents she'd meant to work on. "Would you mind?"

Jolie pointed her brush toward the street. "Go, take a walk—take the afternoon. We'll work out hours later. Get your bearings. With any luck, you'll hear from your mother before you get back."

The moment Adalyn stepped outside, she shuddered at the heat and humidity. She tried to take the heat wave in stride. She wasn't in London anymore, but she didn't want any reminders of her three months there, not right now. She made it to the corner when her father called. "I just got off the phone with Matt Yankowski. Adalyn, what the hell's going on?"

"Where are you, Dad?"

"What? I'm in my office. Where else would I be?"

In bed with another girlfriend? Adalyn chided herself for thinking such a thing. His life was his business—just as her life was her business. She pictured him at his desk in his office a few blocks from the White House. He'd worked as a state prosecutor for years before switching to a prominent DC law firm. She abandoned any urge to needle him. "I thought you might be on a flight up here."

"I'll be there in a heartbeat if you need me."

"Agent Yankowski told you—"

"About this British couple and this man in England who was murdered. Friends of yours. Hell, Adalyn."

"It's okay, Dad. I'm fine. Please don't come. Mom will get

in touch with us when she wants to. If she calls me, I'll let you know. You can do the same if she calls you first."

"She won't call me."

Adalyn wanted to smash her phone on the sidewalk. He was so pathetic. Morose, almost. "Dad, she's fine—you know that, right? Mom's fine."

"Of course she is. You wait, she'll show up safe and sound tonight."

"I hope so." Adalyn realized she was the one who sounded pathetic now. "No, you're right. She will. She picked the wrong time to pull something like this. All she had to do was wait until after dinner to leave on vacation."

"It would be better if we could reach her."

"Understatement, Dad, but going dark was part of her plan."

"I guess."

His heavy tone underscored his obvious uneasiness. He wasn't the type to leap to conclusions, but he had to be tempted. "How are you holding up?"

"I'm okay. I'm sorry about Verity, but I'm optimistic she'll make a full recovery."

"And Graham—"

"He'll turn up," she said. "Did Agent Yankowski call just to update you?"

"He offered to keep an eye on you."

Oh, great. "I'm managing, Dad. Please don't worry. I answered all the FBI's questions."

"Don't lie to them. It's a felony to lie to the FBI. You don't have to talk to them. You have a right to have an attorney present. It's a wise idea to exercise that right."

A bit late now. Adalyn felt like a thirteen-year-old caught sneaking into a six-pack. "Dad, I didn't do anything wrong."

"That's not the point. Next time anyone in law enforcement wants to talk to you, call me."

"Dad—"

"Adalyn. Call me. Promise."

"Okay, okay, I promise, but I don't know anything about the drugs Verity took or why Graham didn't go back to London with her. He's probably just fishing and kayaking in Maine. That wouldn't be Verity's thing."

When they disconnected, Adalyn felt no sense of relief that he'd called, mostly because nothing he said changed anything. She jumped on the subway to Boston, not sure exactly where she'd end up.

Twenty minutes later, Adalyn stood outside Lucy Yankowski's hole-in-the-wall knitting shop on Newbury Street. She started to feel better the minute she arrived at the skinny, classic Back Bay brownstone. She pushed open the glass door and went into the cozy shop with its cubbies of yarn, racks of knitting books, shelves of knitting supplies and a big, red-painted table with mix-and-match chairs for classes and workshops.

Adalyn smiled at Lucy, who got up from an antique rolltop oak desk. She was dressed smartly but casually in slim pants and a linen top. "From clinical psychologist to knitting," Adalyn said. "Works somehow, doesn't it?"

"For me it does. Good to see you, Adalyn."

"Thanks. Isn't Newbury Street expensive for a knitting shop?"

"Rents aren't cheap but it's a great location. We're off to a decent start, but August isn't the high season for knitting projects."

"I imagine it's not." Adalyn flipped open a pattern book on the table. Baby clothes. "I don't know how to knit. My grandmother taught my mother, but neither of them taught me. Gran died when I was in high school. I could learn to knit baby blankets, couldn't I? My friends will be having babies soon. I could get a head start. Knit up an inventory of cute little blankets."

"Start with one small blanket, maybe," Lucy said.

"Can you teach yourself how to knit?"

"People do."

"It'd be more fun to take a class. Maybe I'll sign up for one here this winter, if I have time with work and school." Adalyn moved to the cubbies and eyed a fuzzy twist of raspberry-colored yarn. It'd make an adorable baby blanket. "I'd love just to unpack the yarn and put it on the shelves. Who taught you to knit?"

"My grandmother," Lucy said. "My father's mother."

"Did knitting help you with the stress of your work when you were a psychologist?"

She smiled. "Knitting helps with everything."

"If you know how. I bet it's not any fun if you get your yarn all in tangles and drop stitches and make a mess of things."

"Then you start over."

"Ah, is *that* how it works?" Adalyn grinned, feeling more relaxed. "I probably should take up something less sedentary since I work with documents. I did tons of walking in London. I haven't done as much since I've been back. I've been so busy getting moved in, and it took the longest time for me to adjust to being on East Coast time again after three months. Did you hear about my friend from England who overdosed?"

"Matt told me," Lucy said. "I'm so sorry."

"It's hard to believe. I just saw her and she was fine. Do you have to tell Agent Yankowski I'm here?"

"I don't have to but—"

"But you will." Adalyn immediately regretted interrupting. "I understand. Really. Is it tough being married to an FBI agent?"

"It can be tough being married to anyone, I suppose."

"Now there's an answer."

Adalyn moved to a cubby that contained neutral-colored alpaca yarns. What about llamas? Was there llama yarn? She had no idea. Everything in the upscale shop appeared to be of the highest quality, organic, sustainable—just what you'd want if you were tucked into an expensive Back Bay apartment on a cold night with your knitting needles. She didn't mean to be condescending, but who else would be shopping here?

She shifted from the yarn cubbies to a display of knitting needles. She'd never seen so many. "I'm having a hard time digesting Verity's overdose." Her voice was low, as if she hadn't wanted to say what she'd just said. *What a mess I am.* She fingered a set of wooden knitting needles. "I didn't see it coming."

"It's a shock," Lucy said. "It'll take time to sink in. Be patient with yourself."

"I wish I'd done something. What if it was attempted suicide?"

"She's getting good care. Her doctors will tend to her."

"Do you think Graham knows? Did Matt say anything—"

"I can have him call you."

Adalyn put up a hand. "No, it's okay. I guess I don't need to know, do I? I'm curious, though."

"And you're concerned about your friend," Lucy said.

"Not the best start to being twenty-one, is it?"

Lucy shut the baby clothes knitting book and set it in a stand. "I remember when twenty-one felt so grown-up. Now it seems so young. I wanted everything to be perfect at twenty-one, and it wasn't. It never is."

"Is that what you used to tell your patients?"

"I'm not speaking to you as a psychologist, Adalyn. I'm a friend."

Her way of saying their conversation wasn't confidential. Adalyn hated how irritated she felt. It had to be nerves—shock, fear. Her mother's weird, annoying, inexplicable behavior. She almost wanted something to be wrong, just so Jolie and Rex wouldn't have to know her mother was the type of person to take off without a word and skip her only daughter's twenty-first birthday dinner. It wasn't fair to take out her frustration on Lucy. She was a kind, decent woman married to a hard-driving FBI agent who'd whisked her from her home and work in Northern Virginia to a new life in Boston, running a fabulous little knitting shop, reinventing herself.

"I wish I'd brought Verity here last week," Adalyn said. "She'd love this shop."

"I hope she returns to Boston and I have a chance to meet her then."

"People recover from serious drug overdoses. I know that, but what if she has permanent brain damage? What if she can't walk, can't read—can't hear? I'd rather die."

"That's an understandable reaction."

Lucy adjusted a chair at the table. She didn't seem awkward at all. Her training, Adalyn supposed. "But don't put myself in Verity's shoes, right? That's what my mother would say if she were here. I should go. I should buy something first, though. I've taken up your time—"

"It's okay. Stop in anytime, Adalyn. As you can see, I'm not swamped with walk-ins."

She didn't seem worried about her lack of customers, either. "Thank you, Lucy. I guess I needed to talk to someone. It's soothing to be in here. You're soothing. The shop will do great once word gets out. Tell Matt—Agent Yankowski—I said hi, okay?"

"I will do so." Lucy opened the door. "At least the heat is

supposed to break today. I'm tired of the grumbling. You and I have been through Washington summers."

"This isn't so bad compared to DC, but compared to London—" Adalyn forced a smile. "I could do with a nice, cool, misting London rain right now."

Another quick goodbye and Adalyn was on her way down the stairs. Knitting. She was going to learn and whip up cute little blankets with the coziest yarn Lucy offered that would also be safe for babies.

She checked her phone. Still nothing from her mother.

She shoved her phone back in her bag, resisting the urge to turn it off or throw it into a trash can. Maybe that was what her mother had done with her phone. She felt good about resisting, since the last thing she wanted right now was to think of herself as a chip off the old maternal block.

If not for Verity's overdose, would the FBI have knocked on Jolie's studio door that morning? Adalyn found herself wishing Graham and Verity had stayed in England last week. "Please let Verity be okay," she whispered to herself.

She ducked into a coffee shop. A cold brew and a veggie quiche on her own, and she'd be back to herself. She'd review every word she'd said to Emma Sharpe and Colin Donovan, but she was sure she hadn't lied to them, even if she hadn't told them every single thing. They hadn't asked, had they? She could call her father and go over everything with him, but that was asking for trouble. He'd call some lawyer friend in Boston or be on a plane to Boston himself within the hour, and she just wanted to enjoy her lunch and not think about her mother, Stefan Petrescu and the Blackwoods.

11

Emma took a call from Sam Padgett in the parking lot behind the inn next to Sharpe Fine Art Recovery. Children were tossing stones into the tidal river. A pair of kayakers paddled toward the narrow channel leading to the Atlantic. Most of the working and pleasure boats that moored on the river were out for the day. Emma welcomed the cooler, salt-tinged coastal Maine air, the cry of seagulls, the putter of a lobster boat—familiar, comfortable sights, smells and sounds.

"I texted you and Colin the car rental information for both Tamara McDermott and Graham Blackwood," Sam said. "Tamara rented her car for three weeks and indicated she'd be taking it to Nova Scotia. Graham planned to return his car later today."

"Did he reschedule his flight?"

"Not yet."

Emma edged toward the low hedges that separated the Sharpe backyard from the parking lot. Colin was already up on the retaining wall, looking out at the water. He'd been a marine patrol officer before heading to Quantico. Before that, through high school and college, a lobsterman. "Tamara would probably take a ferry to Nova Scotia."

"We're checking to see if she has a reservation," Sam said.

No surprise. He and the HIT team were thorough. "I

reached the owner of the apartment Tamara rented in Boston. Nothing to offer," Sam added. "I did a quick check on the Blackwoods. Graham started his think tank five years ago and funded it himself to get it off the ground. He keeps it going through speaking and consulting fees and the occasional donation. It has no staff to speak of. He hires virtual assistants and temps when needed. The Blackwoods seem to live beneath their means."

"Oliver said the Blackwood home is nice but not grand."

"Oliver. I didn't mention his name when I spoke to Scotland Yard."

Their British art thief wasn't one of Sam's favorites, either. Emma let it go. "Anything else, Sam?"

"Most of the money's from the Blackwoods. Verity comes from more modest means. Father was a university administrator, mother was a homemaker. No kids."

"I suppose they could be planning to start a family."

"Hope for me yet," Sam said. "Graham traveled to the US twice in the past eighteen months on think tank business. Washington, DC, and New York. Not to Boston. No indication he met with anyone from DOJ, including Tamara McDermott."

"Did you get anything on Stefan Petrescu when you spoke with Scotland Yard?"

"He was an occasional consultant with the think tank on culture and language. He had a wide range of knowledge, but his main expertise was in Eastern European languages and dialects. He was shot on his way home to Oxford from London two weeks ago."

"British police are going to want anything we have," Emma said.

"They already told me that. They believe Petrescu was targeted. He always stopped in the same spot to stretch his legs on the drive home from London. Everyone knew in his circle of friends and colleagues. His friends teased him about it." Sam paused. "The Blackwoods aren't under suspicion at the moment."

"Their friend's death prompted them to come to the US. Any drug connection?"

"Not yet. The detectives will take another look, given Verity's overdose."

"Makes sense." Emma started through the hedges, a route she'd taken hundreds of times to visit her grandparents. "Anything else, Sam?"

"I spoke with Tamara's boss. She's been working flat-out for months and was overdue for a break. She's had threats against her but nothing active or credible. Boss doesn't think she's the type to go off the beam. Does think she's been under personal strain since she and her husband split."

That was all Sam had. "Thanks," Emma said. "We'll stay in touch."

She and Colin met on the soft grass behind the gray-shingled house where Wendell Sharpe had started his art detective business sixty years ago. Where he and his wife had raised a son, indulged two grandchildren and enjoyed more than forty years together. Lucas, Emma's older brother, ran Sharpe Fine Art Recovery now that their grandfather was semiretired in Dublin. He'd had the old house gutted to the studs and renovated it to a high standard. No more offices that felt like bedrooms, or bathrooms with claw-foot tubs. Although small, Sharpe Fine Art Recovery was a state-of-the-art business ready for its next half century.

Emma filled Colin in on her call with Sam. "We can't get tunnel vision," she said when she finished. "Tamara could simply have left early for vacation."

They started across the yard. Emma waved to her father

and brother on the back porch, the one part of the house un-changed since the renovations. She went ahead of Colin up the stairs. Timothy and Lucas Sharpe looked like father and son, but Emma shared the Sharpe fair coloring if not the lanky build.

"Not a bad place to work," she said, smiling.

"We do have the life," Lucas said. "No complaints today, anyway. Talk to me in February."

He'd never expected to run the family business on his own, but he'd taken to the role—although no one would call Wen-dell Sharpe fully retired. Timothy Sharpe, on the other hand, had given up any operational position after a debilitating fall on the ice when Emma was in her teens. He focused on re-search and analysis, and didn't keep regular hours. He and her mother had returned to Heron's Cove that spring after a year in London, a change of scenery they'd hoped would help him cope with the chronic pain he'd endured since his mishap.

Emma gave her father a quick hug, but she could tell from his stiff movements, the tightness around his mouth and the gray cast to his skin that he was in pain. He pointed at three quart-size green cardboard boxes of wild blueberries lined up on a small table by the back door. "You'd think we were expecting you," he said. "I know how much you love wild blueberries."

She laughed. "August in Maine."

"Your mother and I got out early, before the heat built up. She did most of the work but I did all right. We went to the patch out by the beach where we used to take you and Lucas when you were small."

"I remember," Emma said. "They look fantastic."

"You'll have to take two quarts. They freeze well. Lucas isn't interested."

Her brother grinned at her. "I'm interested in you taking a quart and bringing it back as a pie."

"Nothing I'd like better." Pie-baking was her favorite homebody activity to de-stress and enjoy herself. It beat cleaning.

"But it's not why you're here." Lucas nodded to Colin, now his brother-in-law. "You've got that look, Special Agent Donovan."

"It's the suit," Colin said. "How are you, Lucas?"

"All right. Granddad emailed Dad and me a little while ago. He told us about Verity Blackwood, and he said he was flying back to Ireland and not to worry. I can show you the email if you'd like."

Colin motioned toward the back door. "Why don't I check with the receptionist? She'll have it, won't she?"

Lucas nodded. "No problem."

Emma watched Colin go inside. The porch led into the brand-new kitchen. Only the view was the same as when her grandmother had taught her how to bake pies. Lucas had carved out a suite for their grandfather should he ever return to Maine—but he never would, not to live. Dublin was home now. That he hadn't copied Emma on the email didn't offend her. She wasn't a part of Sharpe Fine Art Recovery. He was okay. That was all that mattered.

She'd called ahead. Lucas knew why she was here. But it was her father who turned to her. "The Blackwoods rented a house out by the cove near the convent. We don't know them. Verity stopped here on Friday, and I ran into her on Saturday on my walk."

Emma sat on a chair by the table with the blueberries. "Details, please."

Lucas leaned against the porch rail, his back to the yard and the river. "I wasn't here on Friday. I was at lunch in the village.

Verity dropped in just after noon. She introduced herself to Ginny, our new receptionist. She didn't have an appointment and didn't make one, and she didn't say what she wanted, if anything. Occasionally we get drop-ins who just want to see the place—especially in high tourist season. Granddad would argue the point, but he's something of a legend these days. Ginny says Verity stayed about five minutes, and she was here on her own. If her husband was with her, he waited outside. Ginny didn't see him or anyone else."

"I saw her around eight the next morning," their father said, pacing. He touched a fingertip to a blueberry stain on his knuckle. "I was on my morning walk—I went through the village and out to the convent. It's one of my usual routes. It's quiet roads to the house the Blackwoods rented. I often turn around there, but sometimes I continue onto a trail to the old stone gazebo that used to be part of the estate the convent took over. The trail gets rough. A lot of tree roots and rocks. Cell coverage is spotty out there, so I don't go that far often."

"I know the house you're talking about," Emma said. "Is that where you ran into Verity?"

He nodded. "I'd just gone past the house onto the trail. I was feeling great and wanted to take advantage of the good weather. I don't know if Verity saw me on walks earlier in the week, but she knew who I was. She said she'd seen Faye and me in the village on Friday afternoon when she was at the Sisters of the Joyful Heart's shop. She was looking at pottery and mentioned she'd stopped here. One of the sisters identified us."

Emma picked a tiny leaf out of one of the quarts of blueberries. "Which sister, do you know?"

"I didn't ask. Verity said she was interested in the sisters' work. That's why she and her husband chose that particular house. They were thrilled it was available. We had a brief conversation. I didn't think much of it, to be honest. She said she was returning to London that evening and wanted to get some questions answered about forgeries. It's not my area of expertise." He paused, balling his hands into fists, and cleared his throat. "I put her in touch with Dad—with your grandfather. I gave her his name, phone number and email. I wrote them down. I carry a Field Notes journal and a pencil with me on my walks, in case I have any brilliant ideas. I rarely do, but sometimes I jot down something I think of and don't want to forget, or I sketch a bird or flower I want to look up later."

"Tell me about Verity, Dad," Emma said. "How did she strike you?"

"She wanted answers to her questions, but she didn't appear to be upset. She wasn't obviously under the influence of narcotics." He opened his fists, breathed out. "I'm familiar with the signs, given my own medical history. Except for an interest in forgeries, she seemed like a happy, ordinary tourist enjoying a few days on the Maine coast. She had on a moose T-shirt she'd picked up in the village. She got a big kick out of it. She asked if her sport sandals would be suitable for kayaking. The rental house comes with two sit-on-top ocean kayaks. She said she and her husband wanted to go paddling before they headed to the airport."

Emma found a loose stem in the blueberries. "Did you see Graham, her husband?"

Her father shook his head. "I didn't see anyone else. Verity apologized for interrupting my walk. She said she didn't want to take up my time with her questions." He smiled slightly. "I thought she had kayaking and her last day in Maine on her mind."

Lucas stood straight. "Did she seem troubled to you, Dad?"

"Not really, no. I'd have done more to help her."

"Did she mention any names to you?" Emma asked him.

"Lucas, your grandfather, Sharpe Fine Art Recovery, the Sisters of the Joyful Heart, the name of the shop where she bought the T-shirt and her husband. Do you know how she's doing, Emma?"

She took her tiny leaf and stem to the porch rail and tossed them into the grass. "Doctors are optimistic she'll survive. Graham Blackwood didn't go back to London with her. He canceled his flight at the last minute. We want to find him. Did Verity say anything that might help?"

"No," her father said. "Nothing."

Emma dug out her phone and swiped to a photograph of Verity Blackwood. "Dad, is this the woman you met on Saturday?"

He glanced at the photo and nodded. "That's her."

She slid the phone into the pocket of her lightweight jacket. "Are you both familiar with Fletcher and Ophelia Campbell?"

"Of course," Lucas said. "They've never been clients if that's your next question."

"Could Granddad have worked with them and not told you?"

"It's possible but unlikely. Dad? Is that right as far as you know?"

He nodded, a pinched look to his eyes now. "I don't know why they'd have reason to hire us. What's this about, Emma?"

"What about the name Stefan Petrescu?"

No recognition. Emma didn't provide further details and swiped to a photo of Tamara McDermott. She showed it to her father and brother, but they didn't recognize her and hadn't seen her, certainly not in the past few days. Emma tucked her phone back in her jacket. "If you see her or Graham or discover any additional information on them, get in touch with me right away, okay?"

"Sure, Emma," her father said. He looked spent. He gestured vaguely toward the porch stairs. "Okay if I run along?"

"It's fine. Thanks for your help."

"I'm sorry about Mrs. Blackwood. I hope she pulls through." He blew Emma a kiss and winked, managing a smile. "Love you, Special Agent Sharpe."

"Love you, too, Dad."

Lucas stood next to her as they watched their father limp down the stairs and shuffle across the small lawn, then squeeze between the hedges to the parking lot. "I helped him bring up the blueberries," Lucas said. "He'll be done for the day now."

"Is he in more pain than usual?"

"Probably. All the signs are there. He won't say, and I won't ask."

That was the unspoken agreement between them and their father. If he wanted to talk about how he was feeling, he'd initiate that conversation. He didn't want them asking. He didn't take their *not* asking as a sign they didn't care but as respecting his wishes. He didn't want pain to dominate their relationship. It had consequences, but, as he put it, so did everything in life. He didn't minimize his condition, but he did what he could to manage it in ways that suited him. Acupuncture, yoga, physical therapy, relaxation techniques. Anything to keep him off prescription pain medication.

"Anything else?" her brother asked her.

"Just blueberry related."

He grinned at her. "Take them if you'd like."

"I'll leave a quart for you to give away, unless you get the unlikely urge to bake. I'll freeze at least one quart and make a pie at Thanksgiving."

"Works for me, but there's no chance I'll get the urge to bake." Lucas was visibly more relaxed. "I'll let you know if I hear from Granddad. Keep me posted as you're able, okay?"

She promised she would. She grabbed her two quarts of blueberries and followed him through the kitchen to the office, in the front room where their grandfather had launched Sharpe Fine Art Recovery as a young museum guard and the son of Irish immigrant domestics. Lucas said goodbye and headed upstairs to his office overlooking the water. Colin had gone outside to wait. Ginny Bosko, the newly hired receptionist, confirmed Lucas's version of her story and nodded when Emma showed her Verity's photo. "That's her. That's the woman who was here on Friday." Ginny was in her early twenties, with a strong interest in taking on more administrative duties at Sharpe Fine Art Recovery. "It's good to finally meet you and Agent Donovan."

Emma thanked her and joined Colin out front. He squinted at her in the sunlight. "You came out of this with blueberries."

"They're still warm from the sun."

"I can smell the pie already."

"The Blackwoods rented the last house between the village and the convent."

He nodded. "I know the one."

A stiff breeze caught the ends of Emma's hair and whipped a few strands into her face. She brushed them aside, and Colin noticed her eyes had taken on the blues of the ocean in front of her. Waves washed onto seaweed-covered rocks and submerged tide pools. He was familiar with this stretch of jagged Maine coastline. A trail led through rugosa-rose bushes down to a cove formed, in part, by the small peninsula that belonged to the Sisters of the Joyful Heart. Its buildings weren't visible from where he and Emma stood.

"I haven't been out here in a long time," she said. "I used to take a trail down the hill from the convent, through the woods. It connected with this trail. I'd walk out here and into the village. My father's route in reverse."

"Were you sneaking out of the convent?"

"No. Thinking."

Colin wasn't surprised. She was analytical, thoughtful. He was more reactive, tended to rely on his instincts, tempered by training and experience. Emma could jump into action when necessary.

"I'd visit my parents in the village, walk out to Ocean Ave. to see Lucas, get an ice cream. Sometimes I'd kayak here in the cove."

"In your nun's habit?"

"It was very practical."

"More than this suit. If I'd known you back then, I could have shown you my favorite spots to kayak."

She smiled at him. "I bet you could have."

"Even if I thought you were cute, I'd have respected you as Sister Brigid." He nodded toward the convent, a former Victorian estate the Sisters of the Joyful Heart had purchased decades ago. It'd been crumbling, but they'd gone to work, transforming it bit by bit into the restful, beautiful place it was now. "Who knows, maybe we're dealing with forger nuns."

Emma sighed. "I appreciate your sense of humor. I do."

He grinned at her. "We make a good team."

No argument from her. "We don't know if Verity Blackwood's questions about forgeries have anything to do with her overdose or Graham's decision to stay here—or with Tamara McDermott's behavior."

"Could be a husband-wife situation—a fight over money, art, duplicity, secrets." Colin shrugged, turning away from the water. "Interesting they chose this rental house."

They'd parked in a turnaround on the narrow dead-end road. The house was modern with decks and floor-to-ceiling windows. The ocean views alone would guarantee a high rental or selling price. Emma started across the road. Colin fell in behind her. They stopped at a navy blue Mercedes SUV in the driveway. "Graham's rental," Emma said.

Colin peered through the driver's window. He could see plastic water bottles, a rental agreement, an orange rain jacket. Nothing out of the ordinary.

"Colin." Emma stared at the ground between the car and the house. "That's a syringe."

He moved in closer to her. The syringe lay in the grass by the driveway, as if someone had dropped it on the way inside. "Drugs?"

"Oliver said it looked as if Verity took pills. He didn't see any syringes in her hotel room."

"Maybe the police found some when they searched it."

She stood straight, another gust of wind blowing through her hair. "I suppose Verity could have injected herself somewhere else and tossed the evidence before she arrived at the hotel, but if it was enough for an overdose—" Emma shook her head. "I doubt that's what happened."

"Pills and an injection, maybe. Add a glass of wine, and you've got a deadly opioid nightcap."

"Or she does pills and Graham does injections."

They could speculate the rest of the day. Colin left the syringe where it was and stepped onto a stone walk that led to a side entrance. The door stood wide open. There wasn't a screen door. "I see it," Emma said behind him.

He stood in the doorway. "Mr. Blackwood? Graham? It's Special Agent Colin Donovan with the FBI. I'm with Special Agent Emma Sharpe. We'd like to talk to you. Make sure you're okay."

No response. Colin called again. Still nothing. He glanced at Emma, and she nodded. With the syringe, and Verity

Blackwood fighting for her life in a London hospital, they went into the house.

They checked the lower level. Two bedrooms, shared bath, utility room. Untouched, from the looks of them. They returned to the side entrance and headed up open stairs to the main level. They came directly to a large living-dining room with tall windows and glass doors opening onto a deck that took advantage of the location with its views of the ocean. The only signs anyone had been there were a few out-of-place pillows and rumpled cushions on a large sectional. A dining table, which seated eight, appeared untouched. The kitchen, off the dining area, had a few more signs of life. Coffee mug in the sink, stray grounds and toast crumbs on the counter, gray hoodie hanging on the back of a bar stool.

They didn't linger, instead continuing down a short hall to the master suite. It had windows on three sides, including the front with its ocean view, but the shades were drawn. A suitcase was open on the bed, empty, as if ready for its owner to pack up. A man's clothes were neatly stacked on the bed next to the suitcase. Colin glanced in the master bathroom. Used white towels were draped on the side of the tub and over the door to the separate shower. Shaving gear and other personal items were in a kit open on the sink, ready to be zipped up for packing.

"House is clear," Emma said. "Where's our British tourist?"

They returned to the main room. Colin looked out at the water, choppy with the stiffening breeze ahead of the cold front. No intruder, no one in distress, no drugs out in the open. "It's a nice spot. Naturalized yard in back. Ocean in front. Dead end, so no passing traffic."

Emma stood next to him. "It's early enough he could be taking a spin on a kayak before heading to Boston and a long flight to London."

"That's what I'd do. Is it what Graham Blackwood would do?"

"He hasn't booked his return flight yet. I don't have a good sense of him. The cove is a great spot for kayaking."

They headed back down the stairs and out the side door. They checked a small shed, which, too, stood open. It contained the usual paraphernalia of a Maine summer home.

Emma pointed at a bright orange sit-on-top kayak leaned up against a wall. "Only one kayak. Verity told my father there were two kayaks. Maybe Kevin will have reports of injured kayakers?"

"Yeah. I'll call him in a sec."

She ducked out of the shed. Colin walked with her across the narrow road to the water's edge. He looked down the road toward the village. She looked toward the convent.

Nothing.

"Car's here," Colin said. "If Graham took off on a kayak, he must have launched from close by the house."

"Unless someone picked him up, or stole the kayak, or he wants us to think he's disappeared or—" Emma sighed. "Or aliens beamed him up to their spaceship."

"There's always that."

"If he launched here and he's inexperienced, I would think he wouldn't go too far beyond the cove. It gets rough out toward the tip of the peninsula. It's possible he could have paddled toward the village, but why would he?"

"It'd be a haul," Colin said. "Then again, he isn't here. The kayak in the shed has good stability for ocean conditions. It wouldn't tip over easily. The weather's been decent the past few days. Graham wouldn't have encountered difficult conditions."

"No fog, even," Emma said.

"I've plucked dozens of kayakers out of the water after they got caught in unexpected fog. Kevin has, too. That's not what happened to Graham Blackwood."

"Going to call Kevin now?"

Colin already had his phone out. He gave his brother, a state marine patrol officer, the basics. "Be there in five," Kevin said. He'd get in touch with the local police, too.

Emma had her arms crossed on her chest. She stood on a boulder above the swirling tide. "Are we dealing with a kayak trip gone wrong or something else?" She glanced back at Colin. "If Graham is out on the water, when did he leave? The wind could have caught the door, but why not lock up behind him? Was he in a hurry? Meeting someone? High on opioids?"

"A lot of questions," Colin said. "We'll get answers."

"Maybe a friend of the owners borrowed the kayak and Graham is somewhere else altogether." She stared at the cove as a swell broke onto shore. "Maybe we'll find Graham having a picnic on the rocks. Maybe he walked into the village to buy himself a moose T-shirt."

"Better than getting high on opioids and landing himself in real trouble."

"Where's our prosecutor? She could have stopped here on the way to Nova Scotia to talk to Graham. Kevin and the local police will check, see if anyone noticed her, her rental car—it's not as noticeable as Graham's Mercedes, but this is a quiet area. It might have stood out. Not many people out on the water now. I don't blame them. I wouldn't want to be out on these waves." She angled Colin a look. "I bet you wouldn't mind."

"Not on a day like today. In November, I'd probably mind. What do you want to do, Emma?"

She stepped down from her boulder onto the road. "I'll go up to the convent."

"Do you want to take the car?"

She shook her head. "It's not far. I'll walk."

"If you wait until Kevin gets here, I'll go with you."

"If I wait, he's not going to want me to go up there."

"There's that." Colin decided not to argue with her. "I'll fill Kevin in. He'll get it. The sisters lost one of their own less than a year ago. They won't take well to a man missing so close to them."

"No, they won't," Emma said, her back already to him as she started down the trail toward the cove and her old convent.

12

Sister Cecilia Catherine Rousseau stared at the dense pine and spruce trees on the steep hillside just outside the main entrance to the Sisters of the Joyful Heart convent. Her breathing was shallow, her blue eyes wide with dread, even fear. Emma understood. The young religious sister—her friend—still had scars, physical and emotional, after surviving capture and torture by a murderer last fall, just weeks before she professed her final vows. Her faith, her work as an art educator and her daily routines at the convent—gardening, food prep and cleanup, meditation, prayers, singing—all helped, but healing took time. "This missing kayaker," she said. "Are you worried he's come to harm?"

"We just want to find him. We don't know what's happened."

Sister Cecilia nodded. It was obvious she knew there was more to it. She wore a simple dove-gray tunic and skirt, with thick-soled sandals. A wide black headband held back her white-blond hair. "He's there," she whispered. "I know he is. I can feel it."

She'd been at the main gate when Emma had arrived and explained the situation, and she'd seized on it, plunging along the outside of the black-iron fence that enclosed the convent. They'd stopped at a path that would take them straight downhill to the trail Emma's father had taken on Saturday when he met up with Verity Blackwood.

"It's okay, Cecilia," Emma said quietly. "You can stay here. You don't need to go with me."

"No. I want to go."

"If you want to tell Mother Natalie—"

"She's not here. She won't be back until late. I can go."

"We can go back to the convent."

"No—no, I want to help. I know these woods. I take the trail and wander in the woods all the time to gather things for my art classes. Pinecones, ferns, sticks, leaves—whatever I see provided it's sustainable. I've been learning about mushrooms, but I don't trust myself yet to gather them for eating. It'll be wonderful when I'm confident I know what I'm doing, won't it?"

Emma smiled. "It will be."

She laughed, her pale cheeks taking on a bit of color. "I'll have an expert confirm my haul before I serve mushroom soup to anyone." Her laughter faded, and she took a small step onto the path. "You'd think it's Mordor and we're Sam and Frodo. I'd say I'm more Sam and you're more Frodo, wouldn't you?"

"I don't know about that."

"I met your missing kayaker's wife. She was at the shop on Friday. I don't know her name, but she told me she and her husband had rented the house by the cove and wanted to go kayaking. But she's not missing?"

"No, she's not missing. We don't know for sure he's missing, either."

"But you're looking for him."

"We want to talk to him," Emma said.

"I pointed out your father to her—the wife. Well, she asked me if he was Timothy Sharpe, and I said yes. That was all right, wasn't it?"

"Cecilia—"

"She was gracious, interested in everything—she said she'd heard about us through a friend. I was under the impression she stopped in for that reason rather than as a passerby. She was perhaps a bit self-conscious, but that's not unusual. People are often self-conscious around religious sisters." She grasped her tunic at her chest. "We should go. I need to know."

She plunged down the trail, the first few yards covered with pine needles. Emma dove in after her. Sister Cecilia wasn't impeded by her skirt, lifting the hem as she descended the steep, rough trail, navigating protruding tree roots, rocks, pine needles, pinecones and no small measure of sharp curves. She was going faster than was safe or necessary.

After about a hundred yards, she slowed, pausing at a gnarly spruce sapling. "Sorry." She was breathing hard, her face flushed. "I'd never make a good FBI agent, I'm afraid. I got thinking about orcs."

Emma smiled. "It's that spider that grabbed Frodo that'd get me running."

They both laughed, a short-lived moment of levity. Cecilia pointed ahead, to the spot where their shortcut intersected with the main trail from the cove. Bear right, they'd end up back at the house the Blackwoods had rented. Bear left, they'd end up at the old stone gazebo. "Which way, Emma?"

"I'd like to go out to the gazebo. You can go back—"

"No. I'll go with you. The trail's rough in spots—not many hikers make it as far as the gazebo. Technically it's on convent land, but I doubt we'll ever do anything with it." Sister Cecilia adjusted her wide headband and flicked perspiration off her brow. "It's fairly isolated out here and the trees are dense. It can get spooky, but I promise not to do anything impulsive."

"Good idea." Emma reached for her phone. "I'll let Colin know where we are."

Sister Cecilia shook her head. "You won't get a signal

here. You might have a better chance at the gazebo." She paused, gazing at the narrow trail. "It'll settle my mind, just to know…this kayaker…"

"Stay close, okay?" Emma smiled, hoping to reassure her friend. "I haven't been out here in a long time. I'm not used to these trails."

Emma touched Sister Cecilia's upper arm a few yards from the gazebo. "Hold on, Sister."

She nodded. "I see it."

A bright red ocean kayak was wedged between two boulders below the trail, a few yards from the gazebo, a sturdy hexagon designed as a place to relax and take in the view, the ocean air. The kayak was partially submerged, buffeted by the incoming tide. With the angle of the rocky coast and the tall evergreens, it wouldn't be easily seen by passing boats.

"Emma…is it your missing kayak?"

"It could be the twin of the kayak Colin and I found at the rental house."

She crept down the steep hill toward the wedged kayak. Where was the paddle? Had there been a dry pack? If so, where was it? Most important, where was the paddler? It had to be Graham Blackwood.

"It's a tricky spot," Sister Cecilia said from the trail. "If the paddler ran into difficulty… I hate to think what could have happened."

The kayak looked wedged tightly enough it wouldn't dislodge in the rising tide. How long had it been out here? Had it endured more than one tide cycle? Emma scanned the immediate area—rocks, pine needles, ferns, exposed tree roots—but she didn't see the paddle, a life vest, an emergency whistle or any other gear.

And no signs of anyone having crawled up to the trail.

She checked her phone. Still no decent signal. She rejoined Sister Cecilia, whose face, red with exertion and heat two minutes ago, had lost some of its color. "Let's continue to the gazebo and see if I can get a call or a text out," Emma said.

Sister Cecilia nodded. "If there's no body, it could mean your missing kayaker is okay."

Or it could mean he'd drowned and his body hadn't turned up yet, but Sister Cecilia was accustomed to life on the water. Emma didn't need to tell her the grim possibilities.

They continued to the stone gazebo, part of the original nineteenth-century estate. It occupied a prominent spot almost at the tip of the peninsula, on an outcropping thirty feet above the sea. Emma stood on the edge of the sheer rock face and checked her phone. A seagull caught her eye to her right, down by the water. It flew up and away, and then she saw a body, not quite in the water. A man. Obviously dead.

Next to her, Sister Cecilia gasped. Her first impulse was to rush to help, but Emma caught her by the elbow. "He's beyond our help, Sister. It's best we wait for the police."

"Aren't you—"

"The state and local police will lead the death investigation."

"It's him, isn't it, Emma? The man you're looking for. Graham Blackwood."

"It appears to be."

He lay sprawled facedown among the ubiquitous rocks on this part of the Maine coast. He wouldn't be easily visible from either the trail or the gazebo, or even from passing boats. He wore street clothes—khakis, a T-shirt, sport sandals—rather than swimming trunks or a wet suit. He wasn't wearing a life vest. Emma spotted one bobbing in the water a few yards from Graham's body. Had he taken it off or never put it on? The wind kept any odors from the body from reaching them, but at this distance, she couldn't tell how long he'd been out here.

Sister Cecilia stared down at the body as a wave crashed on the rocks, spraying salt water up toward them. "He wouldn't be the first kayaker to underestimate the conditions out here, but I don't think anyone's ever..." She took in a breath. "Is Colin meeting us here?"

"That's the plan."

Emma tried texting him. Found GB dead by gazebo.

She turned to Sister Cecilia. "Why don't you sit down?" She pointed to a knee-high boulder next to them. "You can look out toward the gazebo." In other words, away from the body. "It won't be long until the police get here."

"Is this a crime scene now, Emma?"

"There'll be an investigation to determine how Mr. Blackwood died. The police will want to speak with you."

Sister Cecilia nodded. "I understand."

An opioid overdose, a mishap, homicide, suicide—nothing could be ruled in or out at this point. Emma remained standing, phone in hand. Why had Graham paddled out here? Had he known about the gazebo? It wasn't on a map or tourist brochure. He could probably see it from his rental house with a set of binoculars.

She felt her phone vibrate and saw Colin had responded to her text. On our way. Ten minutes.

Knowing the Donovan brothers, they'd get here in five.

Sister Cecilia gazed up at the sun, slanting through clouds, and whispered a prayer. The only sounds were the wind in the trees, waves, a distant seagull. She turned, the knife scar from last fall visible on her arm. "'Fill us at daybreak with your love that all our days we may sing for joy.'"

Emma felt her throat tighten. She knew the words Sister

Cecilia recited. They were the motto of the Sisters of the Joyful Heart, taken from Psalm 90. "I'm sorry, Sister."

"No, don't be. It's good I was with you." She paused, staring down at the ground. "I knew he was here."

"Any specific reason for that, or just gut instinct?"

"I heard him."

Colin and Kevin Donovan arrived in under five minutes, as Emma predicted.

An awful ending to their search for Graham Blackwood.

Kevin took charge. He walked up to the gazebo and made calls. The state and local police would confirm the identity of the deceased and lead the death investigation. They'd contact investigators in England who would see to the notification of next of kin—his wife, fighting for her own life in a London hospital.

"The gazebo's not known as a teen or drug hangout," Colin said as he stood next to Emma. "What do you think, does Graham paddle out here to clear his head and gets in trouble because he's inexperienced? Bangs up against the rocks, falls out of the kayak, loses his paddle, hits his head."

"Why no life vest? You always wear one."

"Didn't bother. Cocky. It's hot. Or lands the kayak on the rocks, takes off the vest, wave catches the kayak and he goes after it—falls, and so on."

"I'm not surprised no one saw him out here, even if he struggled and called for help." Emma looked down toward the kayak. "What if he was meeting someone here?"

"You're thinking about Tamara McDermott," Colin said.

"I'm still thinking she could have stopped up here to see Graham. Adalyn told her about Stefan Petrescu at brunch and said her mother was upset. I can see Tamara wanting to talk to him. Maybe he told her on Saturday at the airport he wasn't going back to London with Verity and mentioned where he's staying. She decides to ask him about Stefan—maybe tell him and his wife to stay out of her daughter's life until police made an arrest. Or just get a gauge on Adalyn's new friends."

"Why meet here instead of a cute coffee shop in the village?"

"Maybe Tamara doesn't like cute coffee shops."

"Maybe Graham was meeting someone to buy drugs. Well, we know better than to waste time speculating. It's possible a witness will come forward who saw him on the water before he got in trouble. It could happen fast. Paddling along one minute, bashed up against the rocks the next." Colin rubbed a palm through his hair, sweat dripping down his temples from his hustle to get here as quickly as possible. "I was hoping we'd find him high on opioids and just have to get him cleaned up and on his way home to his wife."

Kevin walked back down the trail from the gazebo. He started to say something to Sister Cecilia, but she shook her head and told him she was holding her own. In a few more minutes, the local police arrived, quickly followed by state detectives. Whatever their British tourist had been up to out here, Emma doubted he'd simply curled up and died of a drug overdose, even if drugs proved to be a contributing factor to his death. The autopsy would determine cause of death and whether other factors were involved—drugs, hypothermia, preexisting medical issues. There was much work to be done.

After giving their statements, Emma walked with Sister Cecilia back up the narrow trail to the convent. They didn't speak until they reached the fence. Sister Cecilia nodded to the wooded hillside. "I told Colin's brother... Kevin... I told him I was investigating wild mushrooms yesterday when I heard a man's voice down the hill through the trees. It was indistinct—I couldn't make out what he was saying. He must have been speaking to someone, but I didn't hear a second voice, maybe because it was too low or didn't carry as well. I thought he was in a boat in the cove—rather than on the trail. I didn't detect any distress or anger. I had no reason to investigate or call the police."

"It might not have been Graham Blackwood, Cecilia."

"I wish I'd gone to check, but the heat and mosquitoes drove me away." She attempted a smile. "I postponed my mushroom education for another day."

"I can walk with you to the motherhouse—"

She shook her head. "No, you have work to do. I'm so sorry about today, Emma. I know what you do can be challenging. Give Colin my best, won't you?"

Emma didn't argue with her. She watched her friend go through the convent gate. She was pale and subdued, but she was where she needed to be—with her small order of religious sisters, resuming her routines and her life at their quiet convent. Emma knew their friendship could go only so far. Sister Cecilia had professed vows that guided her life. When Emma left the Sisters of the Joyful Heart, she'd taken everything she'd learned during her time as a novice with her, along with countless good memories, but she'd never looked back. She'd never doubted her decision to pull off her modified habit for the last time, say goodbye to Sister Brigid and walk through the convent gate into a new life—the life she had now, with Colin.

He drove up to the gate and rolled down his window, his ocean blue-gray eyes on her. "You set?"

She nodded. "Set."

"Rock Point?"

His hometown, a struggling fishing village a few miles up the coast from Heron's Cove. She climbed into the passenger seat. They'd stop at his house—*their* house—and put the blue-berries her father had given her in the refrigerator, and then head to Hurley's, a comfort-food restaurant on the harbor.

Chowder, friends, family.

They were what both she and Colin needed now.

13

Wendell Sharpe gazed up at the late-day sky, relishing the quiet and peace of this spot on the south Irish coast. He could hear the rhythmic wash of the sea across the garden, past an ancient stone wall. Behind him, the O'Byrne House Hotel was bustling. The boutique hotel, once the home of its current owner's uncle, John O'Byrne, was the site of a celebrated, brazen art theft a decade ago—Oliver York's first heist, for which no arrest was pending nor would ever come about. Few people even knew his secret identity as a thief.

"An interesting, complex man, our Oliver," Aoife O'Byrne said across the small metal table.

Wendell smiled at her. She was a beautiful, brilliant artist herself. "Reading my mind, are you?"

"You have that *I'm thinking about my wily art thief* look about you."

He didn't doubt it. He'd chased Oliver for years but hadn't known his identity until recently. Had the Englishman paid enough for his crimes? In Wendell's world, yes. MI5 was extracting retribution from him, and he'd returned the art intact over the winter, save for an unsigned landscape he'd pinched from the O'Byrne drawing room. It was of a local scene, undoubtedly painted by Aoife O'Byrne long before she'd become something of an international sensation.

Kitty O'Byrne, Aoife's older sister, had renovated their uncle's house in the tiny Irish hamlet of Declan's Cross and converted it into a popular boutique hotel. It was booked solid tonight, packed with Irish and American guests. The Americans included a dozen cyclists on a two-night stay on their tour of the south and the west of Ireland. Wendell figured he'd have enjoyed a bike tour back in the day. He liked to walk, even now in his eighties—maybe especially now. This part of the Irish coast offered countless trails and lanes for a good wander.

But that wasn't why he was here.

He'd flown from London to Cork instead of home to Dublin and taken a taxi to Declan's Cross with the dead-certain knowledge this was where he needed to be.

He wasn't like that, really. He was a feet-flat-on-the-floor type. Pragmatic, driven by facts and evidence more than instinct. He'd never been one to hear voices—deities, saints, fairies. When he was a boy, his mother had told him tales about fairies and old Ireland, the one she'd known as a girl. Wendell had never been convinced his mother had believed in banshees, leprechauns, pookas and the rest, but maybe she had.

Ah, he missed her. She'd died when he was in his twenties, but it might have been yesterday.

He was aware of Aoife watching him with concern.

Everything about Verity Blackwood's overdose and Graham Blackwood's death bothered him.

Everything.

Oliver had told him about Graham. *I'm not sure I'm supposed to know.*

That meant Henrietta Balfour or his MI5 handler had told him. Wendell had nothing to add to what he'd told the detectives last night in London, but they had his contact information if they wanted to reach him. Now that Verity's husband was dead, they might.

The police in Maine sure as hell knew how to reach him. His FBI granddaughter would see to it.

Emma and a young nun found him, Wendell.

Oliver had sounded shaken.

Drugs. Opioids. Overdoses.

Not Wendell's world, not his area of expertise.

"My family worries about me if I set foot out of Dublin," he said.

"By yourself," Aoife said. "With someone, perhaps they wouldn't worry so much."

"A chaperone?" He snorted. "That'll be the day. You going to rat me out?"

Aoife smiled, her very blue eyes shining with amusement. "That's not my role in the lives of the Sharpe family, is it?"

"Or anyone's life. You're not a snitch. You've never said you painted that one landscape that remains unreturned."

"It's where it's meant to be," she said.

"You think it speaks to our thief's soul."

"Perhaps."

Wendell raised his whiskey glass. He and Aoife had finished the last of a bottle of Bracken 12 year old. His family kept tabs on him now that he was in his eighties. His eightieth birthday had flipped their worry switch. He'd gone from the eccentric private art detective, father and grandfather on his own in Dublin, no problem, no one bugging him to make sure he hadn't passed out on the bathroom floor, to his family performing regular "wellness checks," as his daughter-in-law called them. It was one of those things in life that was both annoying and comforting—not that they could do much to help from Maine or Boston if he wandered off and couldn't find his way home.

Home being his place in Dublin.

He'd been born in Ireland and lived there until the age of two, but he'd returned sixteen years ago to open up offices in Dublin. His wife had died. He'd needed to make a big change in his life. He'd assumed he'd go home to Heron's Cove one day, but in the weeks before Emma and Colin's June wedding—on his last visit to Maine—he'd discovered it was the other way around. He'd come home to Ireland. He'd die here, when the time came.

"Do you know anything about Fletcher Campbell?" he asked.

Aoife threw one leg over the other and leaned forward. "An intriguing non sequitur. He's a well-known American painter."

"What's he like?"

"We've never met."

"Reputation," Wendell said, sensing she was stalling.

"He's rumored to have an eye for women not his wife. Fletch the Lech. That's what people call him behind his back, not that he'd care. I've never understood artists who use creativity as an excuse for their libertine ways."

"The guy's a pig like any other pig. But no denying he's a great artist?"

"We'll see if his work stands the test of time." She leaned back, looking a bit guilty. "I suppose we should use the past tense. I understand he has advanced Alzheimer's."

"That's what I hear, too," Wendell said. "Any rumors the Campbells were involved in drugs?"

"No, but it wouldn't surprise me. Every rumor I have heard suggests both Fletcher and Ophelia, his wife, were self-indulgent hedonists. I try not to judge, but that lifestyle is so beyond what I can fathom."

Wendell drank more of his whiskey. It was damn good stuff. He knew he probably should stick to enjoying his evening and never mind about the Campbells, but Oliver had asked about them. "You live a fairly solitary life yourself," he said.

Aoife glanced away. "I have Kitty, my nephew, friends." She shifted back to Wendell. "You're in a mood, aren't you? Finish your whiskey, get a good night's sleep, indulge in a full Irish breakfast and then go home to Dublin and have a pint with the lads. It's not a bad thing to retire, you know. You can enjoy your status as an art detective legend."

"For the love of Mary, now I know I've got one foot in the grave."

She laughed. "An art detective of great charm, knowledge and vigor. How's that?"

"Better. Ever hear rumors of forgeries and the Campbells?"

"Oh, my, no, never."

"Such rumors alone could distort the market for their work," Wendell said.

Any spark faded from Aoife's eyes. "Yes, they could. It's awkward to say, but with Ophelia's death and now Fletcher's illness, there won't be any more art from them, and that, as you know, is likely to drive up the value of their body of work, particularly Fletcher's since he's more highly regarded."

"The fire at his painting studio in the US destroyed some of their inventory."

Aoife shuddered. "Terrible to think about. I don't care if my work goes up in price after I'm gone. I won't be around for it to matter. But losing unfinished or recently finished work while I'm here—I wouldn't like that at all."

"But you'd get through it," Wendell said.

"I would."

"You're resilient. Speaking of which, have you heard from our priest friend lately?"

"No," she said, perhaps too quickly.

Wendell decided not to push her. There was something

there between Aoife O'Byrne and Finian Bracken, an Irish priest who'd found his way to a small parish in the struggling fishing village of Rock Point, Maine. Colin Donovan's hometown. "Father Bracken officiated at Emma and Colin's wedding." Aoife knew that, of course. "I'm sorry I didn't stay for it."

"They understood, Wendell. Everyone did."

"And it's done now."

Aoife got up and came around the table to kiss him on the cheek. "Finding that poor woman last night was a shock. Take care, okay? Sean Murphy is at the farm. I'm sure he'll be happy to drive you back up to Dublin. You're just staying the night, aren't you?"

"Just the night," Wendell said. "I don't know about a three-hour drive with an Irish detective."

Aoife grinned. "Oh, no worries, Sean can probably get you to Dublin in two-and-a-half hours."

She winked and headed back into the hotel.

Sean Murphy owned a farm in Declan's Cross and was engaged to Aoife's sister, Kitty, but he was also a senior garda detective in Dublin. He and Finian Bracken were good friends, dating back to Sean's investigation into the untimely deaths of Finian's wife and two young daughters in a sailing accident off the Irish coast.

Wendell tossed the rest of his whiskey into the grass next to the stone patio. Anathema, but finishing it would be a mistake tonight. He felt his weariness straight to his bones. He got to his feet, noticing rabbits hopping in the garden. This part of the south Irish coast was Saint Declan country. He was a healer credited with founding Ireland's first Christian settlement. Some said he was a contemporary of or even predated Saint Patrick. Ruins, holy wells, trails and no small number of miracles were a tribute to his mark in the region more than fifteen hundred years ago.

What mark will I leave?

Wendell shook off the question. He *was* in a mood. He wasn't sure what had gripped him since he'd switched his flight from Dublin to Cork, knowing he had to be here in Declan's Cross. It wasn't fear of his own death. He'd seen his wife die. He'd held her hand as she'd taken her last breath, and he'd thought...*why can't I go with her?*

He left the stone patio, zipping up his lightweight jacket as he slipped into the village with its brightly painted houses and shops.

The brisk evening air and a good walk.

All he needed. He'd be fine by morning.

Wendell expected to turn around after a short walk, but he kept going, past the bookshop and up the hill onto the headland above the village. He worked up a sweat, and his heart was racing by the time he reached the open, grass-covered hill at the tip of the headland. Three ornately carved stone Celtic crosses—taller than he was—commanded an impressive view of the sea. It was dusk now, the light slowly leaking out of the summer sky. He couldn't linger or for sure someone back at the hotel would sound the alarm.

The crosses, an old church ruin, lichen-covered gravestones, pasture, sheep and sea—this was the scene depicted in the one painting Oliver York hadn't returned to its owner. Although Wendell had never seen it, he was convinced it was an early Aoife O'Byrne work.

And this was the spot where Oliver had stayed that November night a decade ago, hiding with his loot, keeping his demons at bay.

Or maybe not. Maybe his demons had followed him out

here. The ruins were similar to the ones he'd escaped as a traumatized eight-year-old.

Two Jack Butler Yeats Irish landscapes, an early, unsigned Aoife O'Byrne landscape and a silver Celtic cross commemorating Saint Declan. Not a bad haul for a night's work, but Oliver had never profited. The stolen art was back where it belonged, in the O'Byrne House drawing room and above the mantel in the lounge. Except for Aoife's painting, of course.

Wendell touched the stone of the first cross, carved with knots, circles and swirls and familiar symbols that represented Saint Declan. His staff, his bell, the boulder that had led him to Ardmore, where he'd built his monastery. To this day, the faithful would come to Ardmore for Saint Declan's healing miracles, particularly with back ailments. Wendell had mentioned it to his son. Could the waters of a holy well or the purported powers of an unusual boulder be any less worthy than some of the other treatments Timothy had pursued over the years? What if one of them helped him, for whatever reason?

As the light faded, Wendell heard a cry that went straight to his bones. It wasn't a seagull or another seabird, or a sea creature—a porpoise, a whale, a seal.

He knew what it was, this strange, terrible keening.

A warning, an alert.

A promise of death coming to someone he loved.

The cry of a solitary banshee.

I'm from the ancient families of Ireland, Wendell. That means you are, too.

His mother, many decades ago. She'd been a hardworking woman. He'd always appreciated her grit and intelligence, but never more so than in his old age. She'd seen so much of life by twenty, when she'd married his father.

Once you hear the wail of a banshee, my boy, you'll know it's real.

He didn't doubt his mother's sincerity, but he didn't believe in such things.

Yet here it was.

The wailing and keening stopped. His soul ached. He held back tears. He exhaled, hoping never to hear such an eerie sound again, whatever its source, whatever its meaning. He walked down the hill and climbed over an ancient stone wall, covered with moss, wildflowers and small trees, out to the lane. He wished now he hadn't come this far, but maybe he'd been drawn up here by the banshee.

"I should have finished my whiskey."

Or had less of it, perhaps.

His attempt at humor didn't help. The lane meandered through a pasture marked off with barbed wire. He clicked his tongue, and a fat sheep lumbered to him. He patted her soft wool. "I don't have anything for you, lass. I'm not here for you. I'm here for myself."

She didn't seem to mind. He left her and continued on his way. If it had been a banshee he'd heard and it had cried for him, he hoped he could wait until he got back to Dublin and die in his own bed.

But as he descended into the village, he knew the banshee hadn't warned of his death. Emma? Was she in danger? He couldn't bear the thought.

"Must have been a trick of the wind."

He wasn't one to mutter to himself, but the night called for it.

When he reached the hotel, he went in through the front door and straight up the stairs, past the drawing room where the two Jack Butler Yeats paintings were back on the walls. There were more recent works by Aoife O'Byrne, too. Rainbows, sunsets and sunrises, seascapes, laundry hanging on a line—the moodiness, the colors, the eye and the skill of the artist lifted her ordinary Irish scenes into the extraordinary.

Or so people told him. Wendell just liked them.

When he entered his room and shut the door, he felt no sense of relief, no easing of whatever had gripped his soul since discovering Verity Blackwood last night.

It was quiet, at least. No banshee.

Housekeeping had been in and done the turndown. Shades and drapes pulled, throw pillows and bedspread placed on a chair, towels changed. Soft music played on the radio. Wendell had made sure he wasn't in any of the rooms Emma and Colin had shared during their visits to Declan's Cross. He hadn't wanted *that* image swirling in his head. They were a pair, suited to each other even if no one, including him, would have put them together. He believed to his core that Colin would love, protect and cherish Emma to the end of his days.

As she would him.

Wendell went to the windows and peeked behind a heavy drape. A wisp of a gray cloud had slipped into the evening sky, appropriate somehow, he thought. He let the drape fall back into place and decided he'd skip a nightcap, the piano in the lounge and laughs with other guests and get some sleep, or at least try.

14

Rock Point, Maine

Finian Bracken had seen to whiskey being poured and de-livered to his table by the windows at Hurley's, a fixture on Rock Point harbor. Colin noticed three glasses as he and Emma joined their Irish friend. "I took the liberty when I saw you come through the door," Finian said. He was in his usual clerical garb, his Kerry accent as rich as it had been his first day in Maine just over a year ago. "I was able to talk Johnny Hurley into stocking a new Bracken Distillers expression. It's been a day, hasn't it?"

Colin sat next to Emma, across from Finian. A few sips of the latest Bracken Distillers whiskey, sent by Declan Bracken, Finian's twin brother in Ireland, were in order. They'd started the distillery together in their early twenties, long before Finian had considered becoming a priest.

Finian had already heard about the discovery of a body out by the convent. Colin wasn't surprised. He picked up his glass. "It's been a hell of a day, Fin."

"How is Sister Cecilia?"

"Shaken but coping," Emma said.

Finian nodded, his eyes serious, warm with compassion. "I'll go see her tomorrow."

He had training in helping people through trauma and his own experience with tragedy. Now, eight years after his wife

and two young daughters were killed in a freak sailing accident, he was the sole priest at Rock Point's struggling Roman
Catholic church. A one-year appointment had turned into
an indefinite stay. A whiskey man turned priest. It worked.
He was educating his FBI friends on the charms of whiskey,
particularly Irish whiskey, and upgrading their whiskey tastes
in the process. Colin sometimes thought it was part of rather
than in addition to Finian's priestly duties.

Finian raised his glass. *"Sláinte."*

"Sláinte," Colin said in unison with Emma as they raised
their glasses.

He heard the crack in her voice, noticed the strain in her
green eyes. He had considerable experience, given his undercover work, in hiding his true feelings, but finding Graham
Blackwood dead had affected him, too. A drug buy gone
bad? An accident, given his inexperience kayaking? Still no
answers, but Colin knew it was early in the investigation. If
Sister Cecilia had, in fact, heard Graham on Sunday while
searching for wild mushrooms, who had been with him? Tamara McDermott was a possibility. She'd have had time to
get there after she'd left Emma. It was a leap, but Colin wasn't
in charge of the death investigation. He could indulge leaps.
What if Tamara had gone to meet Graham and found him
dead? What if she'd killed him? Had she planned to get back
to Boston for her daughter's birthday dinner? Where the hell
was she now? Had Graham's killer grabbed her? Killed her?
Was her body out there for another young nun to discover?

Colin gulped his whiskey. It wasn't like him to bombard
himself with unanswerable questions.

Finian set his glass on the table. He had angular features,
clear, penetrating blue eyes and an amiable manner that made
it easy to forget his own suffering, the depths of his knowledge after six years in seminary and just how damn stubborn

he could be. He was opinionated about whiskey. In his view, after years maturing in a barrel, a good whiskey deserved to be enjoyed on its own, without water or ice. That he and Colin had become fast friends was as unexpected as it was incontrovertible.

"We're not much company," Emma said. "Sorry."

Finian winked at her. "That's why we have whiskey." He ran a fingertip on the rim of his glass. "I have a message for you. Aoife O'Byrne called. She asked me to tell you she had whiskey and a chat with your grandfather."

"In Dublin? I thought she was still in Declan's Cross."

"She is. Wendell is there, too. He's staying at Kitty's hotel."

"Why?"

"He told Aoife to consider him off with the fairies."

"What's that supposed to mean?" Colin asked.

"She thinks finding this woman last night got to him. He asked Aoife about an American artist, Fletcher Campbell. Quite the rake, apparently. She felt guilty for gossiping since he's terminally ill now."

Emma sipped her whiskey. "My grandfather has a knack for getting people to tell him things."

Finian smiled. "I believe many of us have experienced that knack."

She set her glass on the table. "Thanks for letting us know. He didn't mention Declan's Cross to my father and brother, and he blew off my messages altogether. It's late in Ireland now. I'll call him tomorrow. At least he's with people who care about him."

As were they, Colin thought as he tuned in to their surroundings. Hurley's was more crowded than it would be in the dead of winter, but it wasn't a tourist hot spot. It was rustic, set up on pilings, allowing the tide to run under its floorboards. Its busy summer season helped it to stay open during winter. Out-of-town visitors discovered it by happenstance or word of mouth, not through any guidebook recommendations. Most of the food was okay. Some of it was amazing, particularly its doughnuts, chowders and fresh local fish. Right now, though, Colin was satisfied with his good Irish whiskey.

He got a text from Sam Padgett. TM is booked on Portland-to-Yarmouth CAT tomorrow.

Tamara McDermott booking the high-speed ferry made sense but Colin wasn't relieved by the message. It only confirmed what they'd learned about her plans to go to Nova Scotia, and provided a more specific time line. Sam would have someone at the ferry and checking area lodging. Colin didn't have to ask. He glanced at Emma, who'd received the same text. She set her phone aside and picked up her whiskey again. She didn't look relieved, either.

Colin responded to Sam. Thanks. You still at the office?

Yep. You?

Hurley's.

Lousy day. Later.

Colin realized he had no idea how Sam dealt with the aftermath of a day like today. They'd had a few beers and laughs together and Sam had been at their wedding in June, but he wasn't big on sharing anything except his opinions of New England life and weather. Colin swiped to his photos of Tamara McDermott and the Blackwoods. At this point, despite the situation with the Blackwoods, Tamara's vanishing act could be what her ex-husband and daughter had convinced themselves it was—an early departure for a planned vacation.

Colin showed Finian the photos, starting with the Blackwoods. "Do you recognize either of them, Fin?"

He shook his head. "No, sorry."

"What about her?" Colin swiped to Tamara McDermott. "Have you seen her before?"

"I haven't." Finian peered at the photo. "Is one of these photos of the person you found today? I don't know if it was a man or a woman."

Colin slipped his phone into his jacket. "Do you recognize the names Verity Blackwood, Graham Blackwood or Tamara McDermott?"

Finian frowned, then slowly shook his head. "It's disconcerting when I realize you know far more about a situation— a death—than you're telling me. Is there a reason I should know these people?"

"You're the local priest, and a local nun helped us find a body near the convent. Timothy Sharpe walks out there on a regular basis and ran into the woman Wendell found overdosed in London."

"Ah. I see."

No doubt he did. "Fin, if you have any information that can help us—"

"I wish I did."

Their waiter, the nephew of a lobsterman Colin knew, arrived at their table and took their orders for haddock chowder. Colin picked up his whiskey. "Has Oliver York been in touch lately?"

Finian didn't look as surprised as he might have. "Not in several weeks."

"You don't seem shocked I'm asking about him," Colin said.

"I've learned to take things as they come, given the work you and Emma do."

"But?"

"Wendell told Aoife that Oliver and Henrietta were with him last night. I haven't spoken with Oliver myself. I know you two have an unusual friendship—"

"Oliver's not my friend." Colin pointed his whiskey glass at Finian. "You two, though. You're friends."

"Does Oliver have friends?" Finian turned to Emma. "Do you consider him a friend, Emma?"

"He's likable," she said.

Finian smiled at her. "A diplomatic answer. I suppose Henrietta Balfour considers herself a friend. Oliver told me she can knock back the smokiest, peatiest Scotch without breaking a sweat."

"Sounds about right," Colin said.

They shifted the conversation to plans for Andy Donovan and Julianne Maroney's fall wedding. "They've settled on a church wedding followed by a reception at your parents' inn," Finian said.

Colin nodded. His parents had converted an old sea captain's house on the harbor into an inn. His father, a retired police officer, had taken to his role as innkeeper. He loved getting up early to make fresh muffins for their guests. Colin's mother was one of Finian's many parishioners who adored their Irish priest—Franny Maroney, Julianne's grandmother, was another. Colin couldn't think of any woman in Rock Point who didn't adore Finian Bracken.

"Frank and Rosemary insist they're delighted to have two sons marry in the same year," Finian added. "Andy says they've been lighting candles to make it happen. I wondered why your father has been coming to church. I expect Mike will be next. Kevin—he's on this death investigation?"

"Yes," Colin said without elaborating.

The chowders arrived, steaming, bursting with chunks of fresh haddock and potatoes, pats of butter melting into the milky broth. Perfection, Colin thought, noting the steam was turning Emma's cheeks a healthy pink. Chowder was what she needed. The weather was turning cooler, drier. A nice evening on the southern Maine coast. It was almost midnight in England and Ireland, but he'd have no problem getting Oliver out of bed to answer questions. Even if Emma had the patience to wait until morning, Colin didn't. To him, Oliver was an unrepentant serial art thief, no matter his tragic past and the return of the stolen art. Charming and cheeky, though, the man was hard to resist, and he *did* have contacts, insights and expertise that had helped British intelligence with multiple cases, including serious counterterrorism investigations.

They skipped dessert and limited themselves to one whiskey. Finian had walked to the harbor but turned down Colin's offer of a lift to the rectory, instead setting out across the small parking lot. "One day we'll have to bring him good news," Colin said, standing next to Emma.

"He married us in June and danced at the reception. That was a good day."

Colin took her hand and pulled her close. "It was a spectacular day."

"But you want to walk back with him."

He watched their solitary friend cross the parking lot and nodded. "See you back at the house."

"I'll take care of the blueberries."

Blueberries...their visit to Maine had started with freshly picked wild blueberries. Colin sighed, kissed her on the cheek and went to catch up with Finian.

Colin walked with Finian past small houses on the quiet streets above the harbor. "Maine summers are glorious," Finian said. "I'm sorry about this man who died, Colin. I'd rather you and Emma were in Rock Point for a pleasant break instead."

"Her father gave us two quarts of wild blueberries. Emma will enjoy them. He and Faye picked them this morning."

"That's good to hear."

Colin angled a look at his friend. "What, Fin?"

"Timothy Sharpe suffers from chronic pain. It's nothing you don't know. Sometimes it's worse."

"Lately?"

Finian sighed. "Worse. He manages, and then he'll experience breakthrough pain. That's what's happening now. Aoife thinks Wendell knows, or at least senses it."

"Interesting she called you," Colin said.

"She's the one who spoke to him. If it'd been Sean, he'd have called. Sean will take Wendell to Dublin in the morning. If he's hiding anything, Sean will get it out of him. Aoife didn't think he was. She thought he was simply melancholy."

"Finding a young woman near death can do that, and now her husband's dead." Colin left it there as they crossed a narrow street. "Ever think you misunderstood back when you decided to become a priest and God whispered, saying *Aoife O'Byrne* instead of *Father Fin*."

Finian glanced at him. "A calling doesn't work that way, Colin. At least it didn't for me. I also went through a rigorous discernment process."

"Who did the discerning?"

"Colin..."

"Sorry. I'm being an annoying ass when I'm trying to be a friend. I respect your calling, Fin. I respect that you took a vow, but it's not a prison sentence. You can change your mind."

"I'm where I'm meant to be."

"Don't say that because of me, Fin. Because of the work I do. Whether you leave the priesthood or stay, we'll be friends."

Finian paused in front of the rectory. "You're preparing for another undercover assignment."

"Emma and I found a dead man today. His wife's fighting for her life in London."

"If you'd like another drink, come in, but Emma will be waiting for you."

"She's tackling those blueberries."

Finian smiled. "Good night, my friend."

He walked to the side entrance of the rectory, a small Victorian house that needed work. St. Patrick's next door had been built in the nineteenth century as a Baptist church. It, too, needed work. Colin waited until Finian went inside, shutting the door behind him. He could feel his friend's loneliness. Discernment or no discernment, Finian Bracken was far from his home in Ireland—his twin brother who'd gone into the whiskey business with him, his three sisters, his nieces and nephews, friends, colleagues...and beautiful, creative Aoife O'Byrne, famous, dedicated to her art and fighting a forbidden love.

Colin groaned. Where had all *that* come from? It was far more than he wanted or needed to get into. Finding Graham Blackwood had affected him.

Then again, the day such a thing didn't get to him, he'd quit law enforcement.

He continued the few blocks to the small Craftsman-style house he'd bought before he'd met Emma, fallen in love with her, married her. His calling? He'd ask Fin Bracken someday, preferably over whiskey. Like his Irish friend, he knew he was where he was meant to be.

Emma had already put a pie together with one of the quarts of wild blueberries her parents had picked and had it in the oven. The other quart was safely in the freezer for Thanksgiving. While rushing around the kitchen, she'd managed to get flour everywhere, including on her cheeks. In her element, Colin thought with a smile. She'd opened windows. "I want to talk to Oliver," she said. "I want to talk to Henrietta Balfour, too."

"If Henrietta knows anything we don't, she might not tell us."

Emma rinsed off her floury hands at the sink. "MI5, garden design and Oliver York. She does lead a complicated life."

"Think she and Oliver are genuine?"

"Their relationship?" Emma reached for a towel and dried her hands. "Yes, I do. Not that MI5 wouldn't put her up to faking a romance with him. I just think if they tried, she'd tell them to shove off."

"*Piss off* I think is the relevant phrase."

"One you've had used on you by an annoyed British counterpart?"

"More than once. I like Henrietta. I like Oliver, too, for that matter. I just wish he wasn't a thief." Colin brushed his lips across the top of Emma's head, felt the softness of her hair. He could smell the salt in it, faint but unmistakable. And the flour. Not so faint. "Sister Cecilia told me she believes she was meant to find Graham Blackwood's body."

"I wished I'd ordered her to go back to the convent."

"I think she sees today as part of her spiritual growth and healing from her ordeal last fall."

"Wow. I hadn't..." Emma draped her arms over his shoulders. "Thank you."

"Didn't expect such depth and wisdom from me, did you?" He grinned at her. "It's the whiskey."

"You didn't have that much."

"Then it's the by-product of hanging around with priests and nuns and such. So, what do you say—do you want to call Oliver tonight or wait until tomorrow?"

"Tonight."

"Wendell?"

"Still best to wait until first thing in the morning. The second I have half an eyelid open, I'm calling him."

Colin wondered if she'd sleep at all tonight. "I don't have a good feeling about Tamara," he said.

"I don't, either." She sank her head against his chest. "We'll find her. Her office is checking her cell phone calls and talking with friends and colleagues in Washington. Sam's on it, and you know what he's like. He doesn't let go."

"Sam doesn't like being called dogged."

"He is dogged, though. I guess we all are in our own way, or Yank wouldn't have chosen us for HIT."

"He didn't choose me. He shoehorned me onto his team to keep me from getting him in trouble."

"To keep you out of trouble."

"Ha, right." Their levity faded quickly. Colin put an arm around his wife. Hell, he loved saying that word, thinking it...knowing it was a fact now. He and Emma Sharpe were married. They'd be sitting in this spot in fifty years, listening to seagulls and enjoying the breeze through the screened windows. He held her tighter. "Whatever is going on, Tamara hasn't left much of a trail."

"Barely a crumb. Her visit yesterday felt personal, not professional, but I suppose that makes sense because she was inviting us to her daughter's birthday dinner. She didn't mention Stefan Petrescu, but his death and Adalyn's having met him must have been on her mind. I want to know more about Verity's interest in forgeries."

"Do you want to try Oliver on your phone or give him a scare and use mine?"

Emma rolled her eyes and smiled. "You two. I'll use my phone."

"Make it a video call. I want to see the whites of his eyes."

She laughed. "Video calls with Oliver York are my default. I always want to see the whites of his eyes."

Oliver took Emma's call from the living room of his Cotswolds farm. Colin recognized the ugly dog painting above the mantel from his and Emma's visit in June, in the midst of Oliver's reckoning with the two men who'd killed his parents and kidnapped him as a boy.

"Sorry to call so late," Emma said.

Oliver yawned, his tawny hair sticking up in spots. "You caught me dozing on the couch. Do I have dog hair on me? Alfred's been up here. He's incorrigible. Martin spoils him. He blames me whenever Alfred acts up, of course, but it's not my doing. But you don't want to hear about dog hair. It's late here. I'm about to have a good Scotch and go to bed." He leaned closer to the screen. "Oh. I see you're in Colin's dreary fishing village. He's with you?"

Emma smiled. "At my side."

"Better a shedding dog at my side. Hello, Agent Donovan."

Colin leaned to his right so that his face was on Oliver's screen. "Hello, Oliver."

The English thief and MI5 informant—or whatever they called him—went on a bit more about his wire-fox terrier, Irish whiskey and the lateness of the hour. "Henrietta's at her aunt's house. Well, it's her house now, but I can still see Posey Balfour in the gardens. Henrietta said she had hours of deadheading to do. Flowers, Colin. Not people."

Colin didn't smile. He rarely did with Oliver. "She's not still at it, is she?"

"No idea. She's staying at her house. Alfred's itching to be off to Martin's cottage. I'll be here alone." His green eyes, a different, lighter shade than Emma's green, stayed focused on the screen. "It's not as if I'm not used to being alone."

Melodrama, but Colin wasn't as naturally sympathetic to Oliver as Emma was, whether it was her background as a Sharpe, her years with the sisters or Oliver himself. She frowned at him. "You and Henrietta…"

"Childhood mates who took each other for granted and now don't, but we have headwinds. If we didn't, I wouldn't be on a midnight video chat with two FBI agents." Oliver settled back in the overstuffed couch, an updated relic from his grandparents' day. He'd changed little in the house since their deaths when he was at Oxford. He'd immediately dropped out, but he hadn't immediately taken to stealing art—at least as far as Colin knew. "What's on your mind, Emma?"

She started to tell him about Graham Blackwood's death, but he already knew. Emma wasn't surprised given Oliver's relationship with Henrietta Balfour. After last night, she would make a point to know. The Blackwoods were British citizens, after all.

Oliver made a face. "Is this all a sordid drug story? Graham Blackwood buys a stash of illegal opioids in Maine, gives them to his wife, goes off to meet his dealer for more and gets whacked?"

"Have you told us everything you know about last night, Oliver?"

"Yes." He didn't hesitate. "There wasn't much to tell. I doubt Henrietta knows more than I do, but it's always possible. The same with Wendell. We never had the chance to speak with Mrs. Blackwood. I wish we had."

Emma's expression softened. "How is she doing?"

Oliver sighed with what struck Colin as genuine empathy. "She was still unable to speak on the last update two hours ago. I don't know if it's because she's sedated or impaired or what might be going on."

"Who gave you the update?" Colin asked.

"Oh, no one directly involved in the investigation—not the hospital or the police, I mean."

"Henrietta?"

"I don't know if I'm supposed to say." He leaned close to the screen. "MI5 must have this place bugged, don't you think?"

Emma looked mildly amused. Colin couldn't get there. Oliver was growing on him but he still could grate.

"Henrietta has many excellent contacts," Emma said, diplomatic.

"Mmm." Oliver's green eyes were alert, no sign of fatigue. "She's in touch with…well, whomever. She doesn't tell me and I don't ask."

Colin didn't need to follow up. Oliver and Henrietta's relationship with each other and with MI5 was for them to sort out.

"Why did my grandfather go to Declan's Cross?" Emma asked.

Oliver's chin went up. "I wasn't aware he had."

They chatted another minute, but Oliver was clearly fading, given the late hour. "Give my best to Henrietta," Emma told him. "Will you help her with the deadheading?"

"I did a couple of weeks ago and deadheaded the wrong flowers."

"You're only supposed to snip wilted and dead blossoms."

He smiled. "*Now* you tell me. Good night. My best to Father Bracken and your families."

After they disconnected, Emma snuggled close to Colin. He slipped his arm around her, wanting nothing more than to carry her upstairs. "Think Oliver knows why Wendell is in Declan's Cross?"

She shook her head. "No, he seemed genuinely surprised."

"Oliver doesn't like surprises. He likes adventure, risk and high stakes but on his terms, under his control."

"He needed control as a boy and a young man. With maturity you realize you aren't in control—you learn to differentiate between what you can control, what you can influence, what you just have to deal with as it comes." She was silent a moment. The wind kicked up, the shades rattling. The kitchen smelled of baking blueberry pie. "Coming face-to-face with his parents' killers and falling in love with Henrietta were two major surprises Oliver's had to manage this summer."

"Do you think he fell in love with her or just realized he'd been in love with her for years?"

"A little of both, maybe."

"Sometimes you can fall hard and fast and it's right. You know it's right, in your gut." He kissed her, aching for more. "It's forever."

"That's us."

"Yes, it is. How long before that pie's out of the oven?"

He carried her upstairs. It was their thing. Emma relished every step. He laid her on the bed. She held him tight, this man of hers—this one and only husband. "Today was a tough day, but I'm glad we're here together."

"I am, too."

Their clothes went. The house wasn't air-conditioned, and she'd opened the windows while he walked back from Hurley's. The breeze chilled her after the heat of the past few days, and her pie-baking. But Colin's palms smoothing over her bare skin, his long, tender kiss, soon warmed her. He tasted of the salt air, and as he made love to her, and she to him, the troubles of the day fell away. Feeling him inside her, pulling him deeper, she let herself stop thinking and worrying. She coursed her hands up his strong arms and curved them over his shoulders, down his sides...and he rolled over with her, onto his back. He drew her down to him, and she was done, gave herself up to every sensation pouring through her.

Afterward, she did freeze. The wind had stiffened with the cold front and gusted through the screen, curtains billowing. She shivered, snuggling closer to Colin. "Hot then cold, cold then hot." She smiled, his arm coming around her. "I like it."

"Summer in Maine."

She placed a hand on his chest. "I'm worried about Tamara McDermott."

"Yeah. The search is on. The Maine state and local police and the Boston FBI field office are on it." He paused. "Sam."

"He could be his own one-man unit."

"I wonder if Yank wishes Tamara had never invited him to dinner."

Another gust of wind had Emma pulling a lightweight blanket over them. "He and Lucy are friends with both Tamara and her husband. It can be tricky when friends divorce."

"Takes adjusting."

"Yank and Lucy obviously care about Adalyn."

"Adalyn has mother issues," Colin said. "I don't. My mother and I worked everything out when I was twelve. She didn't tell me what to do and I stayed out of jail."

"You're probably not joking." With the wind quieting, Emma drew the blanket down a bit. "My mother and I do well together. We're not as close as we might have been without my father's fall, my flirtation with convent life. Also, she can draw. I can't."

"We're damn lucky with the families we have."

"We are."

Colin shoved the blanket down past his hips. "Do you hear bats?"

Emma laughed, half on top of him now. "No, I do not hear bats."

"I had an ulterior motive for saying that."

"I know you did." She eased on top of him. "You're changing the subject, and you know I kind of like bats."

"And I don't."

"But you don't need me to protect you from them."

"Not when they're outside. Inside..." He kicked off the blanket. "Inside, they're all yours."

"Now, though..."

They had each other, and when the wind gusted again, so hard this time it blew papers off the dresser, she wasn't cold at all. She was where she wanted to be, with this man she loved—and who, she knew, loved her. Whatever happened tomorrow, that wasn't going to change.

15

"What do you want with me?"

Tamara hated the fear in her voice. She *refused* to accept it. If nothing else, she wouldn't give her captor the satisfaction. Unless it helped her situation. Then she'd damn well grovel if it made a difference and got her out of here.

No response.

Maybe she hadn't heard actual footsteps on the stairs. The wind could have caused moans and creaks of pipes and other cellar things—water heater, pump, washer, dryer, freezer.

Vermin. There had to be mice down here.

Tamara sat cross-legged on the smelly yoga mat. Her head was spinning in rhythmic waves. Fear? High blood pressure, given the terror and uncertainty of her position? The after-effects of whatever drugs she'd been given? She kept trying to piece together anything she could remember since she'd been grabbed, in hopes something might help her escape. She'd managed to sleep some. She wanted to be ready for any opening to make her escape. She didn't care about beating her captor to death or discovering who it was. Just get out of here.

She'd left a dim light on above the sink during the night. She'd eaten a protein bar. Drunk the water in the bottle. Refilled it. Balled up the blanket so her dried barf wasn't visible and didn't smell as much. Cleaned up as much as she could without proper toiletries.

Not the Hilton…

Milky light penetrated the thick plastic over the window, presumably from the moon and stars rather than a streetlight or another building. She'd stood on the toilet before it got dark, but the plastic was too opaque and dirty for her to see outside. She had no idea where she was or if anyone would come back for her.

She shut her eyes. The spinning eased. She constantly fought claustrophobia. She wished she'd paid more attention in her anti-kidnapping, what-to-do-if-you're-snatched-by-some-crazy-SOB training, but some of it had stuck—or maybe it was just reptilian instinct at work.

She heard footsteps again.

She opened her eyes. Yes, footsteps. No question now...

They were on stairs on the other side of the door, nearby. Wood stairs.

Why can I not remember stairs?

Were the stairs the only way out of the cellar? Was there a bulkhead? Was anyone else in the building—house, business, whatever it was?

What about weapons? A loaded shotgun tucked in a cellar closet would be nice. Tools on hooks. What she wouldn't give for a good crowbar right now. She'd grown up with two older brothers and a macho father who'd all considered crowbars, hammers, saws, drills and such their domain, but she'd learned a few things. She'd been her dad's "little helper." She smiled, thinking of him.

Law school, Tamara? I thought you wanted to be a teacher.

I could teach at a law school one day.

Whatever makes you happy. You'll make a fine lawyer.

He'd been a state police officer in upstate New York. He'd never had much use for lawyers, but he'd liked that she'd become a prosecutor. He'd died when Adalyn was seven. Tamara blinked back tears. "Oh, Dad. I hope you're watching over me now." Her whisper was hoarse, tight with the fear she hated. "Take care of Adalyn. Let me shoulder whatever she's got herself into."

Tamara didn't see how anyone could have followed her to Graham Blackwood's rental house, and it was unlikely if possible she'd happened upon a stray thug or drug dealer or had been followed by someone related to her work. More likely, her kidnapping involved Graham Blackwood and his reasons for wanting to speak with her.

The footsteps stopped. She focused on her posture on the mat as a way to cope with her fear. She had to stay present. She did her yoga breathing. Deep enough but not too deep. She didn't want to hyperventilate or get nauseated by the odors in the bathroom. Barf and old pee, dank wood, musty wallboard—she figured there had to be nasty mold in the walls.

She heard a shuffling on the concrete floor outside the shut bathroom door.

"Why were you meeting with Verity Blackwood?"

Tamara stayed very still. The voice was male, not male. Female, not female. Deliberately so, perhaps. She licked her lips and pushed back the fear with the same skill and determination she'd used countless times in difficult witness and suspect interviews, before judges, bosses and congressional committees.

The footsteps stopped. Was her captor on the other side of the door?

That close?

She swore she heard breathing through the wood door.

"Why, Tamara?"

Patient, insistent. She licked her lips again. The cuts didn't sting as much as they had at first. "I didn't meet with Mrs. Blackwood."

"You were going to, before her flight back to London on Saturday. What happened?"

She considered her response. "Can you let me out of here and let's talk, clear up any questions you have?"

"Why didn't you meet with Verity?"

"I didn't get a good explanation." Tamara placed a hand on the door frame for balance as she stood, aching with muscle strains and bruises she hadn't noticed until now, probably because of what she'd been injected with. "Verity's husband met me instead. We only talked for half a minute at most."

"About Adalyn?"

She shut her eyes, willing herself not to panic—not to pound her fist on the door in anger.

Her captor knew her daughter's name.

She'd warned herself to expect as much, but she'd hoped she was wrong and this mess she was in turned out to involve only her job after all, not Adalyn.

"You're not Graham Blackwood, are you?"

Silence.

"Where am I? Maine? Boston?"

Again no response.

"Graham told me his wife—Verity—was on her way through security to the gate for their flight. Did he return to London with her after all? He planned to stay." She waited, but again got no response. "Are you still here? Who are you?"

"Was Graham upset with Verity for wanting to speak with you?"

"I don't know. He didn't say. Look, why don't we—"

"Are you worried about your daughter?"

Tamara heard herself gasp. More tears rose in her eyes. She placed a palm on the door and leaned forward, without putting her forehead on the cheap wood. "A mother always worries."

A snort on the other side of the door. No hint of empathy whatsoever. She eyed the fake brass doorknob. What if she turned it? Would her captor start thinking of her as a normal person trapped in a bathroom? How could she humanize herself? She reached for the knob but didn't touch it. A fresh surge of adrenaline made her wobbly on her feet, shaky, as if she had low blood sugar.

She stood straight too abruptly, and her left shoulder rebelled. She moaned in pain but squelched any verbal indication she was vulnerable. No swearing, no cursing, no frantic pleas.

She sank onto the toilet. She'd lowered the lid when she'd tried to see out the window.

Her captor rapped on the door, impatient. "What did Adalyn tell you about the Blackwoods?"

"Nothing."

"That's not true, though, is it?"

"I know about Stefan Petrescu. Did you kill him?"

No response. Tamara had taken it as a good sign her captor had gone to lengths to keep his or her identity from her. Maybe it wasn't. Maybe it hadn't taken any effort once she'd been subdued with drugs. Maybe her captor needed her alive only for now.

Why?

For information? As a hostage? To lure someone to this place?

Then kill her when she was no longer of use.

"You stuck me with something," she said. "Did you drug me? Is that why I passed out?"

She stood and turned on the faucet at the sink. Her captor would hear the running water. She didn't care. She was parched. With her right hand, she cupped water and drank as much as she could. "I have a bad shoulder." She stared at her reflection in the cracked mirror. She looked terrible. Haggard, older than her years, but at least she'd sounded calm. She turned from the mirror. It was just two steps to the door. Whoever was on the other side would hear her just fine. "I can't hurt you. People will be looking for me soon if they aren't already. Let's resolve this now."

Footsteps.

Quick, firm on the concrete floor, with none of the tentativeness she'd perceived earlier.

Then on the stairs. Faster now. Taking the stairs two at a time, maybe.

A door shut hard.

Tamara turned on the faucet again and splashed her face with cold water.

Was her kidnapping a repeat of a previous kidnapping? How had *that* one turned out?

Don't get ahead of yourself.

She returned to her mat and opened the remains of her protein bar. She needed to keep her energy up, bide her time and make her move at the first opportunity. If she had to kill her captor to get out of here and protect her daughter, she would. She'd be ready.

16

Near Stow-on-the-Wold, the Cotswolds, England

Ruthie Burns, Oliver's longtime housekeeper, arrived early to set him up on the terrace with tea, poached eggs, grilled tomatoes from the garden, a rack of toast and a pot of marmalade she'd made herself. She also provided heaps of butter. "My doctor says butter is back," she told him.

"I won't resist, then."

She smiled and disappeared into the kitchen. She was a sturdy woman in her late fifties—maybe her early sixties? Oliver knew he should pay more attention to such things. She had an adult son who worked on the farm, who'd been but a boy himself when Oliver's parents had been killed in London. Charles and Deborah York had been beloved in the Cotswolds village where they'd grown up, his father here on the farm, his mother a few miles away. Until recently, Oliver hadn't realized how much their deaths had affected their friends and neighbors, particularly the children, among them young Henrietta Balfour. She hadn't been raised in the village. When she was a child, her parents would drop her off with her great-aunt while they went gallivanting, telling themselves she'd be bored in Paris or Rome or San Francisco—wherever they were off to next. Truth was, they hadn't wanted to be burdened with a child, have to take into account what Henrietta might enjoy at six or ten or fifteen.

Regardless, Oliver realized he'd been a self-absorbed sod, no matter how broken he'd been, how justified he'd been in choosing his solitary ways. People understood. Henrietta insisted they did. That didn't make it right.

He didn't know why, precisely, but he was less concerned about his years of occasional thieving around the world than he was about his bad form over the years with the villagers. He could make right his criminal past, if not by serving a sentence behind bars. Risking his life, exposing himself to dangerous people, providing information to the intelligence services to save innocent people from attack—if not atonement for his misdeeds, he hoped it made a difference.

He'd returned the art, too.

A perilous undertaking that had been, with Wendell Sharpe and his FBI granddaughter and future son-in-law breathing down his neck.

Jurisdictional considerations helped him elude prosecution, but there was also the matter of the paucity of evidence incriminating him. Law enforcement in the various cities where he'd done his less-than-honorable work had little to go on. Emma and Wendell could probably cobble together a credible case against him and share their findings, but they'd need the cooperation of British authorities—and that they wouldn't get. MI5 had Oliver at their beck and call. How much Henrietta knew about his intelligence work was beyond his grasp, but he wouldn't be surprised if it were everything.

He dug into his breakfast to the sweet sounds and smells of summer, at least until Alfred barreled onto the terrace.

Martin Hambly followed far too many paces behind the wire-fox terrier, who was still a puppy. "He's delighted to see you, Oliver."

"What do I do?"

"Pet him. Reassure him you're a part of his life."

"Am I a part of his life? You're still trying to make me the alpha dog, Martin, and I'm not. You are. I'm like a frequently absent uncle."

It was an ongoing argument, but Oliver did feel a surge of pleasure at seeing the pup on the bright, fragrant summer morning. His grandparents had always had dogs, but he'd never pined for one for himself, much to their consternation and bafflement. He'd loved their dogs in his own way, but he hadn't wanted a helpless puppy to get attached to him. He'd inevitably prove a disappointment. He'd thought much the same about Henrietta, but only got into a muddle when he tried to explain. She wasn't a puppy. He knew that.

Satisfied with Oliver's attentions, Alfred flopped onto his belly in the shade. "He's learning well," Martin said. He'd grown up in the village and had worked first for Oliver's grandparents, then for him. He was in his fifties now, as solitary in his own ways as Oliver was—or had been.

A puppy, Henrietta. Life was changing for them.

"I suppose," Oliver said. "Have you had breakfast?"

"Tea."

"Ruthie cooked too much. Help yourself."

"Where's Henrietta?"

"She'll be along. She's at Posey's house. Deadheading, I think."

The house was a short walk from the York farm. Posey Balfour had died last year in her nineties; she'd been a stalwart fixture in the Cotswolds hamlet for decades. Her older brother, Freddy, an MI5 legend, had owned a small farm adjoining her property. He'd died shortly before a pair of handymen had decided to murder Oliver's parents and kidnap him. He remembered Freddy had liked opera and hated gardening, the latter as if to spite his sister, perhaps the keenest gardener in the village.

Oliver slathered butter on a triangle of granary toast. "Henrietta and I are meeting at the dovecote this morning for a walk."

"Tell me what happened in London with Verity Blackwood," Martin said.

As his personal assistant and irreplaceable right arm, Martin deserved to know more than Oliver sometimes shared with him. Did he deserve to know—need to know—about Graham and Verity Blackwood? No reason *not* to tell him, and Henrietta wouldn't arrive for a bit.

Oliver sighed. "Let's refill the kettle and have a chat, then."

"Someone's died."

"Unfortunately, yes, but not Mrs. Blackwood, thankfully."

Martin helped himself to toast and marmalade while Oliver told him everything he knew about the Blackwoods. As was Martin's way, he listened without interruption. Oliver could tell his friend and assistant was absorbing every word of the sad, dreadful tale and processing the combined impact on the farm, Oliver's schedule, the London apartment and probably a host of other things Oliver wouldn't think of but mattered nonetheless.

Martin poured the last of the tea. "Is MI5 involved?" he asked once Oliver had finished.

"I imagine so."

"Henrietta?"

Oliver arranged his features to make sure he concealed any emotions. "Do you still believe she's with MI5?" he asked.

"She is."

No hesitation. Another area of stubborn disagreement. Martin insisted he knew Oliver couldn't—wouldn't—acknowledge either Henrietta's or his own involvement with the secretive intelligence service. "I don't ask," Oliver said.

"One can draw reliable conclusions from the facts at hand."

"Or make assumptions that later come back to haunt one."
A small smile. "That, too," Martin said.

After breakfast, Martin didn't join Oliver on the walk to the dovecote, instead staying with Alfred and whatever needed to be done at the farmhouse. There was always something. If Oliver had to manage on his own, he'd have to sell the place, hire another assistant—unimaginable—or live in a corner of the kitchen and lock up all the other rooms. And the London apartment? He supposed he could easily find help there, but two contract workers had murdered his parents in the library and kidnapped him to Scotland thirty years ago. Oliver had a low level of trust.

The small dovecote was constructed of the ubiquitous yellow stone that was the hallmark of twee Cotswolds villages. It was a gem on the edge of the farm, above a wooded hillside at the bottom of which ran a stream. Henrietta was fussing with dahlias she'd planted earlier in the summer, when she'd been a garden designer—a career transition that hadn't held and, Oliver suspected, had never been full on. His heart jumped when he spotted her. He was damaged goods—a boy orphaned to violence he'd witnessed, traumatized by his own kidnapping, haunted by a sense of guilt and abandonment he never could explain…and now an MI5 informant or whatever he was, a former thief, a man who would like nothing better, at this moment, than to go for a walk with this woman he'd known since childhood and talk about sheep and wildflowers. But that wasn't to be, at least not yet.

Henrietta strode up the lane, dressed in a long, flowered skirt, a tank top, a denim jacket and wellies that might have belonged to her departed aunt, given their battered state. She smiled that bright, energetic smile of hers. "Good morning, love." She slung her arms over his shoulders and kissed him. "Sleep well?"

"Like a stone." He held her close, relishing the smell of her sweat and almond soap. "More's the pity since I could have done with a couple of hours of nighttime amusements. I had the energy."

"Ah, is that so? You could have joined me in the garden. I've been at it since dawn. I've deadheaded, fertilized, snipped, plucked and yanked."

"What I had in mind—"

"Similar pursuits in their own way, no doubt."

He smiled dryly. "No snipping and such."

She laughed in that way she had. "Posey's place looks amazing. It's in its full summer glory. As you must gather by now, unlike you, I didn't sleep like a stone." She eased onto a bench by the dovecote entrance. "Verity Blackwood is improving. She had a good night. Her doctors are still waiting to determine if she's suffered any permanent damage."

"Is she able to speak yet?"

"Not yet, at least not with the likes of us. Her medical situation is precarious."

"I wonder how she'll take her husband's death."

"I suppose it'll depend on whether she had a hand in it."

There was that. Oliver spotted a wilted blossom on the peach and yellow dahlias he and Henrietta had planted in the old terracotta pot she swore had belonged to his great-grandmother. He had his doubts, but he was positive the dahlia needed to go. Since Henrietta didn't leap up in disapproval when he plucked it, he gathered he was right.

He tossed the wilted blossom into the grass. "Do you have any new information on how Verity got hold of the drugs she took?"

"Not yet. Pills, definitely, not an injection. I'm sure we're right about the herb bottle." Henrietta stretched out her long legs and took in the view of pasture and grazing sheep. "I went to bed early and awoke early, but it was good to work in Posey's garden. I'm afraid I've neglected it. The things I don't want growing are overtaking the things I do want. It's a jumble. I'll need to hire a gardener. Can you imagine? *I'm a gardener.*"

"A garden designer. Not quite the same, is it? You tell gardeners what to do."

"I don't know if I'm any good at it."

"You've done wonders here on the farm."

"It's a start. There's more to go."

"There always is." Oliver brushed bits of dahlia off his hands. "It would help if you weren't also an MI5 officer."

"So you say. I think I've spent far too much time this summer lazing around with you."

"You wouldn't trade a minute."

She smiled, her eyes shining with happiness, at least what he hoped was happiness. He wasn't always good at emotional cues. It could be simple lust. Whatever the complications and uncertainties of their relationship, there were no doubts when they were in bed. He was a bloody brilliant lover if he did say so. And Henrietta…

"Oliver?"

He jerked himself back into the moment and smiled at her. "You're not torn, Henrietta, lazy summer and me aside. You're MI5 through the bone. You're just feeling guilty you've neglected your garden."

"I still think of it as Aunt Posey's garden. I miss her terribly."

He nodded, solemn as he pictured old Posey in her later years. "Missing her is good, Henrietta. Imagine if you didn't. What that would mean about your relationship."

She squinted up at him. "I used to think you were solitary

because you had low self-esteem. One more thing I've been wrong about in recent months."

"I like that you can admit you're wrong. It's not something I always see in you MI5 types."

"I'm ignoring you." She crossed her ankles, a chunk of mud dropping off the bottom of one wellie. "Verity cleared customs going to and from the US without any problem. As we suspected, she has no history of illegal drug use and no history of prescribed narcotics."

"Have you ever taken a narcotic for pain?"

"Never. I've never had serious injury or surgery. I loaded up on whatever doctors would give me when my wisdom teeth were extracted. What a miserable experience that was. What about you?"

"Nothing."

"No surgeries or serious injuries?"

"I wrenched my knee badly in Dallas a few years ago. I had to extend my stay, but I managed with RICE—rest, ice, compression and elevation."

"Tripped helping yourself to a painting or two?"

Three lovely landscapes, actually. They'd been particularly tricky to return to the Dallas corporate offices where he'd lifted them. He'd managed that feat in early winter, not a bad time to be in Texas. He'd celebrated the paintings' successful return with a stay at a five-star Dallas hotel. He wasn't quite convinced Emma Sharpe hadn't known he was in town, despite his fake passport and surreptitious help from MI5.

He smiled at Henrietta. "You know what they say in America. I'll take the Fifth."

"You got a decent look at the Fletcher Campbell painting at the Blackwoods'. It was signed, wasn't it?"

"Yes. That's how I knew it was his work. Why? It's not his work?"

"Just checking," Henrietta said. "They all paint or painted, you know, including Stefan Petrescu. Ophelia Campbell gave him lessons."

Oliver leaned forward. Now this was interesting. "Anything there?"

"An affair, you mean? I suppose it's possible." She paused, her turquoise eyes darkening as she looked down at her hands. Thinking. Not her long suit. She was an all-in or all-out type and a woman of action. Finally, she looked up again. "What if Stefan could tell the Fletcher Campbell painting we saw was a forgery, or he had questions that would lead to it being discovered as a forgery? Who would care enough to kill him?"

"Sometimes caring isn't rational. Graham could care because he'd look the fool. Verity could care because she could think her husband was trying to defraud her. Fletcher could care because it's his work. A collector could care because a forgery could devalue not only that particular painting—obviously— but potentially other Fletcher Campbell paintings."

Henrietta's brow had furrowed as she listened. "Because one forgery would raise questions about other forgeries, or at least cause a ruckus and prompt other owners of his works to have them checked out. Time-consuming, expensive, embarrassing."

"Have you ever bought original art by a well-known painter?"

"No, I could never see spending the money when a trip to IKEA would suit me."

Oliver rolled his eyes. She probably was serious. He adjusted the dahlia pot to give himself something to do. He envisioned his grandmother out here. She'd been a keen gardener. It had been her idea to convert the dovecote into a potting shed—*his* idea, many years later, to add a secret stone-working studio. For a decade, he'd polished small stones he'd selected from the stream below the dovecote and inscribed them with miniature Saint Declan crosses. He'd sent one to Wendell Sharpe after each heist. Later, he'd sent them to his FBI-agent grand-daughter and her mentor, Matt Yankowski.

A mad, frantic business that had been.

He crushed the lump of mud that had dropped off Henrietta's boot under his shoe. "If the drugs Verity took were in her carry-on, tucked in the herb bottle, they went right through security and customs. Is that possible these days? I suppose she could have picked up the opioids or been given them here, but why would she take them *before* her meeting with Wendell? Why not wait until after they'd chatted?"

"To settle her nerves." Henrietta stared out at the pasture, but Oliver doubted she was seeing the sheep and green grass under the sunny sky. "Verity might have been intimidated by Wendell's reputation."

"Or concerned about what she was telling or asking him and where his answers would lead her. Is he under suspicion?"

Henrietta shook her head. "I'm sure he's not, but now with Graham dead in Maine, who knows? I was beginning to think Verity's a garden-variety drug addict and we could bow out of this little drama."

"She still could be, and Graham died supporting her habit."

"Risky to stay behind in Maine for drugs, don't you think?" Henrietta rose smoothly, adjusting her skirt. "Security would have taken a closer look at him even without his wife's over-dose. Easier for her to go home on schedule than for him to explain why he canceled his flight at the last minute and stayed on in Maine. He'd never have sailed through with a stash of drugs. I'm certain of that." She examined the dahlias. "I hope slugs haven't been at them."

"I loathe slugs."

"Well, they love dahlias."

"I didn't dare touch the leaves in case I did something wrong."

"Oh, you won't hurt anything." She stood straight, her cheeks flushed. "Do you have contacts in your world who might be able to help us better understand the Blackwoods?"

His world? But Oliver knew what she meant. "I'm afraid not."

Henrietta nodded thoughtfully. "Just the Sharpes, I suppose, and they're in the thick of this thing. All of them. Wendell, Lucas, Emma." She slipped her hand into his. "Shall we take a walk and let all this simmer for an hour?"

Their walk took them on one of the countless way-marked trails that crisscrossed the rolling hills and pastures of the Cotswolds. This one was mostly along lanes—no muddy footpaths— and very familiar to them since it happened to run through the York farm and wind its way to Henrietta's house. They walked hand in hand but mostly in silence, distracted and preoccupied as they were by recent events. The smells of summer, the sounds of birds, sheep and stream, the beauty of lush pastures and midsummer gardens were soothingly familiar, but Oliver didn't know if he'd arrived at any solutions when Henrietta left him at the table on her garden terrace. She disappeared inside to make tea and take a call.

Oliver watched a butterfly in the garden. He swore Posey Balfour haunted the small house she'd had built to her specifications. It was relatively new by village standards, and constructed of brick rather than locally quarried limestone. He supposed the brick could be local.

He blew out a breath. He felt helpless, useless and faintly annoyed. He had nothing to offer the Blackwood investigation—nothing to help his friends in New England find Tamara McDermott. Henrietta said she understood his mood but she, at least, had contacts, given her MI5 status.

He was relieved when he noticed Finian Bracken texted him. Can you please call me today?

Oliver immediately hit the number for his Irish friend in Maine.

Finian answered after several rings. "Oliver, dear God, it's half five here."

"You said to call."

"I didn't mean now. I'm getting ready for the day."

"What does that entail for a priest, I wonder? Don't answer. I prefer to maintain the mystery. Is it foggy in Rock Point? Bleak?"

"It's a glorious morning. Where are you?"

"I'm in Henrietta's garden watching bees hum in...something purple."

He heard Finian's soft laugh. "Bees are attracted to purple."

"Good for them. Shall I hang up and call you later? Don't tell me you just got out of the shower. I'm glad I didn't ring you on Skype or FaceTime."

"Now is a fine time to talk. I just was surprised to hear from you so soon."

"Well, then. What can I do for you, Father Bracken?"

"I'm worried about Wendell Sharpe. I know about the Blackwoods—the English couple."

"Ah. So now we're down to it. Have you spoken with Wendell?"

"He should be on his way to Dublin with Sean Murphy."

"Not in handcuffs, I hope," Oliver said. Sean Murphy was another law enforcement officer who wanted to arrest him.

"No, no. Wendell was in Declan's Cross without a car."

"Happily for other Irish drivers. He doesn't know anything about Graham Blackwood's death, does he?"

"I don't believe so, no," Finian said. "Aoife said he was melancholy."

Ah. Aoife. Beautiful, talented, testy and in love with Father Bracken. Oliver settled back in his uncomfortable chair. "It can happen after one comes upon a young woman near death of a drug overdose. It's such a waste. Did you meet the Blackwoods in Maine, Finian? Did they confess a dark secret and now you're tortured about what you know?"

"That's not it." Finian sounded long-suffering, as if he'd expected Oliver to say something like that. "I didn't meet them."

"Are you positive?"

"Colin showed me photos of them last night."

"My good friend Special Agent Donovan. Did you have chowder and whiskey at that crumbling restaurant on the harbor? I expect it to collapse into the tide any day."

"There are safety checks, Oliver, and you love it here—and yes, that's precisely what we did."

"I suppose Rock Point would have a certain appeal for tourists who like to get a taste of real Maine life. I doubt the Blackwoods are that type." Oliver kept his tone amiable. "Henrietta's making tea." He wouldn't be surprised if she'd had her garden bugged, but he'd decided to keep that opinion to himself. "Anything else on your mind, my friend? One does worry about Wendell. It's natural, I suppose."

"Yes, I suppose."

Finian didn't sound quite right. Oliver didn't know if he'd offended his Irish friend. He often didn't have the right words at hand and would stumble through emotional minefields. Finian was usually amiable and quick-witted, empathetic and comfortable with people—but it was very early in Maine. "Opiate addiction and abuse are rampant, but I have a feeling there's more to this situation." Oliver felt more at ease with facts. "I've never been to the gazebo where Graham's body was discovered. Have you, Finian?"

"I haven't, no. I visit the convent on a regular basis, but I rarely venture beyond the chapel at the motherhouse. I sometimes lead prayer at their retreats."

"What kind of retreats?"

"Artists, art educators, art conservationists. It depends."

Oliver couldn't imagine. "I can think of a thousand things I'd rather do than attend an art retreat at an isolated Maine convent."

"It's a stunningly beautiful place, Oliver. You could lead one of their retreats. I can see you teaching Celtic mythology, or teaching tai chi as part of a creative life."

"Don't recommend me, please."

Finian laughed, a good sound to hear. "Oliver..." The seriousness returned. "Oliver, do you believe it's wise for you to insert yourself into this investigation?"

"I didn't insert myself into it. I was thrust into it."

"Wendell Sharpe dragged you and Henrietta into it. Do you think he was entirely candid with you?"

"Candidness isn't necessarily a part of my relationship with the Sharpes." Oliver paused, debating how far to go. He didn't have a solid sense of the boundaries of their friendship. Finian Bracken was a priest, and he was friends with two FBI agents, one of them a Sharpe. "What's this call about, Finian? Are you doing a bit of meddling yourself?"

"Perhaps."

Now there was an answer. Oliver sprang to his feet and stepped from the terrace to the garden. "How? What do you know?"

"I don't know anything and I've done nothing. I just..." He didn't continue.

"Did Emma and Colin warn you against speaking with me?"

"Always, Oliver. Always."

"Very funny." Unless he wasn't trying to be funny? Oliver plunged ahead. "I'd like for you to meet Henrietta. You saw her when you visited the farm earlier this year, but it's different now that she and I are…well, together. Let us know when you head back across the Atlantic, won't you? You are always welcome to stay here at the farm."

"Thank you. I would enjoy seeing Henrietta, of course."

Oliver plunged in again. "Is love possible for me, Finian?"

"Oliver…what?"

"After the deaths of your wife and two daughters, you concluded love was no longer possible for you, or God decided for you—however you view it. I don't know. I've never asked. I'm not judging."

"It's okay. You don't have to understand my calling. We are talking about you."

He gripped the phone. "What if my traumatic past means love isn't possible for me?"

"Loving or being loved, Oliver?"

"Not bollixing it up."

"What about Henrietta?" Finian asked quietly.

Yes, what about her? Oliver felt a surge of warmth. That was a positive sign, wasn't it? But then came the crawling sense of panic. "I don't want to hurt her," he whispered.

"That fear comes with loving someone, Oliver. It's a part of it."

"Part of me is still that small lad in the Scottish ruin blaming himself for not saving his parents from two brutal killers. Ah, Finian… Father Bracken… I wish I were a better person."

"Maybe that's a part of loving someone, too." Finian's voice had softened. "Love can help us become a better person if we let it."

"Are you speaking to me as a priest or a friend?"

"I'm a priest and I'm your friend. And, my friend, I think we shouldn't have these calls while you're watching bees and before I've had tea."

"But you called for a reason, and we're dancing around it, aren't we? Did you get the sense Colin and Emma think Verity tried to kill herself?"

"I've learned not to try to guess what they're thinking. Oliver…"

He waited, but Finian didn't go on. "What is it? How can I help you?"

"You can take care, my friend. If there's anything I can do for you, don't hesitate to get in touch."

"You can let me know any developments in the investigation into Graham Blackwood's death, or if you hear any news about the McDermotts and the Campbells."

"Oliver, I'm not privy—"

"It could happen. You're a priest. People unburden themselves to you. I just did, and I didn't mean to. Never mind any of it, will you? It was all nonsense. I finished the Bracken 15 year old last night. I thought I'd finished it last time I was into it, but I found another dram—"

"Taoscán," Finian said.

Oliver could hear the smile in his friend's voice at his Irish word. "Goodbye, Finian. Enjoy your tea and morning devotions."

Once he disconnected, Oliver placed his phone on the table and walked through the late-summer garden. It was Posey's, really, a classic English cottage garden that Henrietta was making her own bit by bit. She surfaced, flicking plant debris off her front. "I thought I might find you out here doing tai chi. Thank heavens you're not snipping anything. You were on the phone?"

"Finian Bracken."

"Regretting he didn't take a parish in Ireland, I imagine. You can tell me about your conversation on the way. We need to return to London. Verity Blackwood's condition has improved dramatically overnight."

"She's awake?"

"Apparently so."

"Has she been told about her husband?"

"She will be soon. Now, that's all I know for the moment. I'll do my best to get us in to speak with her." Henrietta gestured vaguely toward the front of the house and the lane. "You'll drive or shall I?"

"I will." Oliver swept to the terrace. "We'll take the Rolls."

17

Emma could have managed without milk, eggs and bread in the house—there was, after all, a freshly made wild blueberry pie on the counter—but no coffee put both her and Colin over the top. It was off to Hurley's, bustling at seven despite the lobster boats having gone out hours ago to check traps. The day's house-made doughnuts were already running low, given Hurley's four-thirty opening. Just as well, Emma thought as she and Colin joined Finian Bracken at his table by the windows overlooking the harbor. He had his breviary and a pot of tea as he awaited his breakfast. He'd explained on previous breakfasts together how he'd arranged with Hurley's to have grilled tomatoes and didn't mind American sausage and bacon, but he did without mushrooms and puddings for a traditional full Irish breakfast.

It was a gorgeous Maine morning. Bright, clear, dry. Sunlight sparkled on the harbor. Emma wished she and Colin were there under better circumstances. Kevin Donovan had called Colin early, when they were still debating coming down to the harbor for breakfast. Graham Blackwood's death was caused by a blow to the back of his head, probably with a rock. No obvious candidates had been found near the body. It was a needle-in-the-haystack proposition. Rocks weren't exactly scarce in the area. The killer could have tossed it into the water anywhere from the trail. Odds of finding it were remote, but they'd do a thorough, appropriate search.

Emma followed Finian's lead and ordered a full breakfast. Colin did the same. Without waiting for instructions, their waiter had dropped off two mugs of steaming coffee. She dumped half-and-half into hers. Colin took his black. He eyed Finian. "You've got news?"

Finian sighed. "I need to work on my inscrutability. I don't have much news. Sean Murphy let me know he got Wendell safely to Dublin and personally delivered him to his home."

"Does Sean think Wendell has told us everything he knows about the Blackwoods?" Colin asked.

"He does, as a matter of fact, but I didn't ask. He told me, anticipating you'd want to know. He said Wendell was subdued but otherwise himself. He mentioned banshees."

Colin frowned, coffee mug in hand. "Who, Wendell or Sean?"

"Wendell to Sean. Wendell asked if Sean had heard something that sounded like a banshee last night at his farm in Declan's Cross."

Emma waited for more but Finian didn't continue.

Colin set his coffee on the table. "And Sean said…"

"He said he heard the wind. He didn't want to argue whether banshees are real or not real. Sean isn't deep into Irish folklore. Wendell didn't explain further."

"My great-grandmother—Granddad's mother—believed in banshees," Emma said. "I never knew her, but Granddad told me some of the stories she told him when we worked together in Dublin before I left for Quantico. Banshees are one of the solitary fairies. They're always female and mostly known for warning of an impending death."

"Do they cause the death?" Colin asked.

Emma shook her head. "Not according to the tales I know.

A banshee is typically loyal to one family through the generations..." She paused as the waiter delivered their breakfasts.
"Finian, was my grandfather out on the headland when he
heard the banshee?"

Finian nodded. "He walked up there last night."

"Alone? He loves to walk, but that's a difficult route for
him to tackle alone, in the evening." Emma had taken the
lane that wound up the headland from the village a number
of times, including with Colin. "I tell myself if he dies on
one of his rambles, he'll have died doing something he loves.
But, still. He could walk with someone."

"I imagine Sean, Kitty and Aoife were keeping an eye on
him," Finian said. "Your grandfather had a terrible shock.
It's good he's home. Will the police investigating yesterday's
death want to speak with him?"

"Probably," Colin said.

They started their breakfasts and changed the subject to
the weather—always a good topic in New England, Emma
thought—and the latest Rock Point news. She listened, but
she wanted to speak with her grandfather, hear his voice, reassure herself he was all right. Could Verity Blackwood have
told him *anything* that in retrospect could help with understanding why and how her husband was killed, and who was
responsible?

Colin had finished his breakfast and just had more coffee
poured when he received a call. He touched Emma's shoulder. "I have to take this," he said, getting to his feet.

She watched him walk across the restaurant and out the
door. Kevin? Yank?

No.

His MI5 contact, a mysterious man with a tangled connection to Colin through his deep-cover work. Emma had

few details. Information was on a need-to-know basis, and she didn't need to know.

"I spoke with Oliver York early this morning," Finian said.

"Oliver? Why?"

"It was innocuous, but I know how you are with him. Colin, especially."

"I notice you waited until he was on a call to mention Oliver."

Finian smiled. "I did, didn't I? Oliver's sorting out his life. He's allowed the past to dictate so much of what he's done until now."

"Are you two friends?"

"I suppose we are, in a way." Finian's blue eyes narrowed on the harbor, the tide out, exposing mud, stones, seaweed, tiny crabs and periwinkles. "I do my best not to get distracted from my duties here in Rock Point."

"Thank you for your concern for my grandfather," Emma said.

"Did this man yesterday have opioids in his system? Can you tell me that much?"

"I don't know if he did or didn't. The postmortem will include a toxicology screening followed by a full toxicology report. We'll know more then."

Finian nodded, solemn. "I'm not an expert, but I know that what is considered a therapeutic dose for someone who has built up a tolerance can be fatal for a new user."

"My father, for instance."

"I didn't have him specifically in mind."

Emma glanced out at the view. Two kayakers were making their way along the edge of the harbor. She ached to be out on the water, but that time would come. She and Colin had kayaking on their list of must-dos for the summer. She pulled her gaze from the kayakers and turned to Finian. "I don't know if Graham was on opioids, or if Verity got the opioids she took here or in London."

Finian shifted awkwardly in his chair and poured more tea. "The gazebo, the cove, the house the Blackwoods rented—are they known for drug deals?"

"I have no idea," Emma said.

"I'm not aware of any drug dealing anywhere near the convent."

"I'm not, either."

He let out a breath. "That's good. I'll leave the investigating to the detectives." He abandoned his tea and stood, kissed her on the cheek. "I have sick calls this morning to the hospital, but I'll check on Sister Cecilia today. Be well, my friend."

"We'll stay in touch," Emma said.

She watched him leave, wondering if he'd said all he knew or was on his mind—about her grandfather, her father, Oliver, opioids. He'd never even hint at anything told to him in confession. It would be a violation of the seal of confession. Chats with friends were different, but he was still circumspect by nature.

She'd finished her coffee by the time Colin returned from his phone call. "More coffee?" she asked him.

"I'm getting some to go, and I've claimed the last two doughnuts."

"I just ate a gigantic breakfast. I can't eat another bite."

He grinned at her. "Who said I planned to share? Come on. I'll fill you in on my call on our way back to the house. Your folks or the convent first?"

"My folks. I'll bring them the pie."

"Stefan Petrescu was killed with a Rigby .275, a classic English medium game-hunting rifle," Colin said as he and Emma started onto the coastal route to Heron's Cove. She was driving. "Or stalking rifle, as my English friend put it. It was a single shot to the chest with a round-nosed 140-grain bullet. That's the original cartridge for a Rigby. It's fairly accurate up to fifty yards."

"I've seen a Rigby," Emma said. "I've never fired one."

"I have." He didn't elaborate. "It's a classic rifle—the sort one keeps in the family. It's very manageable, and it's perfectly legal in the UK with the appropriate firearms certificate."

"Which would have to be renewed every five years."

"Heavier, more modern bullets are available, but that's not what was used to kill Petrescu."

"Anything else?" Emma asked.

"They haven't ruled out a poacher who hit the wrong target, but it's not the leading theory. There were no drugs in Petrescu's system or found in his possession."

Emma nodded. They passed joggers, bikers, people carting kayaks to the water. A normal Maine summer morning. No one was in yet when they reached Sharpe Fine Art Recovery. She continued into Heron's Cove village with its cedar-shingled shops and restaurants on narrow streets. She turned up a side street, away from the water, and finally stopped in front of her parents' two-story Victorian house. They'd had the clapboards painted a cheerful yellow after her father's fall, as if to say chronic pain wouldn't defeat them—a decorating fork in the eye to the fates. Except for adding a downstairs bedroom, the house was largely unchanged from Emma's childhood.

They'd agreed Emma would speak with her parents alone.

"Give your folks my love," Colin said.

Emma got out of the car, grabbing the pie from the back seat. She headed up the front walk, where her mother was sweeping the steps. She was dressed in a sun hat, a tan linen top and wide-legged tan linen capris. "Emma," she said, smiling. "This is a pleasant surprise." But her smile vanished quickly. "I'm so sorry about yesterday. We were going to drop by to see you and Colin, but we knew you'd be busy. That's Colin in the car?"

"He sends his love. He wanted to give us a chance to talk. We can't stay. Yesterday was a long day and—"

"And you're working. I understand. Is that a blueberry pie under that foil?"

"I claimed some of the berries you and Dad picked yesterday morning."

"Excellent. It's been so hot, it'll be wonderful to have pie. I haven't done any baking since we moved back from London. I've been obsessed with getting the yard in shape. Your father says I look like a pirate in these pants, but they're beyond comfortable."

Emma laughed. "You could do worse than a pirate. Is Dad here?"

"He's out for his morning walk. He went out past the offices. He won't go near the spot where you and Sister Cecilia found that poor man. I don't know how you stand the work you do sometimes. It's still a crime scene, isn't it?"

"Very likely."

Emma watched her mother sweep a pile of debris—mostly leaves and twigs—into the yard, shaded by an ancient sugar maple and an elm clinging to life. The house had served as Sharpe headquarters while the offices were undergoing renovation, but her parents had quickly reclaimed their home once they returned from England. Her mother had added her touches—hanging baskets of begonias and ivy at the front door, a riot of colorful zinnias along the hedges, an herbal wreath. She'd washed windows and curtains and had the rugs cleaned. As far as Emma knew, her parents were thrilled to be back in Heron's Cove.

"Dad says walking helps him more than anything else he does," her mother added.

"How's he doing these days?"

"He's settling into his old routines now we're back here. He did a lot of walking in London, too." She smiled. "He and Wendell have that in common."

One thing, at least. Emma didn't detect any new concern in her mother's tone. "The body yesterday—did that upset him?"

"Heavens, it upset both of us. Lucas, too. The police interviewed us. Ginny and your father met Verity Blackwood but not Graham—the man who died. I didn't meet or even see either of them. We never heard of the Blackwoods or had any contact with them while we were in London, either, that I'm aware of. Do you think this is about drugs, Emma?"

"I don't have any answers for you. I'm sorry."

"People often don't realize how dangerous narcotics are. It's so important to be under strict medical supervision."

Emma set the pie on the steps and produced her phone. She showed her mother a photo of Tamara McDermott. "Have you seen her before, Mom?"

She leaned the broom against the door and examined the photo. She shook her head. "I haven't, no."

"All right, thanks. Did Dad go out to the gazebo on Sunday?"

"He didn't walk anywhere on Sunday. We worked in the yard. Emma, this must be awkward for you—will you get in trouble because Verity Blackwood contacted your family about forgeries?"

Emma gave her a reassuring smile. "No, I won't."

"You used to worry about such things."

"Well, I'm not worried now."

"It's being around those Donovans," her mother said lightly. "Nothing ruffles them."

"They are a hardheaded lot. Mom, I know this situation is upsetting for you and Dad. It would be for anyone."

She inhaled deeply, let out the breath in a rush. "One thing I want to say, Emma. In case it's crossed your mind or another agent or detective's mind. Your father and I don't know anyone local who buys, sells or uses illegal opioids. He isn't on any prescription narcotics himself and hasn't been in some time, and he would never, ever sell or give them to anyone else."

"I've no doubt," Emma said. "By the way, when you were in London, did you or Dad know or meet with a Romanian linguist named Stefan Petrescu?"

Her mother frowned. "Who? No. I didn't, that's for sure. I doubt Timothy did, either, but we don't live in each other's pockets despite appearances."

"Do you recognize the name?"

"No."

"Okay. It's good to see you, Mom." Emma understood her mother's testiness and skipped a hug. "Give Dad my best, won't you? Sorry I missed him. Next time we're in town, we'll have to have pie together."

"That would be nice." Some of her visible stiffness eased. She grabbed her broom and smiled. "You've always baked to relax and think."

"Still do." Emma gave her mother a hug after all, a bit awkward with the broom in her hand. "Stay in touch, okay?"

She returned to the car. Colin was leaning against the passenger door. He waved to her mother. "Hi, Faye. Have a good day."

She waved back. "Wish you could stay for pie."

Emma climbed behind the wheel and started the engine as Colin sat next to her. "Tough conversation?" he asked her.

"Yes."

"Understandable." He clipped on his seat belt. "My mother never gets out the broom when she's upset. Not to sweep, anyway. I think she chased Mike with a broom once."

"Did she catch him?"

"No, but he had to come home for dinner. She'd put the broom away by then."

Emma smiled. "I can just see the two of them."

"They've always been tight in their own way. This sweeping and pie-baking thing, though. They're telling differences between the Sharpes and the Donovans, don't you think?"

Emma eased the car out onto the quiet residential street. This man, she thought. She loved everything about him. His humor, his sensitivity, his ruggedness. "My mother was tense."

"No kidding."

She told him about their conversation, aware of Colin's blue-gray eyes on her. No hint of humor now. "What?" she asked finally.

"Nothing."

"No, tell me. Please."

"It's a question." He kept his gaze on her, unwavering. "Emma, are you worried your father has a secret opioid addiction?"

"No, I'm not." She forced any defensiveness from her tone. "I was just asking my mother questions."

"Fair enough."

"Part of me wants to stay here and help my mother with the yard." She smiled, didn't feel her heart in it. "My inner homebody."

"I get it. I could have gone off with Andy to check his traps."

"But here we are," she said.

18

For thirty years, the tower at the Sisters of the Joyful Heart convent had been Sister Joan's domain. In some ways, it still was, Emma decided as she stood at the entrance. There was no blood there now, but the image of that September morning almost a year ago was seared in her mind.

As it was in Sister Cecilia's. Her breathing was shallow and rapid as she stared at the stone step, but she pulled her gaze away. "Someone was in here, Emma. I'm sure of it."

"Recently?"

"Since I was here last Wednesday. I walk this way once a week to help desensitize myself to the trauma. It's part of my healing. We're not using it as the conservation lab and studio right now. We moved all the equipment to spare rooms in the motherhouse. We're having the tower repainted. We might repurpose it, given what happened here." Sister Cecilia pushed back her wind-whipped hair. "We've decided to sell Sister Joan's desk and chairs—her personal items. It was just too difficult to come in here…"

"I understand."

Emma kept her voice quiet, steady. Sister Cecilia had witnessed the aftermath of the violence that morning, and then had endured her own encounter with the killer. But Emma needed to keep their focus on the here and now. The tower was out at the tip of the peninsula, on its own away from the main buildings of the convent. It was original to the late nineteenth-century estate, an outlook above the sea. Emma noticed lobster boats close to shore, making their way home. A few sailboats were farther out on the water, enjoying the spectacular summer day. Sister Cecilia had met her at the gate and taken her straight here, bypassing the motherhouse. Colin had gone to the Blackwoods' rental house to check in with his brother.

Sister Cecilia pointed at the main entrance. "I think someone might have been inside. The door's locked, but painters were in to do an estimate. Maybe they left it open and someone had a chance to slip in, and then one of the sisters locked up again. I know that sounds far-fetched. I don't think whoever's been in here broke in."

"Sister, why do you think someone's been in here?" Emma asked.

"I saw signs someone was on the outside of the fence. It ends near here." She turned and pointed past the expanse of lawn toward the rocks and sea. "It gets steep, but you can hold on to the fence and then just…take your chances, I guess."

Emma had done that a few times in her late teens. "What signs did you see?"

Cecilia didn't hesitate. "Disturbed brush, footprints and a dropped water bottle."

"On which side of the fence?"

"The other side—not the convent side. It's all convent land, but you know what I mean. I was walking along the fence…" She stopped abruptly and squinted toward the tall black-iron fence, most of it also original to the old Victorian estate the sisters had restored. "To be honest, Emma, I was looking for signs of an intruder. It's a post-trauma stress thing I'm dealing with. I come out here periodically and I check. Yesterday—well, finding that man gave me reason to have a look this morning after my work in the vegetable garden."

Emma could appreciate Cecilia's anxiety. "The signs you saw weren't there the last time you walked the perimeter?"

"No. That was Friday evening, before vespers."

"All right, Cecilia. I'll take a look inside."

She nodded tightly. "The key's in the same place it's always been."

By Sister Joan's decree. Emma fetched it from a gutter and unlocked the door. She pushed it open but saw nothing of concern. She glanced back at Sister Cecilia. "Any specific reason to suspect someone's been in here?"

"Circumstantial evidence only."

Emma heard birds and the crash of waves on the rocks below the tower. It was an idyllic spot, but she knew better than to think the convent was removed from the rest of the world. She remembered realizing that as a novice—a teenager searching for meaning in her life, *for* her life.

"I still think of it as Sister Joan's studio." Sister Cecilia smiled suddenly. "But that would only annoy her, wouldn't it?"

Emma smiled, too. "No doubt in my mind."

She went inside, thankful Cecilia had warned her the studio was in a state of transition. As a rule, Sister Joan had updated only what needed updating, not just for the sake of buying something new. If a piece of equipment worked, what was the point of replacing it with a newer model? That frugality was one of the driving principles of the Sisters of the Joyful Heart.

Sister Joan's scarred oak desk was still tucked against the wall on the first floor of the tower, but it was empty now, ready to be sold. Same with the old filing cabinets and shelves. Emma pushed back an image of Sister Joan with one of her composition notebooks, where she'd jot down everything—phone calls, ideas, snippets she'd pick up from magazines and books. She'd always been thinking, learning, documenting, brainstorming.

Emma took the spiral stairs to the second-floor lab, empty now. Sister Joan had set it up to her exact specifications. Her knowledge and thoroughness had helped with the transition to other experts among the Sisters of the Joyful Heart taking a leadership role.

Trust the process, Sister Brigid. Listen to your heart. Don't be swayed by what you think you should do. Don't worry about people you might disappoint if you profess your final vows or if you choose not to.

I won't, Sister Joan. Thank you for your insights.

This includes me. Don't consider me in your decision. This is your journey.

Brilliant, exacting, dedicated to her convent and its mission, Sister Joan had considered Emma her protégée when she'd become a postulant. They'd put each other through their paces. In the end, when she'd left the convent, Emma had realized Sister Joan had never believed she would profess her final vows and stay.

Not that Sister Joan had ever imagined her protégée in the FBI.

Emma looked out the windows at the ocean. She couldn't get sucked into the past. Sister Joan's murder had nothing to do with Verity Blackwood's overdose, Graham Blackwood's death or Tamara McDermott's whereabouts.

But did the convent's work in art conservation?

Emma descended the stairs and rejoined Sister Cecilia outside. "It's hard to say if anyone slipped inside. We can get the police up here to take a look. Why don't I talk to Mother Natalie? She's back, isn't she?"

"She got back last night."

They walked across the lawn, past the spot where she and

Colin were married in June—where, almost a year ago, he'd deliberately run a borrowed lobster boat onto the rocks as an excuse to get onto the grounds and spy on her after Sister Joan's murder. Emma smiled, picturing him bounding up to her. She'd be lying if she said she'd never imagined such a scene as a young novice. But she hadn't been a religious sister that day she'd met Colin. She'd been an FBI agent who specialized in art crimes.

She and Sister Cecilia continued through the expansive flower garden at the classic late-Victorian house that served as the convent's motherhouse. It was constructed of gray stone, with porches, turrets, multiple chimneys and tall, graceful windows. Bit by bit over the past six decades, the Sisters of the Joyful Heart had created a home for themselves, a place where they could work and play and live their lives as they carried out their mission. Convent numbers had never exceeded thirty-five and often hovered in the low twenties. They didn't fret about whether their order would last another sixty years, a full century—centuries. That was out of their hands.

"It helps to have my routines." Sister Cecilia spoke quietly, as if she'd been lost in thought. "I picked summer squash this morning. We have a good tomato crop this year. I love home-canned tomatoes in January."

Emma smiled at her. "There's a lot to do this time of year."

Gardens—vegetable, herb, flower, meditative—abounded at the convent, a legacy of Mother Sarah Linden, the beloved foundress of the Sisters of the Joyful Heart. More than sixty years ago, the dilapidated and overgrown property had caught Mother Linden's eye for her new order of religious sisters. She and Wendell Sharpe, Emma's grandfather, had been friends early in his career as an art detective. She'd designed many of the convent gardens and had crafted a variety of sculptures herself, from sundials to Saint Francis of Assisi. She'd been an educated, open-minded, loving person devoted to preserving art for future generations and sharing the love of art, confident in its transformative and enriching value for people's lives.

Sister Cecilia glanced back at Emma, a couple of paces behind her as they walked through the garden, passing tall phlox, coneflowers and daylilies. "How's your painting, Emma?"

"I haven't picked up a brush since the wedding. I think about it."

"Thinking counts. When you finally do pick up a brush, I bet you'll realize you know what to paint. Your subconscious is working on it."

Cecilia was a skilled painter and a wonderful teacher. To her, everyone was creative, and it didn't matter if that creativity was expressed in a way that earned a living and kudos or simply whiled away an afternoon. She was giving Emma sporadic painting lessons. Emma loved to dip her brush into a vibrant watercolor and splash it onto a clean canvas, but she had no illusions she'd ever be any good. Sister Cecilia insisted that wasn't the point. *You're meant to create, not to judge what you create.*

They entered a sitting room through French doors off the garden. Mother Superior Natalie Aquinas Williams awaited them. "I'd like to speak with Emma, Sister."

Sister Cecilia nodded. "I'll be in the library."

Mother Natalie turned to Emma. "Please, sit down."

Emma sat on a wingback chair with a view of the garden and sea. It was here in this room where she'd announced she was leaving the convent. Mother Natalie, in her early sixties, a PhD in art history, had accepted Emma's decision with grace. It'd been five years, but she could still feel how tight her throat had been, the sadness she'd felt as she'd faced the reality that the vision she'd had of herself and her life had evaporated like the morning fog on the sea on a crisp fall morning. Only

afterward, walking in the convent gardens, had she felt the
relief, the overwhelming sense she'd made the right choice.
Leaving the Sisters of the Joyful Heart had been an appropriate
outcome to her experience as a novice, not a disappointment,
not a failure. But it seemed like a hundred years ago now—
as if it'd been someone else who'd donned a simple habit and
studied, worked and contemplated in this place.

Chickadees pranced on the branches of a crabapple tree
in the garden. Two seagulls swooped out toward the lawn
where Emma had married the love of her life—the man of
her dreams—in June.

"I was just picturing winter." Mother Natalie turned from
the garden with a smile. "In winter, I'll picture summer. It's
my nature, I'm afraid. It's good to see you, Emma."

"You, too, Mother Natalie."

She glanced out the French doors. "It's such a beautiful day.
To think we were none the wiser that a man lay dead just
beyond our gate..." She shook her head and turned toward
Emma. "I understand you've been out to the tower with Sister
Cecilia. We get more clandestine visitors these days. Trespassers, I suppose. They come up the path from the water. They
want to see the tower where Sister Joan was killed, and the
convent. Curiosity, adventure. We're debating what to do.
It's dangerous to go along the fence and sneak in. We don't
want anyone to get hurt. We're thinking about offering public
tours during the summer and early fall. It wouldn't be every
day. That would be too intrusive."

"Do these people try to slip into the tower?"

Mother Natalie sat on a cozy love seat opposite Emma.
"Not that I've been aware of—at least until Friday."

Emma leaned forward. "What happened on Friday?"

"The police interviewed everyone here yesterday after you
and Sister Cecilia discovered the man by the gazebo. I wasn't

here. I was visiting family in Camden and got back late. I understand this man's death is suspicious. Sister Cecilia is convinced he was murdered." Mother Natalie shuddered. Her gray hair was cut short, and she wore a gray tunic, skirt and simple walking shoes. "Murder makes sense, of course, since you're here, Emma. I don't mean that to sound snarky. It's a fact, given your work. In any case, I have information for you. I'll let you decide if it's relevant to your investigation. On Friday morning, I caught Verity Blackwood and a college student—an American friend of hers—sneaking into the tower. They'd found the key. Sister Joan chose the gutter because it was convenient in case someone forgot a key or was authorized to go in but didn't have one. It wasn't meant to be a secure hiding place."

"I remember that was her thinking. Did you get the name of the student?"

"Her name's Adalyn McDermott. She's studying preservation archiving in Boston. They apologized and explained they'd found themselves on the path up from the water and got carried away. They seemed sincere. I offered to show them around."

Emma eyed the mother superior. "You didn't call the police?"

"No, why would I? There's nothing in the tower to steal. They barely got inside before I spotted them. I showed them the motherhouse, retreat house and the gardens that are open to the public, and wished them a good day. They thanked me and left—through the main gate, I might add. I didn't introduce them to the sisters. They were busy with their duties. I didn't mention the intrusion, either."

"What time did Adalyn and Verity arrive?"

"Nine thirty in the morning. That's when I walk."

"Tell me about your visit," Emma said. "Everything you remember."

"They explained they took the trail from the house Mrs. Blackwood and her husband rented for a few days down past the cove. They walked out to the gazebo first and noticed the trail up the hill on their way back. They decided to take it and see what they could of the convent." Mother Natalie spoke crisply, as if she'd rehearsed her words overnight. "I might be getting ahead of my narrative, but I want to get this out. I'm aware the Blackwoods are friends with Jolie Romero and Adalyn McDermott works for her. It came up on Friday. Sister Joan and Jolie had a solid working relationship over the years, but they were never what I would call friends. I doubt their relationship is relevant to this death investigation. They were two exacting colleagues. Sister Joan didn't leave behind any notes on Jolie. I checked this morning." Mother Natalie paused, gazing at her hands a moment. "We miss her."

"I do, too."

"Of course." Mother Natalie looked up, her clear, pale eyes fastened on Emma. "I didn't sleep much last night. I was informed about the body and the investigation as I was leaving my family. I'm still somewhat rattled, and I'm worried about Sister Cecilia. I wish she hadn't been with you yesterday. A case of twenty-twenty hindsight, but you do have a way of bringing trouble with you."

Emma felt a cool breeze and realized a window was open. She couldn't let Mother Natalie's veiled criticism affect her, or get between Sister Cecilia and her mother superior. She'd let Cecilia explain why they'd gone down the trail together. "Did you show Verity and Adalyn the temporary conservation studio?" Emma asked.

"Yes, I did. They were both knowledgeable about art conservation and what we do here. Jolie's doing, I imagine."

"Did Jolie send Adalyn here because of her work?"

Mother Natalie shook her head. "She said no, she was just here to see Verity. I understood they planned to spend the day together. It was already hot when they arrived, but we had a nice onshore breeze here. We had a good visit. They were just curious about us, our lives here, I'd say. That's not unusual. Adalyn said she was still getting settled into her new job and apartment after three months in London, and took the day to get out of the city heat and see Verity. I gather they know each other from London. Sneaking up here was a spur-of-the-moment decision."

"Any mention of Graham Blackwood?" Emma asked.

"No, and he didn't visit on his own. Normally we ask guests to register, but I didn't bother with Adalyn and Verity. It seemed moot. The police checked the registry book. That's why their names weren't in it."

Emma nodded. "Did they say where they were going when they left here?"

Mother Natalie gave a slight smile. "In search of the perfect lobster roll. Fortunately, it's almost impossible to go wrong with lobster in Heron's Cove."

"Mother Natalie…"

"I understand Verity Blackwood overdosed in London. I saw no indication of drug use when I was with her on Friday."

It wasn't Emma's next question but it was on her mental list. "The detectives will want to interview you. Did Adalyn mention her mother?"

"Not to me, but I overheard her telling Verity that her mother would love Maine."

Emma glanced out at the garden again, the tallest flowers swaying in a stiffer breeze. Adalyn had neglected to mention her trip to Maine. Why? Because she and Verity Blackwood had sneaked onto the convent grounds? She didn't want Jolie to know? "Mother Natalie, can you remember anything else about Jolie's dealings with the convent?"

"I don't think there's much of anything to remember."

"Have you had any contact with Fletcher and Ophelia Campbell?"

Mother Natalie frowned. "I know their names, of course, but no, we never worked with them."

"Might Jolie have consulted with Sister Joan about them?"

"I doubt it, but if she did, there's no record of it."

She'd have checked. Emma eased to her feet and walked to the French doors that opened onto the garden. She glanced back at Mother Natalie, still seated. "How did Verity and Adalyn strike you?"

"What do you mean?"

"Did they get along well? Did either one seem depressed, angry, upset? Did you get the impression they were being forthcoming about why they were here? They did arrive unannounced, and they sneaked into the tower."

Mother Natalie exhaled, then nodded slowly. "I see what you're getting at. It was clear Verity was older and had more life experience. It wasn't a friendship of equals, but they certainly seemed comfortable with each other and got along well while they were here."

"Adalyn turned twenty-one this past weekend," Emma added.

"Now that did come up—on the way out, in a cheerful manner. It was an excuse to have dessert. I recommended our goodies at the shop in Heron's Cove." Mother Natalie rose, smoothing her skirt. "Is there anything else?"

"The detectives investigating—"

"I've already called them." She nodded to the garden. "Please, stay as long as you'd like. Take your time." She joined Emma at the French doors. "Consider all the gardens open to you and

Agent Donovan if he's here with you. Adalyn McDermott and
Verity Blackwood wanted to know as much as they could about
what we do here. They were very knowledgeable. I suppose
that affected my judgment. We'll keep them in our prayers."

Emma thanked her and went out the French doors. She welcomed the gusty sea breeze, the scent of summer flowers, the
sounds of birds—nearby chickadees and distant seagulls. In winter, the sisters would put out bird feeders. She took a meandering stone path through the garden around to the front of the
motherhouse.

Sister Cecilia eased next to her. "Can you tell me anything,
Emma?"

"Sorry, no."

"It's okay. I think I know." She waved a hand. "I didn't do
anything underhanded. Mother Natalie warned us the police would be back up here. I assume she saw the intruders
on Friday."

Emma stopped and turned to her friend. "Sister Cecilia,
please take care of yourself, and don't hesitate to call the detectives investigating Graham Blackwood's death—or me.
Call me anytime."

"I don't want to get you into trouble."

"You won't. Again, Sister, please take care of yourself."

She nodded, pink rising in her pale cheeks. "I was right
about intruders."

"Trespassers, lost hikers, curiosity seekers—not everyone
is an intruder."

"I suppose not. I have to leave for the village. I'm teaching
painting and pottery today."

"Be well, Cecilia. Yesterday was a lot to process."

"I might talk to Father Bracken. He's dealt with trauma,
and he knows—" She stopped, breaking into a smile. "He
understands the life you and Colin lead." The smile didn't

last. "I'm glad you were with me yesterday. I had a feeling about what we might come upon. That helped. It still does."

Emma gave her a quick hug. "Call me anytime. And be careful, okay? The other sisters, too."

"We don't make ourselves targets."

There wasn't a trace of sarcasm in her tone. She was being sincere, Emma realized. "Sister, you didn't make yourself a target last fall. Neither did Sister Joan."

"Sometimes it feels that way, but I know what you're saying. Go on now. You have a job to do. We'll have to schedule another painting lesson soon, before you forget everything I've taught you."

"I look forward to it. I promise I haven't been procrastinating."

"Oh, it's okay if you have." She laughed, looking more herself. "Take care, Emma."

Sister Cecilia turned back to the motherhouse, and Emma continued through tall evergreens to the main gate. Colin was slouched against her car, watching for her. He stood straight when he saw her. She smiled and waved. "Any news?"

"A witness has come forward, claiming he saw a man fitting Graham's description paddling in a red kayak, alone, around two o'clock Sunday afternoon. He was almost to the gazebo."

"It must have been just before he was killed," Emma said. "The cove is fairly easy to navigate, but the conditions are more difficult closer to the gazebo, even for an experienced kayaker."

"Quick study, maybe."

"Could the same person who killed Stefan Petrescu have killed Graham Blackwood?"

"English hunting rifle versus Maine rock." Colin shrugged. "It's possible."

"At this point, anything is possible."

"How was your visit with the sisters?"

"Fruitful."

"A lot of memories for you up here."

"I remembered wondering if I'd meet a rugged lobster-man one day."

"Ex-lobsterman."

"Still rugged."

He grinned. "Come on. You can tell me what you've learned while we get out of here."

He drove, and Emma updated him on her conversations with Sister Cecilia and Mother Natalie. He listened without interruption. As impatient as he could be, he was adept at wolfing down facts and information.

He glanced at her when she finished. "What do we have here, Emma?"

"I wish I knew. Did Adalyn conceal her visit up here on Friday, or did she just not think to mention it?"

"We're looking for her mother, and she didn't arrive until Saturday."

Emma checked in with Sam Padgett. He had a witness, too. "BPD talked to a man who saw Tamara McDermott get into a car that fits the description of her rental. No issues. Nothing suspicious. He described her and then confirmed her photo as the woman he saw. It was just after she'd talked to you. She wouldn't have had time to do anything else between leaving your place and getting to her car—assuming this guy's time line is accurate."

"That means she had time to drive up here and walk into the middle of the mess with Graham Blackwood."

"Or knock him on the head herself?"

To protect her daughter? Emma didn't ask the question aloud. "Let's hope she shows up for the ferry," Emma said.

"She won't."

Emma agreed it was unlikely. "No hotel reservations?"

"None. It's not the time of year to wing it in Maine, but maybe she stayed with a friend."

But Sam obviously didn't believe that. Colin downshifted as they came to the end of the convent's access road. "Ask him if Yank's up to date."

"I heard that, and yes, he is," Sam said. "He's gone up to the Campbell farm."

"Why?"

"Jolie Romero and Adalyn McDermott invited him. They're up there. He's worried about Adalyn. He's aware he's personally involved in this thing. You two are, too. Can't throw a rock and not hit a Donovan or a Sharpe or someone they went blueberry picking with up there. Sorry. Rock's a bad analogy."

"Yank went alone?" Emma asked.

"Yeah. It's a personal visit, but is anything ever personal with Matt Yankowski?"

No answer necessary to that question. When Emma disconnected with Sam, Colin glanced at her. "Where to?" he asked.

"The sisters' shop in the village and Lucas's office. Adalyn must have been with Verity when she stopped at both places on Friday, even if she didn't go inside. Maybe someone saw her. It might not help but I'd like to know."

"If Tamara McDermott thought her daughter was in over her head with the Blackwoods and their problems, she could have come up here to talk to Graham—"

"What if he grabbed her? He's dead. If she's hidden somewhere, he didn't leave behind any evidence of where she might be."

Colin sped up on the main road to Heron's Cove. "With any luck, she'll be on that ferry to Nova Scotia this afternoon."

19

Finian Bracken was at the shop run by the Sisters of the Joyful Heart, tucked on a narrow side street in the village. Colin had been to the shop a few times. It sold student and professional work and offered classes in its upstairs studio in painting, pottery, scrapbooking and a few other arts and crafts. Finian looked out of place even among the gray-habited nuns. He'd come to Rock Point last June as a freshly minted priest. He and Colin had met on the harbor. Finian had left Ireland— his home and family—for an uncertain future in a struggling Maine fishing village. Colin had been taking a break after an intense, long-term undercover investigation. He and Finian had become instant friends. They didn't have heart-to-heart talks. No confessionals, that sort of thing. Mostly they talked about whiskey and life in Maine and Ireland.

"What is this, do you suppose?" Finian held up a chunk of pottery. "Not something one of the church ladies did in pottery class, I hope."

"I've no idea what it is, Fin."

"A pen holder, perhaps? Sally wanted the girls to take pottery lessons after we returned from our sailing vacation. She loved handcrafted works. We had pottery vases and flowerpots."

Colin had stayed at the Brackens' stone cottage in the Kerry hills. It had stunning views across Kenmare Bay, and lots of flowerpots. Finian hadn't stayed there himself since entering seminary a year after the deaths of his family.

He moved to another display. "What can I do for you, my friend?"

"I want to talk to Tim Sharpe. Know where he is?"

"I don't." Finian stood still. Finally, he looked up. "He's in pain, Colin. He's always in pain."

"Is he addicted to pain meds?"

"No. He was dependent for a time but not addicted. There's a difference."

"A distinction," Colin said. "I'm not sure there's a difference."

"Dependence is manageable with medical supervision. An addict has a compulsive need for drugs. Timothy no longer takes prescription pain medicine, but as I mentioned last night, he's enduring a period of breakthrough pain right now."

"What exactly does that mean?"

"It's when pain breaks through his management protocols. It goes from chronic but tolerable to acute and intolerable. That's how he explained it to me, at least. I'm not a medical professional. He's doing his best to manage with non-prescription NSAIDs and his yoga and walking and such."

"He didn't tell you this in confidence or you wouldn't be telling me," Colin said.

"That's right. He doesn't talk much about his ordeal but only because it's one of his ways of managing it. He's not hiding it. You know I don't judge either addiction or tolerance and dependence, Colin. I battled alcohol abuse at one time. Timothy believes this episode of breakthrough pain will pass."

"Poor bastard." Colin sighed, held up a hand. "I know he hates pity."

A small smile from his Irish friend. "He's a Sharpe, isn't he?"

"Does he keep close tabs on any meds he has on hand?"

The question obviously surprised Finian. "I have no idea, but I would assume he does. I've run into opioid addiction in my work here, Colin. It's a terrible thing. I have only compassion for those suffering. If you're suggesting Timothy is contributing to the epidemic—"

"I'm not. I'm not suggesting anything. I'm just asking questions."

"Do you think someone could have stolen some of his medication?"

"I don't think anything."

"The man who was killed—"

"I can't talk about that."

"Of course not. Sister Cecilia is due here any moment. I planned to stop at the convent to see her, but I'll look in on her here, informally."

"The nuns—they've been straight with the police? They've all told the detectives everything they saw and heard this past weekend?"

"I have no reason to think otherwise. Do you?"

"No." Colin examined a deep brown pottery bowl. It looked like a salad bowl to him. "I'm just trying to find a missing prosecutor and figure out why a couple who was here last week ended up dead and near-death."

"Is there a Sharpe connection?"

"There's always a Sharpe connection, isn't there?"

"Maybe so." Finian pointed at Colin's bowl. "That is your mother's work."

"Seriously? Not bad."

"I should go. I have weeding to do at the rectory. Soul work, Sister Cecilia calls it."

"My mother says the mallow's taken over there."

"Mallow?"

"It's pink. It spreads. You've got too much going on in the

rectory garden. Stick to one or two colors. Get rid of everything that's not those colors."

"And you decided I wouldn't choose pink as one of the colors?"

Colin grinned at his friend. "I made it easy for you. You can blame me if any parishioners get on your case."

"How do you know about mallow?"

"Emma had me get rid of it the last time we were up at the house. That was a good weekend."

"No murders and missing prosecutors."

"Mallow-plucking followed by whiskey."

Finian smiled. "It was a good weekend. We'll have another one again soon, my friend."

"Yeah, Fin. We will. Who am I to argue with a priest?"

Finian scoffed. "You argue with me all the time."

Despite Finian's attempt at humor, Colin could feel his friend's uneasiness as he walked away—and his own. They hadn't spent much time around Timothy Sharpe and weren't used to his struggle with chronic pain. Colin reminded himself he didn't know what, if anything, his father-in-law's troubles had to do with the Blackwoods and a missing federal prosecutor.

Emma joined him by the display of pottery bowls. "Adalyn was with Verity Blackwood on Friday but she didn't come into the shop. One of the sisters was arriving to teach a brush lettering class and spoke with her outside. Adalyn asked about the class. It was an innocuous conversation, but the sister remembered Adalyn because she mentioned her friend had rented a house out by the convent."

"Did the sister speak with Verity?" Colin asked.

"Just a nod as Verity was leaving."

"Brush lettering. Calligraphy? That'll be next for my

mother." He pointed at the pottery display. "She made that salad bowl."

"It's not a salad bowl, Colin. It's a decorative work."

"Oh."

She smiled. "You knew that."

"Good for Mom, though, getting down here to take pottery lessons." They went outside, got back in the car. The streets were crowded with tourists enjoying the beautiful day. "I'd rather be on the water if I were a tourist, but I'm sure the shop owners appreciate the business."

"People are lining up for tour boats," Emma said.

Cap'n Colin. His road not taken. Sometimes he thought Emma had actually taken the road that should have remained one not taken in becoming a nun, but he was glad she'd gotten Sister Brigid out of her system. "On to Sharpe Fine Art Recovery?"

"I want to hear what Lucas has to say about Granddad and his banshee, and if he's heard from him."

"Still nothing from him?"

"A text telling me he's fine."

"Maybe he is fine."

She glanced at him, her expression tight. "I hope so."

They found Lucas on the docks behind the Sharpe Fine Art Recovery offices, almost to the marina next door. Colin spotted him first. Emma, he knew, wouldn't be looking for her brother down by the boats. He was a runner, and dedicated to his work with Sharpe Fine Art Recovery. But he nodded to a good-looking cruiser. "I'm thinking about buying a boat. Surprise, huh? Nothing fancy. I've lived in Heron's Cove all my life, and I've never owned a boat."

"We Sharpes aren't known for our boating skills," Emma said.

Her brother grinned. "That could change. Maybe I'll get you to go in with me."

"More likely Colin would. I can watch you sail off while I set up my easel on the back porch."

"I did say you could paint there anytime."

"I'm a terrible watercolorist, but Sister Cecilia says she has hope."

"You enjoy it," Colin said.

"A neutral answer if ever there was one," Emma said.

"Painting's meditative for you," her brother said. "It takes just enough concentration your mind can't wander off too far into the weeds or get too deep into the stress that comes with your job."

Colin didn't comment. Emma had told him she painted as much as possible when he was away, working undercover. Not a gibe. Just a fact.

"Great day today," Lucas said. "I hate to be inside. I went for a long run early. But you're not here to talk about running or the weather. Do you want to talk here or go up to my office?"

Emma leaned against a post in front of a Boston whaler that had seen better days. "Have you heard from Granddad today?"

"Text on my run. He said he'll be at his pub with the lads soon and not to fret."

"Did he mention hearing a banshee?"

Lucas frowned. "No, why?"

"It came up with Sean Murphy. What about you? Have you heard a banshee recently?"

"Me? Not recently, not ever. Granddad would hear one before I did. I'd pass it off as the wind or a bird even if I did hear one."

"Banshees are said to be loyal to one family."

"Yeah, great. Emma, what's this about?"

She shook her head. "I don't know. Worried about Grand-dad, I guess."

"That'd just piss him off, but I get it. He's not himself. I think this woman's overdose Sunday night got to him. She's lucky to be alive—and she is alive thanks to Granddad's persistent nature. He could have gone to bed. Housekeeping would have found Verity Blackwood dead in the morning. Did she intend to overdose or was she trying to get high and went too far?"

"Police are still investigating," Emma said.

"Granddad doesn't believe she was deliberately trying to harm herself. He believes someone set her up to take the drugs, hoping she'd die or be incapacitated. It's hard for Granddad to fathom that a young woman with so much to live for would do that to herself."

Emma nodded. "I hope it's never easy for any of us to fathom, no matter who it is."

"Agreed. Hard to fathom someone slipping her opioids, too."

"What about Dad? How's his mood?"

"We spoke last night, after the detectives took our statements, and he stopped by a little while ago. He didn't mention hearing a banshee if that's your next question."

"He's struggling with pain," Emma said.

Her brother sighed. "It's obvious but you know how it is. We don't talk about it. That's the deal, because it just draws his mind to it—even if I can see he's in pain he might not be thinking about it. He said he wants to walk out to the gazebo once it's released as a crime scene. He thinks he might remember something, but I think he just wants to go out there. He's worried he missed something. Bothers him that the Black-woods were in such distress and he didn't see it."

Colin touched the thick rope that tied the whaler to the

post. "Did you check the Sharpe files for any references to the Campbells or Stefan Petrescu, the Romanian linguist who was killed on his way back from London a few weeks ago?"

"I did. Zip."

"Would you have everything?"

"You mean would Granddad have met with them and not told me? It's possible, but I think he'd have said something by now. Do you think this linguist's murder is related to Graham Blackwood's murder?"

"I didn't say Graham was murdered."

"It's all over the village." Lucas was matter-of-fact as he squinted out toward the ocean. "He was friends with Stefan Petrescu. I checked with my mother, too, and she doesn't recall meeting any of them when they lived in London—Petrescu, the Blackwoods or the Campbells."

"Where's your father now?" Colin asked.

"I don't know. He might have headed to the gazebo." Lucas hesitated. "He doesn't have regular hours. I've offered him an office but he doesn't want one. When he's here, he'll find an empty desk, sit at the kitchen table or go out onto the porch. He and my mother have only been back from London a short time. We're still sorting things out. Anything else?"

Emma shook her head and thanked him. She eased next to Colin as they watched Lucas jump up to the retaining wall to the Sharpe backyard. Lucas was steady and analytical, like his younger sister, but he and their grandfather shared a decided impatience.

A tour boat chugged past them toward the channel that would take it out to the ocean. Its upper and lower decks were crowded with passengers. Colin heard the guide on the loudspeaker. He was explaining what a tidal river was, but he'd go into the history of Heron's Cove and point out the expensive houses on Ocean Avenue, talk about what kind of wildlife they would see on the ocean, the various types of boats—whatever might interest people visiting the Maine coast.

"Not a bad life, being a tour boat guide," Emma said next to him.

He slung an arm over her shoulders. "Not a bad life at all. How are you, Mrs. Donovan?"

"I want to head to the Campbell farm and talk to Adalyn McDermott."

"Yank should be there by now. Do you want to try your grandfather again?"

"He'll be with his buddies at the pub soon. He knows I want to talk to him, but he also knows I'll have spoken with Lucas and Finian—and that I'll call Sean Murphy if I feel the need."

"No place the poor bastard can hide," Colin said with a grin.

She smiled back at him. "Damn right."

"Would the sisters know much about forgeries?"

"They would recognize an obvious forgery, but they wouldn't know much if anything about the contemporary market for forgeries. An artist might copy a work of art or imitate a particular artist to learn technique or even to sell what they produce—but never by passing it off as someone else's work."

"Signing the painting must make a difference."

Emma nodded. "My grandfather has dealt with forgers and forgeries both past and present in his career. I don't know how much my father and Lucas have."

"So it would make sense for your father to put Verity Blackwood in touch with Wendell."

"That's right."

"Got it," Colin said. "Drop me off at the Blackwoods' rental house. I'll check in with Kevin while you check in with Yank and Adalyn. We'll stay in touch."

"Sounds good. It's only a thirty- or forty-minute drive to

the Campbell farm. I can be back here in time for chowder at Hurley's. And whiskey," she added, "to celebrate Tamara McDermott's safe landing in Yarmouth."

20

London, England

A blur of people…beeps…tubes…

I'm in a hospital bed. I have an intravenous tube running out of my arm. Not just one tube. Multiple tubes. Why? I don't understand.

"What's happened to me?"

I hear my hoarse whisper, but I don't know if anyone else can. If anyone else is here. What if I'm not in hospital? What if I'm dead?

I shut my eyes. The lids feel swollen and heavy, as if they're filled with fluids. I try to lift my arm but I can't, or I just don't. I'm not sure which it is.

Transient damage…

Where did I hear that?

No permanent damage to the brain, lungs, liver, kidneys.

"Mrs. Blackwood should make a full recovery."

I remember now. That's what the doctor said. I'm sure of it. I didn't dream it.

I'll be all right.

But what happened to me?

Oxycodone.

I'm propped against pillows in my hospital bed. I'm sure the doctors said I overdosed on oxycodone. They're worried I did it on purpose.

A suicide attempt.

Me.

I wouldn't want to kill myself, would I?

Why would I?

Is there something I don't remember? Can't, because of the over-dose?

Panic surges through me, unexpected, vicious. It's as if I'm being grabbed by my feet and yanked underwater. I can't breathe. I want to rip the tubes out of me. I want to run.

"Graham!"

A nurse appears at my side. I see now that my IV tubes are hooked up to a machine that takes my vital signs, and there's oxygen... I was given oxygen... I remember now...

The nurse asks me how I'm doing.

My panic eases. "Graham. My husband." *My voice still is little more than a hoarse whisper.* "Where is he?"

"Just try to relax, Mrs. Blackwood."

"He stayed in Maine and I returned to London." *I pause, sinking into my pillow. I try to grab snippets of memory, put them together— make sense of where I am. Figure out what's happened to me.* "I'm in London, yes?"

The nurse nods. "Yes, you're in London. You're doing well."

She's pretty. She has bright red hair and freckles. She seems so young.

I feel myself drifting off.

Graham...

Did my husband try to kill me?

21

Oliver hadn't been in a hospital since he was eight, after his escape from his would-be killers. His grandparents had died peacefully at home. He often wondered if they'd made sure of that, given his trauma. Verity Blackwood looked distraught and shaken though she was sitting up, the thin white hospital sheets and blankets neatly tucked around her, only the shoulders of her gown visible. Her color was less deathly than on Sunday night, but she nonetheless looked seriously unwell, if improved since they'd found her at Claridge's.

Oliver was perfectly happy to let Henrietta take the lead. She gave Verity a brisk yet kind smile. "Thank you for speaking with us."

"My doctor said it would be all right provided I don't over-tire myself. She understands that I need answers, and I want to help. Graham…" Verity cleared her throat. "I know he's dead."

"I'm very sorry, Mrs. Blackwood," Henrietta said.

"Me, too. It's hard to believe. I understand you're friends with Wendell Sharpe. If not for him—for you and Mr. York—I might not have been found in time. Thank you." Verity's gaze remained fixed on Henrietta. "You administered CPR?"

"Mmm. One of those things one learns these days. How are you feeling?"

"Strange. It's the only word I can think of at the moment. Where is Mr. Sharpe?"

"He's returned to Ireland," Oliver said. "He sends you his well wishes."

"Thank you. My husband..."

Verity seemed to want them to tell her what had happened to him, but Oliver wasn't touching *that* one. He was confident Henrietta would skate past it, too. They'd promised the doctor and the police they would avoid mention of Graham Blackwood's death. Henrietta had promised, at least. Oliver had gone for coffee. He suspected she'd used her MI5 credentials to get them in to see Verity, and he didn't want to muck things up.

Henrietta placed a vase of flowers on Verity's bedside table. Grabbing the bouquet had been Oliver's idea, actually. Gardener though she was, Henrietta was in MI5 mode and had breezed past the flower shop without a second thought.

She picked a brown-edged leaf off a cheerful gerbera daisy and tossed it in a small bin. "We won't keep you long, Mrs. Blackwood."

"Verity," she whispered. "Please."

Henrietta smiled. "Of course. If at any moment you want us to leave, we will. Say the word or lift your hand, and we'll be gone. Oliver and I stopped at your house in Oxford yesterday. We both have homes in the Cotswolds. The back door was open—Oliver thought he smelled gas and we went in to check. We noticed you own a Fletcher Campbell painting."

"My husband bought it. The painting you saw isn't Fletcher Campbell's work." She gasped, her eyes widening. "I didn't mean to say that out loud."

"But it's what you believe?" Henrietta asked calmly.

Verity sank against her pillows. "Yes."

She reached for a water glass with a cover and a straw. She fumbled a bit but managed. She took a sip and set the glass back on her table, almost missing. She settled back against her pillows.

Henrietta waited a few beats, but Verity didn't go on. "Is the painting the reason you wanted to talk to Wendell Sharpe?" Henrietta asked finally.

Verity nodded but didn't elaborate.

Oliver appreciated Henrietta's smooth manner, caring without coming across as insincere. She had impressive skills, but she also drew on her nature, her core decency and generosity of spirit. "Verity, what do you know about the painting in your drawing room? It's signed by Fletcher Campbell."

"He might have signed it. That doesn't mean it's his work."

"Was it a gift?"

"No. Graham bought it. I had nothing to do with the purchase. He didn't consult me. He insisted it's one of Fletcher's last works."

Henrietta pushed Verity's water glass back from its precarious position at the edge of the table. "How did you conclude it's not authentic?"

"That's my theory. I don't have proof. I became suspicious a few weeks ago at a dinner party we hosted at our house. We invited Rex—Fletcher's son—and Jolie Romero, a mutual friend, and Adalyn McDermott, a young intern." Verity shut her eyes, sunken, as if she'd never get enough sleep again. "And Stefan... Stefan Petrescu."

"The Romanian linguist who was later killed," Henrietta said.

"A week later. Yes." Verity opened her eyes and fastened her gaze on Henrietta. "Stefan said something..." She faltered, turning so that her right cheek was against the pillow. "It doesn't matter now. I didn't tell anyone I had questions about the painting. Graham was happy with it. I didn't know if he realized it might not be Fletcher's work and simply didn't care."

"You used the word *forgery* with Wendell," Oliver pointed out.

Verity nodded. "A forgery is illegal. An imitation, fake or a copy might not be. That's how I think of it. I was going to get into more detail with him when we met." She sat up abruptly, her breathing rapid, as if she'd just run a hard 5K. "I assure you I wouldn't kill myself over a fraudulent painting. I didn't attempt suicide. I don't know what happened."

"Did Fletcher paint other scenes of the River Cherwell?" Henrietta asked.

"I think so, yes. He said he wanted to do a series. I don't know how far he got with it." Verity adjusted her position, her hair stringy as it dropped down her front. "I finally told Graham I had questions about the painting on Saturday as we were leaving Boston. He found out I was meeting Tamara McDermott, Adalyn's mother, and wanted to know what was on my mind. I suggested we get the painting appraised—get an independent, expert, objective opinion. I never assumed anything nefarious had happened. I thought it might just have been a mistake and Graham picked up the wrong painting."

"But you were leaning toward fraud," Henrietta said briskly. "How did Graham react when you told him?"

"He was very understanding, but he said asking questions and an appraisal would be a waste of time and money. He wasn't going to do anything about it even if the painting wasn't Fletcher's work. He wasn't going to stir the pot. Those were his words. Then he asked me not to meet Adalyn's mother. I agreed. He went to tell her I wasn't coming. Then he didn't get on the plane with me."

Henrietta considered a moment. "Graham bought the dis-

puted painting after the fire? Ophelia was gone by then and
Fletcher was very ill."

"No, no—Graham bought the painting last fall when
Fletcher was still working on it, but he only picked it up in
July, a couple of weeks before Rex returned to England to
start closing up the cottage." Verity paused, grimacing. "We
hoped Fletcher and Ophelia would get back to Oxford after
the winter, but she went downhill and died in April. The
shock and strain took a toll on Fletcher. Graham walked
over to their cottage and collected the painting himself. We
have a key. It was the only River Cherwell painting there.
If Fletcher did others, he must have taken them back to the
US with him. Maybe he ended up only painting the one."

"Except he didn't paint it," Henrietta said.

Tears formed at the corners of Verity's eyes. Oliver was impressed with her clarity under the circumstances. "I'm afraid
that's right. Graham adored the Campbells. He was distressed
to see them go through so much. He wanted to help them
if he could."

Henrietta moved closer to Verity. "Whose idea was it to
go to Boston and then to Maine?"

"I don't remember who suggested it, Graham or me, but it
was a mutual decision. We wanted a change of scenery after
Stefan's death and decided to visit Fletcher while he still might
recognize us. My questions about the painting weren't at the
forefront of my mind. I'm fond of Adalyn and wanted to see
her, too—how she was getting on with Jolie Romero. I knew
Rex had hired Jolie to work on the fire-damaged paintings."

"How was your visit with Fletcher?" Henrietta asked.

Verity adjusted her blanket. She had more color in her face,
if only because of the energy she was expending to speak
with her two guests. She glanced out the window, as if she
was watching a scene play out, a memory—her husband and

a brilliant artist whose mind was deteriorating. "It wasn't as sad as I thought it might be," she said finally. "Fletcher didn't recognize us at first, but he came round, or at least he pretended to. Rex brought him up to the farm for our visit. We talked about the heat wave and how beautiful New England is. Graham was so good with him." She licked her lips, her eyes puffy, more tears welling. "It feels strange to talk about him in the past tense."

Oliver noticed Verity's increasing fatigue. Henrietta picked up the water glass and handed it to her. "You can stop at any time, Mrs. Blackwood. This is entirely voluntary on your part."

"I just want to understand what's happened." Verity's arms collapsed at her sides, the modest strength to keep them in her lap clearly no longer available to her. "I'm sorry. The nurse gave me your surnames but not much else. Who are you? Why are you asking me these questions?"

Oliver took on that one. "I'm Oliver and this is Henrietta. We were with Wendell on Sunday. He wants to help if he can."

She accepted his response without argument. "That's decent of him after he found me…in distress. I still can't figure out how oxycodone tablets ended up in my possession. I didn't think twice when I took them. I don't know anyone on pain medication. I'm not, obviously. The doctor indicated I'm a 'naive' patient—not as in innocent and oblivious but someone new to opiates. A habitual user might have managed better with the dose I ingested. One builds up a tolerance." She shuddered. "I never want to. The tablets I took…"

"Were they in the bottle on your bedside table?" Henrietta asked.

"Yes—I thought they were herbs. I remember wondering why they were white tablets instead of green capsules, as most of my herbal remedies are—the ones that aren't tinctures, of course. I take several tinctures, too. I don't remember, but I must have decided they were different because we bought them in America."

Henrietta stood, her expression gentle. "Where did you buy them?"

"Graham got them for me from a chemist in Heron's Cove. I stopped to see Lucas Sharpe—but you know that already, don't you? I have a feeling you're police. You are, aren't you? Maybe the doctor said. It doesn't matter. I have absolutely nothing to hide. We had our visit with Fletcher, had a wonderful dinner with Rex, Jolie and Adalyn and drove to Maine to enjoy ourselves for a few days. We took walks and ate ourselves sick on clams and lobster. I told myself friendship was as good a reason as any to buy a painting, but I wanted to talk to Wendell Sharpe in case I was missing something. In case Graham and I both were missing something."

"Then you don't think your husband—"

"I love and trust my husband, Miss Balfour, and I don't think he was trying to pull a fast one on anyone, including me." Verity sniffled and brushed her fingertips under her eyes, catching tears. "Loved and trusted. Oh, God." She sniffled. "That doesn't mean he wanted my advice, or anyone else's for that matter. Not Graham's style to seek advice."

Henrietta smiled. "I know the type. Did he take any meetings while you were in the US? Did he see anyone associated with his think tank, for example?"

"No. We didn't see anyone else. Adalyn, Jolie, Rex, Fletcher, the Sharpes, townspeople."

Oliver spotted a nurse frowning at them from the doorway. Henrietta either had an instinct they were about to get the boot or had spotted the nurse, too, and wrapped up with Verity, who was visibly done in. "Please thank Wendell Sharpe for me," Verity said. "I'll thank him myself soon. I know he's elderly. I hope my situation didn't cause him too much distress."

"Wendell's a tough old bird," Oliver said. "He's seen it all in his lifetime. No worries."

Verity looked relieved, but a tear slid down her cheek. "I'm sorry."

"You're done in," Henrietta said. "We'll go. Do take care, Mrs. Blackwood."

"Come back if you have more questions." Verity shut her eyes, visibly fading. "I want to help in any way I can. Graham... I know he was murdered. I just know it."

"Mmm. We'll give Wendell your best."

"Adalyn's mother..."

Henrietta turned again. "Tamara McDermott?"

Verity was half asleep. "Graham was worried she'd meddle. He called me when I was at the gate about to board and said he'd reassured her all was well. Then he told me he'd decided he wanted a few days to himself. He was going to learn to kayak."

"How did you take that?" Henrietta asked.

"Not well. I suspected he was going to follow up with Adalyn's mother and make sure she didn't cause trouble, but I didn't argue with him." Her voice was barely audible. "I just went home to London."

"And when you arrived in London, you immediately rang Wendell Sharpe."

"Yes, I did."

Oliver was about to drag Henrietta out of there, but she said farewell to Verity and spun around, exiting ahead of him. He caught up with her. She glanced at him with those turquoise eyes. "Forgeries and such are out of my area of expertise. Yours, Oliver?"

"I don't know about forgeries."

"Of course not. You only stole works of real value."

"Why would anyone want to steal works of no value?"

"Or hang a forgery in their drawing room. I don't think Verity lied, but I'm not convinced what she told us is complete."

"She never said why she believes the painting is a fake."

"She didn't, did she?" Henrietta hooked her arm into Oliver's. "We'll let her rest, and then we'll see if she'll answer a few more questions."

They slipped into a traditional tea shop that served cakes, scones, soup and light sandwiches—and a wide variety of tea—and sat at a table in a quiet corner. Plain scones, gooseberry jam, cream, English Breakfast tea. For two. Henrietta hadn't asked Oliver what he wanted. Obvious, he supposed, that he, too, preferred to keep things simple.

"I wonder how far we'll get into our scones before I'm hauled in for a tongue-lashing," Henrietta said when the tea and scones arrived.

Oliver lifted the sturdy pot and poured the tea into the two cups. "I thought you had permission to speak with Verity."

"Yes, well..." Henrietta didn't finish.

"How would MI5 know? The flowers were my idea. They couldn't have been bugged."

She ignored him and picked up her tea, closing her eyes as she breathed in the steam.

Oliver was still on the case and couldn't relax. "What if Graham Blackwood knew the Campbell painting was a fake and wanted to talk to Tamara McDermott about it? What if he was afraid it had something to do with Stefan Petrescu's death? What if the painting was payment somehow for taking out Petrescu?"

"I don't see the Campbells as assassins, Oliver."

"The son? Jolie Romero? Graham, Verity—"

"Alfred the wire-fox terrier puppy? Let's throw him into the mix."

"I'd be his first victim," Oliver said, but he didn't feel any humor. "We could be trying to connect dots that might have nothing to do with each other. Are you going to check into Mr. Petrescu's MI5 and MI6 connections?"

Henrietta slathered gooseberry jam on half a scone. "I'm starving. I could eat fish and chips but scones will do for now."

"Henrietta?"

She sighed. "Any intelligence work he might or might not have done isn't why he's dead."

Oliver felt her frustration. "Law enforcement here and in the US will do their work, Henrietta. Emma Sharpe and Colin Donovan won't leave a stone unturned. You know what they're like."

Her rich turquoise eyes settled on him. "And you, Oliver?"

"I want to hold your hand and walk with you to my apartment and enjoy this fine summer day. It's London, Henrietta. We can't let the day go to waste."

"Not any day," she said, smiling at him as she popped her scone into her mouth. But the moment didn't last. She sighed as she reached into her pocket for her phone. "Here's my tongue-lashing now."

Oliver started into his scone while she took the call in the toilet. She rejoined him moments later. "It was about something else, not a tongue-lashing after all. I suspect we're being left alone."

"Is that good or bad?"

"Depends on the outcome, doesn't it? I want to talk to Verity again, after she's had a chance to rest."

"Is that wise?"

"Necessary. Wisdom isn't always a consideration for me."

That incisive gaze of hers settled on him. "That's something we have in common, isn't it, Oliver?"

"That and a love for dahlias."

She rolled her eyes. "You didn't know what a dahlia was until I showed you."

"I didn't know their name. There's a difference."

"You are incorrigible."

They finished tea and returned to the hospital. Verity had tea and scones of her own on her table. "Please, come in. I'm feeling better. Speaking with you helped everything feel real and chased away some of the fog in my brain. I've never been so sick in my life. And Graham... I can't believe he won't be coming home."

"It's dreadful," Henrietta said. "Do you mind speaking with us again?"

"If you think I can help."

"What else can you tell us about the Fletcher Campbell painting? Did Graham commission it, for instance?"

Verity shook her head. "Fletcher didn't take commissions. Graham said Fletcher took his easel to the river and painted what he saw. He didn't always work that way."

"Did you ever witness him painting at the river?" Oliver asked.

Verity broke off a piece of scone. "In fact, I did. The Campbells' cottage is a short distance from our home. I'm an early riser. I take the dog for a walk first thing."

"I didn't see a dog at your house," Oliver said. "What breed?"

"Springer spaniel. She's with friends. She needs considerable exercise."

"I have a wire-fox terrier." Oliver smiled, having discovered talk of puppies usually eased people's tension. "I should say Alfred has me. I doubt he considers himself in anyone's care."

That brought a smile to Verity. She looked less drawn than she had earlier. "Alfred is establishing terms early, then. I can't say I'd roll out of bed before nine if not for walking the dog. Graham and I take turns…" She caught herself. "She was his dog. There'll be an adjustment without him."

"You'll have each other," Oliver said. Henrietta gave him a look, as if she hadn't expected such a comment from him. Now that he'd done the job of settling Verity down a bit—perhaps a first for him—he hoped Henrietta would dive in and take charge of the interview.

"What did you see that morning while out walking?"

"Only where Fletcher was and that he was painting a river scene. That's why I didn't question at first that the painting Graham bought was authentic." She slowly put her piece of scone into her mouth, as if she needed to buy herself a moment to think. She chewed, swallowed, took a sip of tea. "As I explained earlier, Graham didn't do due diligence," she added, returning her tea to the table.

"What prompted you to question its authenticity?" Henrietta asked.

Verity's shoulders slumped. She stared at her scone. "Stefan told me at the dinner that he noticed small differences between it and a similar painting he'd seen at the Campbell cottage. He wouldn't go into detail. I was going to talk to him after the dinner, alone, but then he was shot to death. He was such a lovely man." She placed her hands at her sides and pushed herself up. "I can't imagine who killed him, or why, but his death has nothing to do with the painting."

"Mmm." Henrietta's tone was neutral—obviously wasn't going to argue with Verity. "How well did Stefan know the Campbells?"

"We were all neighbors but we seldom socialized together. Graham and I hosted the dinner because Rex, Adalyn and Jolie were in Oxford. It was Rex's first visit since his mother's death and the fire and putting his father in a care home."

Henrietta touched a bright daisy, tracing a blossom with the tip of her finger. "Did Stefan have anything else to say when you two talked about the painting?"

Verity didn't answer at once. Finally she cleared her throat and sat up straighter. "He said if it's genuine its value would increase, given the fire and Fletcher's illness. The fire reduced any inventory, and the Alzheimer's meant he wouldn't be painting any more. He asked me if I agreed. I said I did."

"But he suspected your painting wasn't authentic."

"That's right. Stefan was observant—he paid attention to the tiniest details. It's one reason he was so good with languages. He could discern the smallest differences in dialects. I never could. Everything sounds the same to me."

"When did he see the other painting?"

"Last fall sometime."

"Did he tell anyone else what he noticed?"

"I don't know. I asked him not to. At first I wasn't sure what to make of his observations—that's what he called them. He didn't offer a definitive take on the painting. He simply was trying to reconcile the painting he saw in the Campbell cottage with the one he saw in our drawing room. Honestly, for all I knew there was an innocent explanation and it really was Fletcher's work."

"You didn't tell police about Stefan's comments," Henrietta said.

Verity reached for her tea with such force she almost fell out of bed. "I didn't, but I haven't lied to anyone. How could Stefan's fussiness about a few potentially misremembered details of a painting possibly have anything to do with his murder?"

Oliver leaned against the door. Should he state the obvious? Yes, he should. "Given what's happened, I would think a connection between Stefan's and Graham's murders and the painting isn't outside the realm of possibility."

"A possibility isn't a probability or a certainty," Verity said, ready with an answer.

He shrugged. "True enough."

"You went from uncertain about Stefan's take on it to convinced," Henrietta said abruptly. "Why? What happened? What finally convinced you the painting isn't authentic?"

"It was something Fletcher said when we saw him last week," Verity said, her voice just a whisper. "I asked him about the river painting, and he remembered Stefan liked it. It wasn't much, I know."

"But it was enough," Henrietta said.

"His tone, his eyes—I think he knew we ended up with a fake."

"Oliver and I aren't detectives, Verity. We're as mystified by what's going on as you must be." Henrietta smiled, her amiable manner easing the palpable tension in the room. "What was your relationship with Stefan?"

Tears shone in her eyes. "I admired him. He was a kind, good man."

"But nothing—"

"No, there was nothing between us beyond mutual respect. He was pleased Graham had found someone after his first marriage fell apart. That was years ago. The pressures of his long absences wore out his first wife. I've never met her." Verity inhaled deeply. "It'll come out sooner or later—Graham had a brief affair with Ophelia Campbell before we met."

"Ah," Henrietta said. "What happened there?"

Verity squirmed, averting her eyes. "I shouldn't have said anything."

"No, go on, please. It's a difficult time, Verity. I don't need to tell you. Talking can help. Getting things out. How do you know about the affair?"

"*Affair* might be too strong a word. Ophelia told me. She assumed I'd find out through idle or malicious gossip, and she wanted me to know it was nothing. She was much older than Graham, but she was an incredibly alive and sexy woman right up until the end. She knew how to make a man feel special. I imagine Fletcher was like that with women. He's eighty-one now and his mind's gone. It's sad, really. Rex and Jolie are good with him, but you can tell he misses Ophelia. She was only sixty-nine when she died..." Verity's voice trailed off. "I never told Graham I knew about their affair."

Henrietta glanced at Oliver, but he kept his face expressionless. He was out of his realm when it came to extramarital affairs, illicit relationships—the lot. "We're not here to judge," she said.

"I'm not sure it would have worked between Graham and me if not for Ophelia. Fletcher had multiple liaisons. I wouldn't call it an open marriage, but they were devoted to each other in their own way."

"Did Fletcher know about Ophelia and Graham?"

Verity shrugged. "It wouldn't have mattered."

"What about their son—Rex?" Oliver asked. "Was he aware of his parents' extramarital affairs?"

"I wouldn't know but I can't imagine he wasn't aware. Everyone knew, and Rex has managed their business affairs since he left college. Discovering unseemly human behavior is one of the hazards of working for family, I suppose."

Verity drank more tea, some of it dribbling down her chin. She brushed at it with a hand. Oliver glanced around the quiet hospital room. He'd love to go another thirty years before he entered a hospital again. "Verity," he said gently, turning to her. "When did you notice Fletcher's mind was beginning to fail him?"

She gave a tight shake of the head. "I didn't notice."

"Even if his illness was rapid onset, there likely were early signs. His wife must have noticed."

"Ophelia would never have told anyone if she had noticed."

"Not even Graham?" Henrietta asked.

Verity hesitated. "I doubt it, but I couldn't say for certain."

Henrietta leaned forward, toward Verity. "Is it possible Ophelia painted the landscape Graham bought and kept the original? Perhaps she realized she was dying, and she saw Fletcher's mind was failing. She knew they'd never saved for a rainy day, but now one was upon them. She couldn't count on him to keep producing salable works. This way she could profit twice—let Graham buy the fake and then sell the authentic version. She could pretend it was part of a series. She knew Graham wouldn't ask questions."

"Could she pull it off?" Oliver asked. "Could Ophelia imitate or copy her husband's work?"

Verity's face drained of color. "Honestly, I wouldn't know. If it got around she did or even considered it, that could undermine the value of all his paintings. But I'm sure this was a one-off and has nothing whatsoever to do with what's happened." She thrust her chin up, defiant. "I'd look to Stefan's and Graham's work with the British intelligence services if I were the police."

"Well, I'm sure they are doing just that," Henrietta said briskly. "Does Graham own a rifle, by chance?"

Verity frowned, clearly caught by surprise—as Henrietta intended, no doubt in Oliver's mind. Finally she bit down on her lower lip, thought a moment and responded. "He inherited an old stalking rifle from his father. I believe it's the only gun he owns. I never knew his father, but I understand he was a great sportsman. Graham was never that interested in hunting, but he'd go off with friends once in a while to target shoot."

Henrietta raised an eyebrow. "Stefan? Fletcher?"

"I didn't pay attention," Verity said coolly.

"Last question," Henrietta said. "Was Stefan involved in opioids, Verity? Buying, selling, using? Helping a friend or loved one who was dependent or addicted?"

"I didn't get a whiff he was involved in opioids in any capacity. If you don't mind…" Verity pulled up her blanket. "I'm worn out."

"Of course. Thank you for speaking with us again. You'll be sure to tell the police everything you told us, won't you?" Henrietta smiled in that gracious, all-innocence way she had. "They'll be annoyed with us as it is."

"Good," Verity said, the slightest flicker of amusement in her eyes. "Dare I ask who really you are?"

Henrietta pretended not to hear the question, and Oliver followed her lead. Verity, fading rapidly, didn't press for an answer. Henrietta wished her well. "If you need anything, Verity, please let the police know. Don't hesitate a moment."

But Verity was already asleep.

Henrietta was raging by the time they reached Oliver's apartment. "Who would care enough to kill Stefan Petrescu and Graham Blackwood over a forgery? I hope that isn't what got them killed. It's not worth it."

"What was that bit about a rifle?"

"Your FBI friend Colin Donovan asked your MI5 friend whose name I shall not utter for ballistics information on Stefan's death."

"Our friends not just my friends."

She waved a hand. "Whatever. Was your grandfather a hunter?"

"In his younger years he liked to go out for a day of bird shooting. He left me a relic of a stalking rifle. I keep up the license, but the rifle's locked in a vault. I've never touched it. Did Freddy leave you any weapons? He would have had access to an arsenal."

"My grandfather listened to opera at home."

"One can listen to opera and enjoy game hunting."

"Well, he didn't leave me any weapons."

"Not even a poison-tipped umbrella?"

"Oliver..." She sighed. "Sometimes you can be terribly inappropriate, you know."

He grinned. "Perhaps Martin can socialize Alfred and me at the same time."

"I suspect you're both incorrigible."

"What's next?"

"The police need to search the Blackwood house for Graham's rifle."

"You'll tell them?"

"As if they'd listen to me. I'm a garden designer."

"Mmm. A wonder we got in to speak with Verity Blackwood about forgeries, murder and overdoses."

22

Dublin, Ireland

Wendell entered his favorite Dublin pub with his phone stuck to his ear, something he'd always sworn he would never do. But Oliver needed to talk to him. "Can you find out if Graham Blackwood owned other paintings that are copies of the original? Could he keep the original in a vault and display the copy?"

"Anything's possible but why bother?"

"I'm alone in the library with an obscure lowlands single malt. Henrietta's been whisked off to Thames House. That's my assumption. A car came for her."

"At least it didn't come for you," Wendell said, easing onto his favorite stool at the bar.

"I have an evacuation route."

No doubt not an exaggeration, given his history as a thief. "Sounds as if you two have been busy. Care to fill me in?"

He did so, obviously in shortened form. Wendell listened carefully. He had a good mind, but his hearing wasn't what it once was, and he hadn't dismissed that creepy banshee shriek from his mind. He didn't interrupt Oliver, waiting until he finished before speaking. "We need to know who else Stefan Petrescu talked to at that dinner," Wendell said finally. "Did he share his observations about the Campbell painting with anyone besides Verity? Fletcher Campbell's a fine painter, but it's anyone's guess if his work will appreciate in value over time."

"He's no Picasso, as Martin would say—who dislikes Picasso, by the way."

Wendell smiled. He liked Martin Hambly. Oliver was fortunate to have such a dedicated, capable assistant and good friend. Wendell found himself longing for dinner with his family. Timothy, Faye, Emma, Lucas. What he wouldn't give for his wife to be there. He missed her every day, but less so here than in Maine.

Colin. Hell, he'd have to invite his grandson-in-law. Good guy. Solid.

"Wendell?"

"Sorry. Figure this out, and maybe MI5 will let you off the hook."

"Decide I've served my time?"

"Something like that. Thanks for calling, Oliver. I'm glad Verity Blackwood's going to make it." Wendell paused, trying to pin down what he wanted to say. "I think her husband was trying to help people, and it got him killed."

"Any evidence to back that up?"

"I'm an old man having a pint in Dublin. What would I know about evidence?"

Oliver snorted. "Right. Enjoy your pint."

"And you enjoy your Scotch."

After Wendell rang off, the barman placed a pint of Guinness in front of him, having anticipated what he'd want. He'd sit here awhile and hope it helped him dismiss his unease. Some of the lads from the neighborhood would be arriving soon, telling stories, laughing at life's latest absurdities, shaking their heads at its latest outrages or just rattling on about hurling and Gaelic football. They'd snort with amusement if Wendell told them he'd heard a banshee last night. Even if they believed in banshees, they'd all lived too long and seen too much to fear death. Some were men of faith. Some weren't.

It wasn't his own death he feared, Wendell knew.

He pictured Emma, always in the thick of her FBI investigations. He trusted her training and her abilities, but sometimes he wished she'd become a golf pro.

The barman sighed. He was in his fifties, celebrating a new grandson. "Are you going to stare that pint into your stomach, Wendell?"

He picked up the glass and tipped it. *"Sláinte."*

He drank, but he'd missed that first, fresh taste of Guinness. He'd let it sit too long, but it was still good. He set his glass down and wiped the foam off his mouth with the back of his hand.

"All right, Wendell," the barman said. "Who's died this time?"

"I saved a woman's life in London the other night."

"A pretty woman?"

"As a matter of fact."

"It'd be a good deed to save an ugly one but more fun to save a pretty one, eh?"

Irreverent humor. It was what he needed. "You can get into trouble nowadays for that kind of talk."

"Go on, then. Drink up. Tell me about this woman whose life you saved."

"She overdosed on opioids."

"Ah. God bless her, Wendell. God bless her."

He remembered then, the barman—Francis was his name— had nearly lost a son to drugs. "A scourge, these drugs. Have you ever heard a banshee shriek, Francis?"

"The night my grandmother died. I was just a lad. I'll never forget it."

"Do you believe the banshee was warning you of her death?"

"There's no belief to it. It's what it was." Francis, a red–faced, portly man, paused, gazing at Wendell. "Did you hear a banshee?"

"Last night near Ardmore."

"You'd better drink up, then, and I'll pour you another pint."

23

Adalyn made coffee in the Campbells' fantastic country kitchen. It was huge and homey, with big windows, scarred counters, a giant pine table. So perfect on such a lousy, miserable day. The weather was fine. Sunny, pleasant. It wasn't that. Her father was on his way to Boston. There was no stopping him, but she hadn't really tried. Graham's death had put him over the top and freaked her out.

She'd driven up to the Campbell "farm" with Jolie, who'd stayed out late with friends last night and admitted she'd had a bit too much to drink. Verity's overdose and now Graham's death had upset her, too. Rex had visited his father, convinced he would sense his friend had died and need comforting. Adalyn felt it was the opposite, that Rex needed comforting.

But she loved his family farm. It hadn't been a working farm in the forty years the Campbells had owned it, but it was a spectacular place, on a hillside within easy driving distance from the University of New Hampshire, Portsmouth and Boston. And Maine, Adalyn added silently, thinking of Graham out on the rocks by the convent for who knew how long. A detective had talked to her on the phone last night but wouldn't reveal many details. He'd probably want to talk to her, Jolie and Rex today. Adalyn had the advantage of having a prosecutor and criminal defense attorney for parents, but she still was unnerved. And so, so sad, she thought, flip-ping on the coffee maker.

Matt Yankowski was on his way to hang out with her until her father got there. She didn't mind having an FBI agent keeping an eye on her. He made her nervous, but it was okay. Right now she just wanted her mother to turn up safe and sound. Her father had checked with a friend in Halifax who was expecting her tonight. All she had to do was show up, and Adalyn could go back to being mad at her for being so thoughtless. What she wouldn't give for *that*.

She sank onto a white-painted chair at the table while the coffee brewed. Her father would camp out on her sofa until police made an arrest, her mother got in touch and their lives returned to normal. She was pleased and grateful for his concern, but she was torn about having him fly up here. *I'm twenty-one now.*

Her stress was palpable. It was as if it was in the air. A won-der the rest of the place didn't catch fire just from her tension. She'd been open with her father about how she felt. *I know you and Mom deal with stress, but you're better at coping than I am.*

It's difficult when it's friends...family...

Verity and Graham were a lovely couple, Dad. Verity's going to recover, but her life...

She'll figure it out. She has friends who will help her.

She listened to the hiss of the coffee maker. It was an old one. She liked that. As well-off and sophisticated as the Camp-bells were, they hadn't adopted every trend of recent years. No fancy espresso maker. She'd worried the house would have a feel of death and illness about it, but it didn't. Ophelia's cheer-ful watercolors hung in the kitchen. A large Fletcher acrylic landscape of the surrounding hills hung in the living room. Otherwise the stark white walls were unadorned, making the house feel clean and bright, showing off the wide-board floors and exposed beams. Rex had said their Oxford cottage was quite different—more contemporary and colorful. Adalyn would have liked to have seen it, but one day in Oxford hadn't been enough time to get to everything.

She jumped up two minutes after sitting down and grabbed mismatched mugs off an open shelf. She set them on the counter. Rex and Jolie had gone to the barn that had been Fletcher's studio—or what was left of it. It hadn't been condemned, but Adalyn had been shocked at the extent of the damage. Rex hadn't decided whether to raze the studio altogether or rebuild it. He was debating what to do with the property as a whole now that his mother was gone and his father was in a memory-care home.

Adalyn hated to think about such things. Rex had assured her he could cope. He'd grown up in private schools and had always known his parents as international people, with this place as their base. It felt like a real home to Adalyn, but Rex said he didn't have a huge emotional attachment to it. She figured he'd sell it and buy a condo on the Boston waterfront.

Yank knocked on the screen door. Adalyn jumped, clutching her chest. "You startled me," she said. "I didn't hear your car."

"I parked down the hill by the—guest cottage?"

"That's right."

"I walked up. Nice place. I parked next to a white van. Rex's?"

"Jolie's, actually. She and Rex have both been using it to clear out the barn now that it's burned." Adalyn smiled, opening the door. "Come in, please."

He stepped inside, the screen door snapping shut behind him. He wore a lightweight gray suit. Dressed for work, Adalyn thought, her heart racing. Her knees buckled, but she managed to steady herself.

"Where are Rex and Jolie?" he asked.

"At the barn—Fletcher's studio. I'll bring them coffee when it's ready."

"Right."

Yank steadied his gaze on her, and she stood back, grasping the edge of the counter, unable to breathe. "You know about my trip to Heron's Cove."

"Tell me about it, Adalyn."

Why tell him when he already knew? But it wasn't a question she articulated to him. The mother superior who'd discovered her and Verity must have said something. They hadn't seen any other nuns or workers at the convent. "Mother Natalie remembered us?"

"Seeing how you sneaked onto the property and broke into the tower, yes, she remembered you."

"You make it sound worse than it was. It was my first time in a convent. It's beautiful but I can't imagine that life."

Yank glanced at a watercolor of a vase of lilacs, one of Ophelia Campbell's paintings. "Whose idea was it to go up there? Yours or Verity Blackwood's?"

"Verity's, but I wanted to—she didn't have to persuade me."

"Did she tell you why she wanted to go there?"

"Curiosity. I believed her. We both were interested in their work in art conservation, and their convent is in such an incredible spot. We didn't hurt anyone, do any damage or take anything." Adalyn hoped she didn't sound too rehearsed, but she'd spent a good chunk of the night planning what she'd say if asked about their visit. "We stopped at the Sharpe offices in Heron's Cove, too—except I didn't go in, just Verity. Then we had lobster rolls at the restaurant across the street and visited the sisters' shop in the village."

"Did you see Graham on Friday?"

"No."

"Did Verity mention kayaking to you?"

"She did, as a matter of fact. She said there were two kayaks at their rental house, and Graham was obsessed with learning how to kayak. He'd been in canoes. Is that what happened to him? He fell off his kayak and hit his head or drowned?"

"It's an ongoing investigation," Yank said, turning from the painting. "You should have told us about Friday, Adalyn."

"I didn't think of it. Will the Maine detectives get mad at you for talking to me?"

"Probably." He didn't seem concerned. "How did Verity strike you on Friday?"

"Honestly? Frayed. She's not usually like that, but she... I don't know. She was tense. She pretended all was well but it wasn't. I could see that."

"Did you tell her so?"

Adalyn shook her head. "I just tried to make it a fun day. She had ulterior motives for everything we did, though, didn't she? The convent, the Sharpes, the sisters' shop. What was she after, do you know?"

"Did she strike you as suicidal?"

"Not for a second."

"She and Graham—"

"No marital problems if that's your next question. She didn't kill him. He didn't drug her. It wasn't a murder-suicide."

Yank smiled grudgingly. "Detective McDermott."

She relaxed, at least enough to feel less combustible. "I think my parents like the idea of my being an archivist."

Yank seemed more relaxed, too. "Are you seriously considering art crimes?"

"Not committing them."

He grinned. "Smart aleck."

"Agent Yankowski...my mother..."

"We'll find her. Did you tell your mother about your excursion to Maine?"

"No, I didn't tell anyone, even Rex and Jolie. I only told my mother about Stefan Petrescu. I wasn't hiding my trip to Heron's Cove. I just didn't think to tell her. I thought it might come up at dinner." Her voice cracked. "I will get a chance to tell her about everything that's happened since Sunday, won't I? Did Dad get in touch with you about her friend in Halifax?"

"He did. I'd like to talk to Rex and Jolie."

"I'm supposed to bring them coffee. I don't like it in the barn—the painting studio. That's why I volunteered to make coffee."

Yank nodded to the mugs on the counter. "I'll help. Cream and sugar?"

Had he ever helped with coffee? Adalyn pointed at a pottery pitcher and sugar pot on the counter. "We need spoons, too," she said.

He winked at her. "You got it."

Yank didn't want coffee himself. Adalyn smiled. Why wasn't she surprised? They set three mugs, cream, sugar and spoons on a tray. She insisted on carrying it herself. They went through an herb garden at the back door and across the lawn to the barn, painted a classic red despite the addition of windows and skylights.

Rex greeted them at the side door, the only safe entrance. "Coffee, perfect." He took the tray from Adalyn and set it on a table he'd set up by the door after the fire. He nodded to Yank. "Good to see you, Agent Yankowski. Any word on Adalyn's mother?"

"Not yet," Yank said.

"She'll turn up. Jolie's inside. She thinks she's found more papers for you, Adalyn. My parents were disorganized, but I swear they kept everything." Rex added cream to one of the coffees. "Jolie and I are both devastated about Graham.

He and my father were good friends. Maybe just as well the Alzheimer's has advanced to the point Dad wouldn't retain that Graham is gone."

Yank picked at peeling paint on the door trim. "How long did your parents know the Blackwoods?"

"They knew Graham for twenty years at least. Verity's only been in the picture for a couple of years. I'm sure you know my parents didn't have a monogamous marriage, but my father and Verity never had an affair." Rex picked up his mug and sipped his coffee. "Trust me, I'd know if they did."

Adalyn slopped cream into another of the mugs. "Your father was forthright with you about his extramarital relationships?"

"Notches on the belt," Rex said without any apparent animosity.

She couldn't imagine. Her father at least had been embarrassed about his affair.

"My mother was more discreet if that's your next question," Rex added. "Also less prolific an offender. It's just who they were. I gave up trying to understand them a long time ago. It's not how I'm wired, thankfully. But I don't know what this has to do with the Blackwoods."

"This place and Oxford their only homes?" Yank asked.

"They rented the cottage in Oxford. They own the farm. They often spent part of the winter in Portugal, New Mexico—they'd do a short-term rental. I became their unofficial travel agent."

Yank moved to a damaged painting on an easel in light shade. "You'd go with them?"

"Often but not always."

Adalyn shifted awkwardly by the easel. She had no idea if Yank was making idle conversation in a difficult situation or if he had an agenda. *An agenda. FBI agents always have an agenda.*

"This your father's work?" Yank leaned forward, looking

more closely at the canvas, whatever image was there now covered in soot and grime. "Some kind of landscape?"

"Dad's work, yes. It's in Oxford. He started a series of paintings of the River Cherwell last year, before he and my mother came back here. She knew she was terminal, and then he was diagnosed with Alzheimer's." Rex stared at the painting. "I think Jolie can save it. The underlying work is sound."

Yank stood straight. "It's finished?"

Rex nodded. "My father took it home from Oxford and finished it last fall, before he had to stop painting. This is one of my favorites, maybe because it's one of his last paintings. I'd hate to sell it. My parents were as reckless with their finances as they were with their personal lives, but I managed to get hold of the money reins in time—all is not lost." He grinned easily. "I don't have to get a real job yet."

"The painting Graham and Verity have by your father is a landscape of the River Cherwell," Adalyn said. "When did he paint that one?"

"Last fall, in Oxford," Rex said. "Graham bought it before my parents came back home, but he didn't pick it up until July. I think he held out hope they'd get back to England. Given the circumstances, the painting's value is likely to increase. Supply and demand, right? I don't blame Graham if he wanted to make sure I honored his agreement with my father—which, of course, I did."

"You handle your parents' business affairs as well as their finances?" Yank asked.

"If you want to call it that. They often sold works without my involvement. I wouldn't find out until after the fact. My mother was never the artistic or commercial success my father was. Graham wasn't a fan. She was too feminine and lowbrow for his taste, not that he was any kind of art expert. Verity is more knowledgeable. I never got the impression she was particularly interested in my parents' work. She's an old masters type. She organized art exhibitions before she married Graham."

Yank moved back from the easel. "Did she give up her job voluntarily?"

"Yes, as far as I know. Men don't demand their wives quit their jobs these days, do they? That'd be an asinine thing to do. Graham was a fair bit older than Verity, but he wasn't a control freak or a dinosaur."

"Did he buy just the one painting by your father?"

"I think so. If he bought another, I don't know about it."

"I asked at dinner," Adalyn said, pleased to have something to offer. "Graham told me it was only the one. He joked about needing some artist friends who weren't as well-known so their paintings would be cheaper."

Rex set his coffee back on the tray. "As I mentioned, the painting he owns is likely to increase in value now that my dad is no longer able to work, although who's to say whose works will be valued in a hundred years. Won't matter to us. Barring major advances in medicine, we'll all be dead by then."

Yank glanced at the old barn again before shifting back to Rex. "Back to last week. You were with the Blackwoods when they visited your father. How'd he do with them?"

Rex bit down on his lower lip, took in a breath and finally nodded. "He was having a good day. He recognized them. They had a normal conversation for a few minutes." He cleared his throat. "And then it wasn't normal, and they left and I took him back to his home. It's just down the road. It's small and private."

"How did the Blackwoods handle seeing him?" Yank asked.

"They're decent people, Agent Yankowski. They weren't embarrassed for him, or for me. They know he's ill. Alzheimer's isn't a character flaw."

"Did your parents have anything to do with Graham's think tank?"

"No, nothing. They were apolitical if that's your next question. They were way too wrapped up in themselves to notice what was going on in the rest of the world."

Yank raised his eyebrows. "Matter-of-fact about it, aren't you?"

"Resigned," Rex said. "They were what they were. I like to think I inherited the good without the bad, but I'm not perfect by any stretch. Dad was fifty and my mom was thirty-eight when they had me. They were set in their ways by then. So many changes to absorb these past few months."

Adalyn hated to hear the sadness in his voice. "Graham was a fantastic guy," she said.

"Yeah." Rex rubbed the back of his neck as if in pain. "He was energetic, smart, determined. You couldn't help noticing that about him when you were in his presence. You look at photos of him and you might not get that from them. He's sort of milquetoast looking. Was. Damn." He lowered his hand, his gaze on Yank. "I'm having a hard time believing he's dead. He and my father were men who loved being men and who loved women. Whatever people want to say about my dad—and it's probably all true—he would totally focus on any woman he was with."

"How do you know this?" Adalyn asked.

"My mother told me. She said she understood why other women were attracted to him. It was an amazing experience to be with him." He reddened. "You know? I hate to admit it, but some days I wish I had half my dad's luck with women."

Adalyn drank her coffee, wishing she'd kept quiet. But she couldn't help wanting to know more. "What about Jolie? She never…you know…" She shook her head. "Never mind. It's none of my business."

Rex laughed, incredulous. "Jolie? No chance. Not each other's type. Trust me. I should go find her before her coffee gets cold. Is there anything else, Agent Yankowski?"

"Do you paint?" Yank asked casually.

"Not what my parents would call painting, no. I've dabbled. My mother tried to teach me when I was in elementary school. I was hopeless. Nonetheless, I paint every morning from five to six but only for myself. Instead of journaling, I paint."

"What did you paint this morning?"

"I don't even know. The sunrise, I guess. I looked out the window and painted what I saw."

"Original work, then," Yank said.

"If you want to call painting a sunrise original. I wasn't copying anything, if that's what you mean."

"Have you ever copied a work of art?"

"Tried. It was garbage. I don't have that spark my father had. My mother didn't have it, either. She worried about it. I don't."

"A good copyist wouldn't worry about it," Yank said.

"I wouldn't know. I have no interest in that sort of thing. Why?"

Jolie came out of the barn, a bandanna tied over her hair, dirt and bits of cobwebs on her dark gray tunic. She looked hot, sweaty and yet, Adalyn thought, totally in her element. She loved this art rescue mission. She brushed her hands off on her hips. "I've heard of collectors who display copies of valuable art and keep the original under lock and key. It's not forgery—it's all aboveboard. Sorry, I wasn't eavesdropping, just overheard you."

Adalyn sat cross-legged in the shade as Jolie grabbed a mug. The coffee was at best lukewarm by now but she didn't seem to mind as she took a huge drink.

Yank watched her a moment before turning again to Rex. "Have you or your parents had copies done of your father's work?"

"No, Agent Yankowski, we haven't. We've never had an issue with forgeries if that's your next question. Anything else?"

"Where do you paint?"

"In the study at the house. Fortunately, the house was untouched by the fire." Rex glanced at his watch. "I should get busy. It's been a rough couple of days with Verity's overdose and now Graham's death."

"Adalyn was in Maine on Friday," Yank said. "Did you know that?"

"No."

Jolie looked surprised, too. Adalyn felt like a snake. She glared at Yank. Wasn't he supposed to be on her side? But she wasn't going to say that out loud. She rose, adjusting her top just to give herself something to do to keep herself from running. She didn't even have a car. She couldn't leave if she wanted to. She turned to Jolie. "Verity and I visited the Sisters of the Joyful Heart convent and Sharpe Fine Art Recovery and had lunch in Heron's Cove and wandered around a bit."

"No crime in that," Rex said, obviously in her defense. Somehow that made it worse—as if she needed a defense.

"Did you go up there?" Yank asked him.

Rex shook his head. "I didn't, either," Jolie said. "I was working at the studio."

"Graham and Verity wanted a break," Rex added. "It didn't occur to me to intrude on their time in Maine. Adalyn—" He sighed, shifting to her. "You and Verity are friends. It's different for you. I'm really sorry about what happened to her."

She didn't know what to say. Her father would remind her Yank was an FBI agent and she should err on the side of not saying anything. She watched Yank pluck a dandelion long gone to seed, but there was nothing casual about him. "Have you two ever visited the Sisters of the Joyful Heart?" he asked Rex and Jolie.

"I have," Jolie said. "Not since Sister Joan's death, though. I've never been to the Sharpe offices. I'm aware of their work, of course."

Rex was shaking his head. "Not me. Convent, Sharpes. All new to me."

"Heron's Cove," Yank said. "Ever been there?"

"Probably. I've been all over the southern Maine coast on weekends. Heron's Cove is one of those precious towns with shops and clam shacks, isn't it? I must have been there."

Adalyn plucked her own dandelion. She wished she could walk through the fields and woods without a care in the world. It was so beautiful up here, but she and her friends were being questioned by an FBI agent. That was what this was, too. If Yank had come up here as a friend, he was also very much a federal law enforcement officer. Did he think her trip to Heron's Cove had something to do with her mother's behavior? Why she hadn't been in touch, why they couldn't reach her? Adalyn shut her eyes a moment, calmed a surge of panic. She'd be glad when her father arrived. She hated to admit it, but it was true.

"What about your parents?" Yank kept his gaze on Rex. "Sisters of the Joyful Heart, Heron's Cove. Sharpe Fine Art Recovery offices."

"No idea," Rex said. "You can try asking my father. I don't know if you'll get a coherent answer from him never mind a reliable one, but it's a start. He has good days and bad days. He's a very sick man."

Yank nodded. "I'm sorry to hear that. He's at the home?"

"No—he's here." Rex pointed vaguely down the hill. "He's

taking a nap at the cottage. I fetched him before you got here. I won't be able to bring him up here for much longer. I thought... I don't know what I thought."

"We thought he might be able to help with our salvage operation," Jolie said softly.

"Yeah. He spent a lot of time in his studio. He remembers things I never knew." Rex waved a hand vaguely. "I should check on him."

Adalyn hadn't realized Fletcher was there. She supposed she wouldn't, since she'd been in the kitchen making coffee. She felt like a fifth wheel but told herself it was to be expected. She didn't know Jolie or the Campbells well.

"I would like to talk to your father if he's up to it," Yank said.

"I'll let you know."

"Thanks for answering my questions. Mind if I take a look inside the barn?"

"Of course not," Rex said. "Be careful, though. It's not condemned, but it did sustain considerable damage in the fire."

Yank started to duck into the barn with Jolie, but paused as he glanced back at Adalyn. "Join us?"

Adalyn didn't like being in the barn. It was sad, smelly—overwhelming. It made sense for her to tackle as much document research here, on scene, as possible, but, emotionally, she'd rather have everything back at Jolie's Cambridge studio. She shook her head. "I'll bring the tray back to the kitchen."

"Hang out here," Yank said. "I'll only be a few seconds."

He made her *so* nervous. She plopped into the grass and pulled a dandelion out by the roots. The ground was soft enough it came right up. How would Rex ever manage this place on his own? Why would he want to? Sell it, move to the city. That was what she'd do. Maybe Rex didn't have a choice. She supposed the property still belonged to his father. She had no idea how that worked with Fletcher's mental incapacity. She hadn't gotten into that kind of personal detail with Rex.

She debated ignoring Yank's instructions and taking in the tray, but Rex waved to her from the stone walk that led up to the barn from the cottage and lower parking area. "My dad's wandered off. Check up there, will you? I'll check down here. He could be heading back to the home. I'll call there."

He spun around and ran down the walk, veering off to the parking area, out of Adalyn's view. She jumped to her feet and poked her head into the barn. Even now, months later, the smells of the fire were strong. "Fletcher's missing," she shouted.

Jolie and Yank were just inside the door and joined her back outside. Adalyn relayed what Rex had told her. "Do you think he sneaked into the barn?"

"I'm sure I'd have noticed," Jolie said. "I'll look. Does Rex want to call for help?"

"He didn't say. Fletcher's sick. We should help find him."

Yank smiled at her. "I think you're more like your mother than you want to admit. Come on. We can take a look around the property."

24

Tamara heard no sound in her tiny cell except for a few loud birds and clanking pipes. She had no idea what kind of birds or pipes. The stillness felt eerie. She didn't live on a busy road, but she was used to hearing cars. She hadn't heard any traffic since she'd woken up in the nasty bathroom. *But this is good*, she told herself. She'd be more likely to hear the arrival of any cars, wouldn't she?

She hadn't screamed for help in a while. Hadn't done any good, just made her hoarse.

She stood up from her mat—if anything, smellier—and marched in place to get her heart rate up. After a hundred paces, she put the lid down on the toilet and climbed up. She'd absolutely never fit through the window, but maybe she could alert someone she was down here. At least try to get some fresh air and ease her persistent, crawling claustrophobia.

She poked at the thick plastic and pulled on it, but it'd been up there forever and didn't budge.

"Don't be a wimp. Work harder."

She was at an awkward angle, but she fit her fingers under a slightly curled edge of the plastic and tugged on it, cutting herself on a nail hammered in crookedly. She swore at the pain and ignored the blood, continued to work at getting a proper hold on the plastic. Who the hell had banged in so many damn nails? There had to be one every three inches. On a cellar window.

A section of the plastic dislodged, throwing her off balance. She lost her footing on the toilet and grabbed hold of the window frame. She didn't get a good purchase and dropped to the floor.

She caught the side of her hand on another nail, but she didn't care. She hardly felt any pain, and the blood was worth it, a signal of her determination, grit and progress.

I'll get out of here.

She felt a surge of optimism and energy knowing she could break through to the outside world.

She checked her cut hand. She didn't need stitches or anything. The blood could coagulate on its own. It wasn't as if there was a first-aid kit in the gross little bathroom.

Next she tackled the door. She wished she'd done some forcible-entry training. Of course, then she'd have appropriate padding and equipment. Now she was in a dress suitable for tramping around in Boston on a hot summer day. She didn't want to wreck her shoulder, but what were her options? She didn't know if her captor would be back, or when. She wouldn't run out of water, but she'd run out of food soon. She knew she could manage for a long time on just water…

I've got to get out of here.

Adalyn…

She ached to see her daughter. To find out if she was all right.

With a renewed sense of urgency, Tamara slammed herself into the locked door, throwing her body weight into it, magnifying it with as much momentum as she could muster in the small space. The door opened into the bathroom. That worked against her.

She thought it gave way, at least a bit.

She sank onto the toilet, catching her breath. Her shoulder ached. Her cuts stung and throbbed. Slamming into a door hadn't done her injuries any favors.

She knew guys in real life who were like Liam Neeson in the *Taken* movies. Colin Donovan was one. Hadn't Liam Neeson smashed through a door and walked into a bunch of bad guys with guns? Tamara didn't want to do that. He'd killed them all, but he was trained.

Maybe that was a different movie.

Tamara was familiar with Colin's lethal capabilities. She wouldn't be surprised if she knew more about them than his wife did. Emma, the ex-nun.

As she stood again, Tamara placed a hand on the wall for balance. She noticed a drop of blood on the floor. She checked her hand, realized it was bleeding more now. She grabbed a towel, pressed it to the wound. She'd let herself get out of shape the past year, with work—with Patrick. Did he know she was missing? Did he give a damn?

He'll see to Adalyn.

He would. That much Tamara knew.

She sank onto her mat. She was so damn tired. Hungry and sick to her stomach at the same time. What if she managed to break open the door? Then what?

I'll find a way out of here.

She shot to her feet with a burst of energy and pushed on the door with both hands. It didn't budge. She shoved it with her aching shoulder, then shoved harder. Maybe she'd loosened it and she could pull it open now. She yanked on the knob.

Zip. Nothing.

She swore. "Let me out of here! Help! Someone, help!"

She gave up. Maybe someone would hear her now that she'd managed to peel back some of the plastic, but there had to be someone out there. She climbed back onto the toilet, reached for her bloody towel, wrapped it around her hand

and smashed at the plastic and glass. If the glass broke, maybe it would tear up more of the plastic. It was damn tough stuff.

Nada.

She climbed down from the toilet and tossed the towel into the sink. She hadn't cut herself further, but she was spent. She was alone. No one knew she was here. Her captor had left her.

I'll die here.

She should never have helped Adalyn go to London. She couldn't have done it without financial support. Tamara had discussed her misgivings with Patrick. *Three months, Patrick. London is expensive. It's such a big city.*

Adalyn's used to Boston and Washington. She'll be fine.

If Tamara hadn't gone along with the plan, she'd have alienated Adalyn—and Patrick would have shouldered the cost. She'd compromised, asking Adalyn to adhere to a few simple precautions and protocols. Adalyn had been disgusted, of course. *You're paranoid because of your job.*

Probably true.

She loved her daughter with all her heart, but that didn't mean their relationship didn't have its ups and downs. The divorce had put tremendous strain on both of them. Patrick was happy as a damn clam playing the single, high-powered Washington defense lawyer.

Not playing. He was one.

"I'll kill you if you hurt my daughter." She raised her voice, yelling as if her captor was on the other side of the door or out by her window and could hear her. "I promise you. I'll kill you." Tamara shut her eyes, fighting tears. "I'm so tired."

This last was a hoarse croak. Her throat was raw. She heard the defeat in her voice, felt it to her bones. Never in all her life had she felt so alone.

She heard a noise outside the window.

Voices.

"Tamara? It's Yank."

Yank! She went still, listening. Nothing now. But she was positive she'd heard something.

"Mom—Mom, are you here?"

"Oh, my God, Adalyn." She reached up and held on to the sink as she pulled herself onto her feet. "Hello! I'm in here. Help!"

She climbed onto the toilet. She'd stick her face against the plastic and yell. But why were Yank and Adalyn here? *Where am I?*

A gunshot ripped through the silence.

She was so startled she fell off the toilet, wrenching her knee as her momentum smashed her into the wall.

A man swore nearby, just outside her window. Yank?

Her daughter screamed. Tamara recognized Adalyn's voice, felt her terror.

Another gunshot.

No, no, no...

Tamara didn't know what was happening. She lunged at the door. She had to get to her daughter. She heard footsteps— someone half running, half falling down the stairs outside the bathroom door.

"Tamara. Tamara, it's Matt Yankowski. Adalyn's okay."

Her heart leaped. She pounded on the bathroom door.

He pushed it open, collapsing onto the floor just across the threshold in the cellar. He clutched his right shoulder. Blood oozed through his fingers. She swore, kneeling next to him. "My God, Yank. Is Adalyn..."

"I'm here, Mom."

Tamara looked up, saw her daughter crouched by an empty clothes rack. "What happened? Who shot Yank?"

"I don't know. I think Fletcher Campbell got hold of a gun.

Yank—he saved me. He saw something or heard something and he grabbed me…"

Those details could wait. Tamara knew they had to focus on the immediate situation. "Where is the shooter?" she asked sharply. Her daughter stared blankly at Yank. Shock was setting in. "Adalyn. The shooter."

She shook her head. "I didn't see anything. Rex said his father was asleep in the guest cottage but wandered off. Then he went to look for him."

"Guest cottage?"

"That's where we are, Mom. The Campbells' guest cottage on their farm."

Not Maine, then. Tamara pushed back her questions. Yank still had his gun in his right hand. She knew better than to ask him to give it up to her. He tried to speak but Tamara stopped him. "Don't talk. Let me help you. Adalyn, can you grab some towels? We need to stop the bleeding."

Adalyn leaped into action, running into the bathroom. In a moment, she returned with a hand towel. "He'll be okay, won't he?"

Tamara took the towel and pressed it against Yank's wound. He winced and lowered his hand. "Be still, Yank. It looks like a through-and-through wound." It did, but she had no idea if she was right. She just wanted him to stay optimistic. "We need to get help. How did you get down here?"

"We went through the bulkhead," Adalyn said. "It's still open. We heard you. We thought Fletcher…" She gulped in air. "We didn't know. Yank was trying to protect me."

He shifted despite Tamara's instructions to stay still. "My phone's in my right jacket pocket. See if you can get a signal."

Tamara managed to dig out his phone, but she saw *no service* on the screen and set it aside. Yank slumped, still managing to keep a decent grip on his nine millimeter. She didn't have a plan formulated yet, but he needed medical attention. Soon.

"Mom, he's not dying, is he? Verity overdosed and Graham is dead…"

"Adalyn. Listen to me. We need to stay calm. Who else is here?"

"Rex. He's looking for his father. Jolie. I don't know where she is. Fletcher."

"Did you actually see Fletcher?"

"No," Adalyn said. "He's sick. He has Alzheimer's."

Tamara had no idea what to do next. Had an old man with Alzheimer's shot Yank? Was he out there now with a gun? How would he get a gun?

No.

Something else was going on.

"Mom…" Adalyn's breathing was noticeably shallow. "Those are drugs."

Tamara followed her daughter's gaze to a box by the washer. Pill bottles, syringes, patches. And painting materials, in another box. "That's for later," she said quietly. "Adalyn, can you keep the towel pressed against Yank's wound?"

She nodded, her face pale. "Yeah."

"We're going to be okay. We'll figure this out."

Tears glistened in her daughter's eyes. "I guess you're not on the ferry to Nova Scotia."

Tamara managed to smile. "No, I guess I'm not."

Emma parked next to Yank's sedan at the Campbell farm, a spectacular place with sloping lawns, a white clapboard house with black shutters, a red barn and what she assumed was a guest cottage, also white. Yank hadn't responded to her text on the forty-minute drive from Maine. She checked her phone again when she got out of the car. Not much of a signal.

A stone walk led up to the main house, the climb steep enough there were intermittent steps. She noticed the driveway circled up from the cottage parking area to the barn. She couldn't see if anyone was parked there. The house blocked her view. A pleasant breeze wafted through mature maple trees that dotted the sloping lawn. A plaque by the cottage's front door noted it had been built in 1811 by an Elias Jones. An empty pottery flowerpot on the doorstep was the only indication of the troubles the property had seen in recent months, with Ophelia's death, the fire and Fletcher's decline. Rex probably hadn't had time for flowerpots.

As she started up the walk, Emma heard a noise to her right, by the cottage. Jolie Romero waved to her from a narrow spot between a cedar tree and the side of the cottage.

Emma crossed the grass to her. "Is something wrong?"

Jolie placed a finger on her lips. "Shh." She didn't budge from her spot. "I swear to God I heard gunfire. I ducked behind the first tree I saw." She spoke in a whisper. "I was looking for Fletcher. He's on the loose. I don't know how he'd get hold of a gun. I would think Rex would have any weapons locked up."

"Where's Agent Yankowski?" Emma asked.

"He and Adalyn went to help look for Fletcher. It's a big place."

"Before the gunfire?"

Jolie nodded. "I could be wrong. Maybe it was just a car backfiring." She motioned vaguely behind her. "I heard something back there. The bulkhead's open. Maybe Fletcher's hiding in the cellar. He's probably scared and confused. Don't shoot him or anything."

"Keep your hands where I can see them, Jolie."

"Of course. Will do."

Emma quickly patted her down but didn't find a weapon.

As she stepped back, a frail-looking, elderly man stumbled toward them, from behind the house. He had a small .22-caliber pistol in his right hand, pointed at the ground.

Jolie gasped. "Fletcher. Jesus…put that gun down."

He dropped it at once. Emma eased over to him and grabbed the weapon. "Let's see your hands, Fletcher." He splayed his hands in front of her, and she quickly patted him down, not finding any other weapons. He had on baggy jogging pants, a hoodie and sneakers. She stepped back. "My name's Emma Sharpe. I'm with the FBI. You're Fletcher Campbell?"

A curt nod. "I know who I am."

"Did you fire this weapon, Fletcher?"

"What weapon?" He looked helplessly at Jolie. "Do I know you?"

"I'm Jolie, Fletcher. Jolie Romero. We're here to help you. I heard a gunshot—do you know what happened?"

He stared at the gun in Emma's hand. "We went shooting with Graham. I hated it. Ophelia and Rex loved it. They never killed anything. Birds. Graham's father shot birds. No, no." He looked pained and confused. "I heard a gun go off."

"Where did you get this gun?" Emma asked.

"That's not my gun. Rex locked up my guns. He doesn't trust me. He's always grumpy." Fletcher stared at Emma and then at Jolie, confused, frustrated. "Who are you? Where's Ophelia?"

"It's okay, Fletcher," Jolie said gently. "We'll get you home. Emma is here to help. Have you seen Rex?"

"Rex is here? Where is he?" Fletcher stared blankly at Emma. "Who are you?"

Jolie glanced at her. "We aren't going to get anywhere with him. Even if he tells us something, it won't be reliable."

"I see that," Emma said. "Did Agent Yankowski come in this direction?"

Jolie nodded. "Yes, with Adalyn. Maybe they ducked into the cottage cellar when they heard the gunshot? If Fletcher woke up confused and scared and saw people he didn't recognize—strangers..." She looked helplessly at Emma. "He's not in his right head. You can see that, can't you?"

"Where's Rex now?" Emma asked.

"My van isn't here," Jolie said. "I assume he took it and went to Fletcher's nursing home to see if he's there or making his way there. The home's just a mile up the road."

Emma peered around the corner of the house. She could see the open bulkhead. "Yank? Adalyn? It's Emma Sharpe. I'm here with Jolie and Fletcher."

She heard a moan. Then Yank crawled out from the open bulkhead, falling onto the grass. "Emma..."

Tamara McDermott poked her head out. "He's been shot." She scrambled out of the bulkhead and knelt next to Yank, her eyes fixed on Emma. "He won't bleed out but he needs an ambulance." Tamara pressed a blood-soaked towel to Yank's shoulder. He still had his gun in his hand. She gave Emma a faltering smile. "He won't let me touch it."

Adalyn burst up the bulkhead stairs past her mother. She gulped in air. "Emma—Agent Sharpe, I told Agent Yankowski about the convent. I know you found out I visited Verity in Heron's Cove on Friday. I'm so sorry I didn't say anything. I didn't think it mattered. It didn't get anyone hurt, did it?"

"Let's focus on getting Yank medical attention," Tamara said.

"Mom—"

"It'll be okay."

"You don't know that." Adalyn pivoted back to Emma. "Mom was held in the bathroom in the cellar. There are drugs down there. By the washer. Patches, pills. Syringes."

"Ophelia," Fletcher said softly. "She's been sick a long, long time. She likes her pills. Rex keeps track. He doesn't want her to overdose." He stared at the ground, as if he was trying to figure out if what he'd just said made sense. He looked up. "Where is Ophelia?"

"They aren't legal meds, Emma," Tamara said. "There are painting materials down there, too. They're in boxes mailed from Oxford in the UK."

"I want to go home," Fletcher said. "Would that be okay?"

Jolie took his hand. "Of course. We'll get you there as soon as we can."

Emma had a weak signal, but she managed to call 911. She identified herself to the dispatcher and gave her the rundown of the situation. They needed an ambulance, and they needed to put out an alert to find Rex Campbell.

Adalyn sniffled and collapsed onto the grass. "Yank saw a shadow or heard a click or something. He shoved me to the ground. He took the bullet..." She raised her chin to Emma. "He saved my life."

Emma turned to Fletcher. "You did a series of paintings of the River Cherwell in Oxford."

He squared his thin shoulders and shook his head, adamant. "One painting. My last one. I told Rex. He paints better than he lets on. He likes Oxford. He painted the river, too. Copied me. Cheater."

"Hell, Fletcher," Jolie said. "Has Rex been faking your work?"

The old man didn't answer. He sat next to Adalyn and patted her knee. "You'll be fine, dear. What's your name?"

Emma shifted to Jolie. "What do you know, Jolie?"

"Nothing, but I've been uncomfortable since I got back from England. I blamed it on Stefan Petrescu's death. It was so upsetting. Fletcher knew he was failing last fall. Ophelia was very sick by then. They never saved any money. He did one fantastic painting of the river in Oxford before they came home. Then he worked off photographs to do a series. He was obsessed. He started at least ten different paintings, but every single attempt was crap. He never finished any of them."

"What happened to the one that was good?"

Jolie sighed. "That's the one Graham bought."

"And the attempts? Where are they?"

"Burned up in the fire, mostly. Ophelia and Rex wanted to put together an inventory to help with finances, but it was too late. Rex took it in stride. For all he did for his parents, they left him with nothing but debts and problems." She paused. "Only two of Fletcher's paintings survived the fire. They're not in great shape but they should sell. One of the crap river paintings survived, too. I haven't had the heart to tell Rex it's worthless. Fletcher didn't keep much inventory. It's lucky there were even two solid works that survived. They're authentic. I'd swear to it. I know Fletcher. I know his work."

He was still sitting in the grass next to a shaken Adalyn. His chin popped up. "Rex copies me all the time. Pisses me off. Ophelia told me to lay off him."

"Where did you get the gun?" Emma asked him again. "Can you remember?"

His eyes lit up. "Rex. Rex gave it to me. I was scared. I heard a gun go off. He didn't want me to be scared. All my years here…" He frowned, glancing around him. "What is this place? I want to go home. Jolie, can you take me home?"

"Of course, Fletcher. Just sit tight, okay?"

"When did Rex leave here?" Emma asked her.

"Thirty or forty minutes ago."

Time enough to get to Heron's Cove. "Tamara," Emma said, "where were you when—"

"I was in Heron's Cove. I went up there Sunday afternoon to meet Graham Blackwood at his rental house. I never saw him. Someone grabbed me and shoved me into the back of my rental car. Next thing I knew I woke up in the cellar. I had no idea where I was. Have you found my car?"

Emma shook her head. "It isn't here."

Tamara frowned. "It's not? Then where is it? Still in Heron's Cove? I was transferred to another vehicle, then. I don't remember much, sorry. I was injected…" She paused, licked her chapped, cut lips. "Opioids, I suspect."

"We found opioids at the Blackwoods' rental house," Emma said.

Tamara didn't look surprised. "Planted," she said without hesitation.

Emma tried Colin, but the call didn't connect given the lousy signal. She texted him. It's Rex. He could be in Heron's Cove.

But why?

To plant more evidence. He didn't plan to take the blame for what he'd done.

She clutched her phone in her hand. "Fletcher mentioned Rex went shooting with Graham," she said, addressing Jolie. "Is that true? Does Rex know how to shoot a rifle?"

Jolie shrugged. "Oh, sure. He's a damn good shot."

Yank stirred at the sound of sirens from the vehicles of the approaching first responders. Tamara kept pressure on Yank's wound as she gave her daughter a weak, encouraging smile. "We'll get through this, Adalyn. We'll get through it together."

"I liked Rex, Mom," Adalyn said softly.

"We both did," Jolie said. "He took my van on Sunday. The bastard's going to try to pin everything on me."

"Tough to give up the goodies," Yank mumbled, stirring as the first police cars arrived. "Emma?"

She heard the emotion in his voice and understood what he was asking. "We'll see to Lucy, Yank."

"Thanks," he said, and passed out.

25

Heron's Cove, Maine

"There it is."

Sister Cecilia pointed at Tamara McDermott's rental car, tucked behind a garden shed down the hill from the convent vegetable garden. Colin had arrived at the convent's main gate to meet Kevin when she intercepted them. They followed her down a dirt lane to the shed on the opposite side of the peninsula from where she and Emma had found Graham Blackwood's body.

"I didn't find the car myself," Sister Cecilia said. "Another sister discovered it a little while ago when she came down here to dump compost. We collect it from the gardens and kitchens and then dump it here every few days."

Colin took a look inside the car. He wasn't surprised to see opioid patches and syringes on the front passenger seat.

"I'll call it in," Kevin said. He turned to the young nun. "Did you or the sister who found the car touch anything?"

Sister Cecilia shook her head, adamant. "We're familiar with basic police procedures." She glanced at the car. "Unfortunately."

"Understood," Kevin said.

"Sister Bernadette—she's the one who found the car—told me she saw a small van coming out of here Sunday afternoon, probably a bit after I heard the voices down on the water by the gazebo while I was looking for mushrooms. She didn't think anything of it. Someone turning around, lost. It was a white van with Massachusetts plates. Do you want me to get her?"

"That's okay, Sister," Kevin said. "Let's wait for the detectives."

Sam Padgett had checked in to let Colin know Tamara McDermott didn't get on the ferry in Portland. Made sense now that he and Kevin were looking at her car. Colin noticed Sister Cecilia was squinting past him toward the lane that led to the convent's main gate. "What is it, Sister?" he asked her.

"I saw Timothy Sharpe on the trail to the gazebo."

"When?"

"Just now."

Kevin frowned at her. "What were you doing there?"

She scrunched up her face, a touch of defiance about her. "I was looking for mushrooms."

"Mushrooms, huh?"

Sister Cecilia flushed. "Yes, Officer Donovan. I can't be afraid to look for mushrooms. I live here. It's my home. I went alone. I shouldn't have, I know, but I did. Mother Natalie asked us to go about our routines in pairs, at least until you make an arrest." She paused, still with that look of defiance. "You being the police, I mean."

Kevin crossed his arms on his chest. "You weren't doing a little detective work of your own?"

"No, I wasn't. Anyway, I didn't get far. Sister Bernadette came and got me about the car. Mr. Sharpe passed me on the main trail. I was still on the path down from the convent."

"Did you see anyone else on the trail?"

"No, and I didn't speak with Mr. Sharpe."

Colin shifted to Kevin. "Can you stay here with Sister Cecilia? I'll go see what's up with Timothy."

"Meet you there as soon as I get free," Kevin said.

Sister Cecilia sniffed. "I don't need anyone to stay with me."

"I meant free of the detectives," Kevin said with a wink. "Easy, okay?"

"Sorry. I woke up..." She paused, thinking. "Angry."

Kevin nodded. "Good."

Colin left them. Sister Cecilia had gone pale again, but she was handling herself well. Kevin wasn't easily ruffled. Colin followed the dirt lane back out to the gate and walked along the black-iron fence that enclosed the main convent grounds. He almost missed the path to the waterfront trail, but Sister Cecilia had left a small basket of mushrooms tucked on the roots of a pine tree. He picked up his pace once he was on the rough trail, feeling a sense of urgency he couldn't define. Had Tamara parked the car by the sisters' shed herself? Had someone else? Was she hidden on convent grounds, somewhere else in the area—would the police find her body when they searched the area around the car?

When Colin reached the water, he turned toward the gazebo. Best to get his father-in-law out of here. He continued on the wider trail out to the gazebo where Sister Cecilia and Emma had discovered Graham Blackwood's body. The tide was rising, a cormorant diving off the point. Colin welcomed the steady, refreshing breeze off the water. He'd like to be taking this walk under better circumstances—with Emma, checking out tide pools and seabirds instead of with a man's death and a woman's disappearance weighing on him.

The trail wound through tall spruce trees. Their pungent scent mingled with the saltiness in the air from the sea, his own sweat. He trusted his instincts, but knew better than to jump ahead of the facts. When he reached the gazebo, no one was there. He noticed a six-inch length of yellow crime scene tape that had been left behind, but otherwise there was no sign a man had died here.

He stood on the ledge above the water. A Rock Point lobster boat was working its string down toward the cove and the house the Blackwoods had rented. The New York couple who owned the house had gotten their cleaning crew in to scrub it top to bottom. They were lining up painters. They didn't want any reminders of the tragedy with the British couple who'd stayed there a few days.

Colin checked his signal to call Emma but stopped abruptly. Directly below the ledge, a man was facedown in the water. His head popped up. He gasped for air, reached forward with one arm as if he were trying to swim or grab hold of something.

Timothy Sharpe.

He rode the back of a wave into the face of the ledge. He flailed, but he couldn't get a decent grip on the steep, wet rock. Another wave smashed into him, pulled him away from the ledge.

His bad back, the cold water even in summer—he was in trouble.

Colin shoved his phone into his jacket pocket. "Timothy! Hang on. I'm coming."

He ran down the trail, away from the gazebo and the ledge. He cut through trees to the water's edge. He looked around for a branch, something he could use to help pull Timothy into shore. How the hell had he ended up in the water?

Rex Campbell suddenly appeared from behind a spruce tree on the edge of the water. He was up to his knees in the incoming tide, balanced precariously on rocks. He lunged as if to jump into the water. Colin grabbed him, yanked him up off the rocks and threw him facedown onto the ground. "Keep your hands where I can see them and don't move."

"I wasn't attacking you. I was going to help Timothy Sharpe. He's in the water—"

Colin patted him down but didn't find a weapon.

"I haven't done anything. I'm not your problem. I saw Timothy Sharpe on the trail. I wanted to talk to him to find out if he saw anything on Sunday, but he fell in the water. Is he high on opioids? It's not his fault. My mother—I saw what can happen with these drugs."

Kevin appeared and eased down to them. "Hold on to him," Colin said, handing Kevin his gun. "I need to get Timothy out of the water. He'll drown if I don't."

"I've got Rex," Kevin said. "State guys heard from Emma. She's been trying to reach us. Rex here is our guy. The rest can wait. Go."

Colin pulled off his jacket, tossed it onto a dry rock and plunged into the cold Maine water. He couldn't wait for rescuers. Kevin would get them here as soon as possible. He could hear his brother placing Rex under arrest, reciting his rights.

Rex wasn't shutting up. "You're wrong, wrong, wrong. I haven't hurt anyone! It's Jolie Romero. It's *all* Jolie. She provided my mother with illegal painkillers. She used what was left over after her death to set up Graham and Verity. She wanted Timothy Sharpe to take the blame for the drugs. She knows he's had problems with opioid abuse. Graham was suspicious, too. He told me so." Rex paused, breathed. "Graham was going to get Adalyn's mother involved. Jolie couldn't have that. She came up here on Sunday and killed him and grabbed Tamara. I left her and Adalyn with Special Agent Yankowski at the farm just now. My dad, too. I had to get up here. I'm telling you, I'm innocent. She's framing me."

Colin heard everything Rex said but didn't break stride. He caught a swell and rode the back of a wave toward Timothy, who was clearly losing motor control with the cold and the effort to stay afloat and grab on to a rock, a tree root—anything. The water was deeper below the ledge, and Colin swam the last few feet to his father-in-law. He got hold of him, his thin body slack with exhaustion, and pulled him to a flat boulder and then up and out of the water.

Timothy lay on his back, his lower legs dangling off the boulder as another wave crashed against the ledge, spraying salt water. Colin checked Timothy's carotid for a pulse. His skin was cold, bluish, but he was alive.

"Tim…it's Colin. Can you speak to me?"

"I fell." He coughed slightly, shivering. "I slipped."

"Are you hurt?"

"Bruised. My leg and my back. Doesn't matter. I'm okay. I just need to get my feet under me." He grabbed Colin's wrist and tried to raise himself up. "Emma?"

"She's fine. She's with Yank at the Campbell farm." Close enough, anyway. "Sit tight. Help's on the way."

Timothy managed a faltering grin. "Not going to carry me on your back?"

"We need to get you warm."

Kevin had Rex in handcuffs and tossed Colin his jacket. He tucked it around Timothy, who was suffering from at least mild hypothermia. He tried to hold the edges of the jacket, but his fingers didn't cooperate. "I keep a stash of OxyContin at the house. My doctor prescribed them. Last one I took was—" His lips trembled with the cold. "It was more than a month ago, after your wedding. I didn't tell Faye. It was just the one pill."

"We can talk later, Timothy. Conserve your strength and get warm."

"I don't know how many pills were left. Ten, maybe. Someone could have taken some of them and slipped them to Verity Blackwood. I didn't give them to her or to Graham. I didn't know them in London. We didn't talk about drugs. I'd have told you."

"I know, Tim. Just relax."

"Help's three minutes out," Kevin yelled to them.

Timothy struggled to speak. "I'm not in pain. I didn't take any drugs. Must be the cold water." His eyes fluttered shut. "I lost my footing."

"Did you see anyone else?" Colin asked him.

"Fletcher Campbell's son. He wanted to talk to me. I slipped. Colin..." Timothy opened his eyes. "I have a bad heart. If I don't make it, make sure my family knows... I tried, but I'm okay. I'm okay."

Kevin splashed toward them. "Local officers are here. Rescue crew is still sixty seconds out. How bad, Colin?"

"He's weak. He's lost a lot of body heat. He couldn't get himself out of the water with his back injury."

"I'm throwing out the pain pills when I get home." Timothy's eyes were shut again. "I don't think any were stolen. They're a crutch I don't want or need."

"It's okay, Tim," Colin said. "I'm here for you. I'll meet you at the hospital. I'll get Faye. Don't worry."

Two EMTs arrived in helmets, with rescue gear and a stretcher. A marine patrol boat eased around the point. Colin had to back off while they got his father-in-law onto the stretcher. He went with Kevin back to Rex, who was in the custody of a female officer Colin recognized from Rock Point.

Rex raised his gaze to Colin. "You two have this all wrong, Agent Donovan. Jolie betrayed her friendship with my parents. My mother was dying. My father was losing it. He did one last, good painting of the river in Oxford, and she decided to make it the first in a series, with his help. Graham bought that painting, but he picked up one of Jolie and my father's collaborations."

"Is that what you call it?"

"That's what it was. She needed to be up front about it, but a collaboration wouldn't be worth as much as a solo work. Stefan Petrescu figured it out, but he thought it was a mistake and gave me forty-eight hours to straighten things out. I had no idea what he was talking about. I mentioned it to Jolie. She panicked, I think. Her reputation. What people would do when they found out." Rex paused, all innocence as he looked up at Colin. "She killed Stefan. At first I didn't think his death was related to his questions about the painting. Honestly, I didn't. Then Verity and Graham showed up in Boston, and she overdoses and he's killed—I think Jolie did something to Adalyn's mother, too. You have to believe me."

Colin shook his head. "Why would Jolie do all that, Rex?"

He didn't hesitate. "She's devoted to my father. She's the one woman he never had in bed. It's a source of pride for her. As if he respected her too much to sleep with her. She wanted to help. I think she felt sorry for me, too. Thought I wouldn't manage on my own. I let her stay at the farm whenever she wanted after the fire. She was there last night. She told Adalyn she was out with friends, but she wasn't. I played right into her hands by being stupid."

Kevin shook his head in disbelief. "This guy, Colin."

Yeah, Colin thought. This guy. "It wasn't Jolie Romero, Rex. You killed Stefan Petrescu, you slipped Verity Blackwood opioids, you killed Graham Blackwood and you grabbed Tamara McDermott and took her to your family's farm. Why bother with Tamara? Did she surprise you and you needed to find out how much she knew about what you'd done?"

"No, no, no," Rex said, shaking his head, adamant. "None of that's true. Did you find Tamara's car? It's not on the farm. It has to be out here somewhere. I found the key while I was looking for my father. It's in my pocket. I took it with me.

I brought him up to the farm this morning. I let him take a nap in the room in the guest cottage where Jolie stays. The key was on the bedside table. I freaked out when I saw it. I knew what she was up to."

Kevin angled a skeptical look at him. "Figured you'd plant the key here at the gazebo?"

"No. I'm not planting anything. I was in a panic."

"I bet," Kevin said. "Having Tamara's rental car key on you isn't in your favor."

"That's what I'm saying. She's framing me."

"You've been doing a lot on the fly, Rex," Colin said. "You hid Tamara's car by the nuns' shed and transferred her to Jolie's van. What did you do, drug her with some of your mother's meds?"

"Jolie did," Rex said calmly. "It'll all come out. You'll see."

"The police are searching for Graham's old hunting rifle," Colin said. "They'll match it to the weapon used to kill Stefan. Hope you have an alibi for where you were that night."

Rex stared at Colin and, for once, was quiet.

Colin squished some water out of his shoes. "What if I told you someone saw you out here on Sunday?"

Rex didn't hesitate. "I was here. I admit it. It was part of her plan. Graham called me that morning and asked me to meet him. I told her. I was doing a run to Cambridge in Jolie's van and detoured up here to see him. I parked at the convent and walked down the road to the cove and got onto the trail. I don't know this area. I got a bit lost. Graham didn't show up. He'd said he was going to kayak out to an old gazebo. I was already running late and didn't want to wait. So I left. I didn't see Adalyn's mother."

"Where was Jolie Romero?" Colin asked.

"I thought she was at the farm, but she must have followed me. She probably took my father's car since I had the van.

He doesn't drive anymore, obviously. Did she drug Graham? Is that how she killed him? Or was it just a contributing factor? She could do it. Kill Graham, kidnap Adalyn's mother. You've seen her. She's tough. She hauls paintings. She used to go shooting with Graham."

"You're all over the place now, Rex," Kevin said without sympathy. "You should pick a story and stick to it. You don't have much working for you."

"I see everything so clearly now, but I'm the one who looks guilty."

Kevin sighed. "That's because you are guilty, Rex."

"What did you do with the rock you used on Graham?" Colin asked.

Rex smacked his mouth shut and looked away.

"You threw it in the water," Kevin said. "That would make sense."

"You don't understand." Rex gave a long-suffering sigh. "Jolie manipulated my parents. All of us."

"It's over, Rex," Colin said.

Kevin got him up. "Let's go."

The EMTs got Timothy onto the marine patrol boat. It was the fastest way to get him to a hospital. Colin gazed out at the water. The lobster boat had gone. Bright buoys bobbed under the clear sky. He walked up to the ledge, where he could get a decent signal, and called Finian Bracken. "Meet me at hospital. Bring Faye and Lucas."

He'd get Emma and bring her there himself.

26

Emma finished up with the state and local police at the Campbell farm. She stood outside of the barn. She'd finally taken a look inside and had seen the damage from the fire. A wonder no one had been killed. The art in the studio had been Rex's last hope for maintaining his lifestyle. It included his attempts to imitate his father's work with a River Cherwell "series," based off that one last painting Fletcher had done in Oxford in the fall. Rex had substituted it with a similar painting his father had started and he'd finished. He'd left the fake for Graham to collect from the Campbell cottage.

The genuine Fletcher Campbell painting burned in the fire.

What a blow that must have been for Rex, Emma thought. He'd have sold it when the price of his father's work had increased to his satisfaction. Since it was the first in a series, who would ever question the authenticity of other River Cherwell paintings, including the one in the Blackwoods' drawing room?

Stefan Petrescu, for one. An observant friend.

Increasingly desperate and entitled, Rex had spiraled out of control, and now he was under arrest in Maine, thanks to Colin and Kevin.

Emma felt no sense of relief.

Yank and Tamara had been transported to the hospital. Tamara seemed to be in good shape—worried about her daughter and desperate for a change of clothes. Sam Padgett was escorting Lucy Yankowski to meet her husband. Yank needed surgery, but he'd managed to make a statement to police as EMTs were loading him onto a stretcher. No question Fletcher hadn't shot him. Yank had spotted him seconds before getting hit. Fletcher had pointed past Yank, into the trees where Rex must have been, and yelled something about a gun. It was enough for Yank to draw his weapon and protect Adalyn.

Of course, Yank was mad at himself for not having seen through Rex sooner.

Emma hadn't told him about her father. She'd head to the hospital in Maine where he was as soon as she could get her car out. It was still blocked by emergency vehicles.

She noticed Jolie Romero edged toward the row of sunflowers by the barn. "They reseeded themselves," she said quietly. "Rex didn't plant them. He got rid of the property manager this spring. That should have been a damn clue money was tight, but I didn't pay any attention. He was scrambling to figure out what expenses he could cut, what he could sell."

"I'm sorry, Jolie," Emma said.

"Yeah. Thanks." She touched a yellow sunflower petal. "Happy flowers, aren't they? Rex—he's in custody, the police said. He did everything, didn't he? Killed Stefan, set Verity up to overdose, killed Graham, kidnapped Tamara. Sociopathic SOB. Any word on your father?"

"He's in the ER."

"He has family with him?"

"My mother and brother. My husband. I'll get there as soon as I can."

"Rex shot Agent Yankowski, too. He ambushed him and then gave his own father the gun. He said it was me and I set them up to take the blame. He didn't care what happened to Fletcher. Rex would never have managed to get away if he hadn't fired at Yank and Adalyn. It was a risk because you FBI agents are armed, but Rex is a good shot." Jolie shuddered, rubbing her upper arms as if she were cold. "One of his English gentleman skills. He liked playing the role. He had a good time being Fletcher and Ophelia Campbell's son, but ultimately, he gave up everything for self-absorbed parents with talent and no limits. I loved them, but I did see that about them. He should have walked away at eighteen."

"He didn't have to kill anyone," Emma said.

"No." Jolie propped up a tall sunflower bent over in the afternoon heat. "I was fooled, Special Agent Sharpe. One hundred percent. I wasn't a part of this scheme. Rex didn't risk trying to finish off Agent Yankowski and kill Tamara— kill Adalyn and me—but he had his fake alibis and fake motives and whatever lined up so he could pin everything on me. Bastard. Narcissistic psychopath. Those are the ones who fool you, aren't they?"

"We'll do a thorough investigation."

"A nonanswer answer. Sorry if I'm jabbering, but I just had the living daylights scared out of me, and a young man I trusted..." She blew out a breath at the sky. "I bet killing felt good to him. It was a release. Empowering after living in his parents' shadow. Get rid of threats against him at the same time. Win-win."

"I'll never understand how taking a life is empowering," Emma said.

"He slipped opioids left over from his mother into Verity's herb bottle and planted them at the house she and Graham rented. I can't believe he killed poor Stefan. Where'd he get a gun in England? The Blackwoods? Graham had this old relic..." Her lower lip was trembling now. Shock, adrenaline. "It's the gun Rex used, isn't it? Never mind. I know you can't say."

Henrietta and Oliver had been in touch with Emma. The police had searched the Blackwood home in Oxford and discovered a Rigby .275—the weapon used to kill Stefan Petrescu. They were in the process of searching the Campbells' Oxford cottage.

Jolie looked up at the sky as if somehow it could provide answers, or at least understanding. "I was so focused on saving what paintings I could after the fire. I just didn't see anything else." She swallowed, turning to Emma. "I'm still putting the pieces together. Rex grabbed Tamara because he needed to know what she was up to with the FBI and the Blackwoods. He took my van in order to frame me if it came to it. Here I was *helping* him. I gave him a break on the salvage work I was doing. The ingrate."

Emma said nothing. Let Jolie ramble.

"I didn't notice anything off about the painting that night at dinner with the Blackwoods. Maybe if I had..." She shook her head. "Rex would have killed me, too. He kept telling everyone Fletcher was doing a series of River Cherwell paintings. More lies."

"Rex dug himself deeper and deeper into a hole," Emma said.

Jolie nodded, still obviously trying to process what had happened. "He thought he'd get away with it. The easygoing son of intense, spendthrift artists who's actually arrogant and aggrieved. I wonder if he'd have turned violent if his parents hadn't squandered his inheritance. Well, it was their money. That was what my mother used to say about her money. Rex was free to earn his own income."

"Did he ever hold down a job?"

Jolie shook her head. "Not really. He was at his parents' beck and call. He never believed he would measure up to his father either as an artist or a lover."

"Worshipped or hated him?"

"Both. Fletcher was a larger-than-life type, and now he's been brought to ground by Alzheimer's. He's human after all. I thought Rex was coming to terms with his father as someone he didn't have to hate or worship. I was wrong about that, too."

A detective drew Jolie away for more questions. Sam Padgett joined Emma. "Yank will make it. They took him straight into surgery. Lucy's knitting in the waiting room. Hell of a day. How's your dad?"

"He's still in the ER. I adore my father, Sam. He's a regular guy. He never wanted Lucas and me or anyone else to worship him. I think Fletcher Campbell wanted Rex to worship him. Do you worship your father, Sam?"

"Nope."

"Is he still alive?"

"Yep. We talk every Sunday. He always thinks it's about to snow up here."

"Is he retired?"

"My dad will never retire. That's what he says. Hell for him is an umbrella on a beach. He owns his own business. Construction. My brother and sister work for him."

"And you went into law enforcement," Emma said.

He grinned at her. "Someone had to be the black sheep." His grin didn't reach his eyes.

"Yank will need time to recover. What do you think this means for HIT?" Emma asked.

"We carry on," Sam said.

"Unless the director shuts us down."

"Yeah. There's that."

"I need to get to the hospital."

"Want me to drive you up there?"

She shook her head. "It's not far. I'm okay. My car's here."

"I'm sorry, Emma. Be with your family." He kissed her on the cheek. "Keep me posted."

As she started for the parking area, she recognized Andy Donovan's truck as it pulled up next to her car. Colin got out. He was wearing what he liked to call Rock Point clothes. Cargo pants, sweatshirt, running shoes. "You went in the water after my father," Emma said.

"Andy brought me dry clothes when he picked me up at the hospital. You good to go?"

She nodded. "Dad?"

"He's where he needs to be." His eyes connected with hers, and he seemed to understand what she was trying to ask. "It wasn't Rex. It wasn't suicide. He lost his footing. It's a tricky spot. He wasn't reckless."

"You'll tell me everything he said?"

"Everything. Come on. I'll drive."

Adalyn sat next to her mother on uncomfortable chairs in the surgical waiting room. Lucy Yankowski had stepped out to get coffee, leaving behind her knitting. She was working on a sweater made with gray-blue alpaca yarn. She'd told Adalyn about it, had shown her the pattern—a coping mechanism while her husband was in surgery. He'd lost a lot of blood. Lucy had stared at Adalyn and her mother, the blood on their clothes, stuck in their fingernails. Adalyn had scrubbed and scrubbed in the bathroom in the ER waiting area while doctors examined her mother. They'd cleaned up her cuts and scrapes, checked her vitals and released her. Just like Tamara McDermott, wasn't it? Drugged, kidnapped, held for almost three days…and just fine.

Jolie had finally called and said she was going home to drown herself in vodka martinis. *I never saw it coming, Adalyn. Never. I just thought Rex was a lot of fun and didn't have a care in the world.*

Adalyn couldn't imagine going back to work on the Campbell paintings. Jolie probably couldn't, either.

First things first.

"You need to find a new place to live, and a new job, Adalyn," her mother said, as if reading her mind. "Too much baggage working for Jolie Romero. I don't care if she was oblivious to what was going on. Two men were killed. She has a lot to sort through—emotionally, professionally. You're only twenty-one. You just don't need that. You don't need to ask that of yourself."

Adalyn nodded, stretched out her legs. Her mother could be so imperious but right now, she didn't mind. "I have friends looking for someone to share an apartment. I thought it'd be romantic—different—to live above an art conservation studio. It'll be okay. I never got settled."

"You know I try not to put my foot down very often."

"Huh?" Adalyn grinned at her. "Seriously?"

Her mother smiled, patted her on the shoulder. "Compared to what I want to do, I don't put my foot down often. Better? It's your life, Adalyn, but, damn it, all I could think about when I was locked up in that nasty, awful little shithole of a bathroom was…" She bit back a sob. "Was you."

"I know, Mom."

"And you—were you scared?"

"More and more, but mostly I thought you took off early for vacation."

"You were pissed at me, then."

"Yeah."

Her mother hugged her, kissed her on her forehead. They weren't the hugging-and-kissing types, but it felt okay. Natural, even. "I'd never have missed your birthday dinner," she whispered. "I'll make it up to you."

"Mom…it's fine. I got to have dinner with two stud FBI

agents and a brilliant art crimes FBI agent and see them go into action."

"You're not considering—"

"A career in the FBI? No. I'm over that. I'm looking forward to classes starting." She saw Lucy chatting with a nurse outside the waiting room. "I've taken up knitting. Well, I've got yarn, and knitting needles—and I picked out a pattern. A baby blanket."

"You're not—Adalyn, don't tell me—"

"No! Mom, I'm not pregnant."

"Phew. I just survived the worst ordeal of my life. I can't take any more surprises."

"I heard the doctor. She says you're as strong as an ox."

"Those were not her exact words."

Adalyn laughed. They'd be all right, her and her hardheaded, hard-assed mom. "I don't want to abandon Verity. I'm going to write to her and see her when I go back to London. Which I will. I have to. I can't let my life be tainted by Rex's actions."

"I have faith in you to figure out what's right for you," her mother said.

"You have good friends in the Yankowskis, Mom."

She smiled, leaning toward Adalyn. "I'm still not going to start knitting."

Adalyn jumped to her feet when she saw her father through the glass door. He poked his head in the waiting room. "Okay if I say hi?"

Her mother sniffed. "Did you bring your girlfriend?"

"No, no, I—"

"It's okay if you did. I was just asking. I'm glad you're here for our daughter."

"I am, too. I wish I'd gotten here sooner." He walked into the room, kissed his ex-wife on the cheek and then Adalyn.

He was a handsome man, fit at forty-seven, with graying hair and dark eyes, and he had a great career as a criminal defense attorney. Right now, though, he looked haggard, the effects of the past few days bringing out the lines and shadows in his face. "Thank God you both survived."

Adalyn fought tears, but her mother waved a hand. "My office is going to have a field day over my being held in a bathroom. They'll want to hear all the details, and I'll have to tell them I stood on a toilet and slept on a smelly yoga mat and..." She sucked in a breath. "It was awful, guys. It was truly awful, but it's done and we're here."

"I'll go with you on vacation," Adalyn said.

"No, you have school, you have to find a place to live, a job. You have your own life. I planned to meet friends in Nova Scotia. I can fly up there once I get free of the FBI and various detectives."

Adalyn smiled at her father, who winked at her. "At least your mother never thought it was me who had her stuffed in a cellar bathroom."

"Oh, but I did. It was one of the scenarios that ran through my mind. *That damn Patrick McDermott finally snapped.* It made me laugh, at least." She turned to Adalyn. "We get angry sometimes, but your dad and I are friends and always will be. We share you. That's a good thing, the best thing in our lives. I'm sorry about your friends. At least Verity will be okay. She wanted to talk to me, but her husband turned up instead. It was a red flag. Then you tell me at brunch about this linguist's death. I figured I'd talk to Graham and get together with my FBI friends that evening and, if warranted, see what they had to say."

"At my birthday dinner," Adalyn said. "Only you, Mom." She grinned. "What?"

Lucy Yankowski entered the waiting room. "Matt's out of

surgery. It went well. He'll need time but he'll make a full recovery. This has been my nightmare for fifteen years, but he'll be fine. I can see him for a few minutes. Would you—" Her voice cracked. "Would you hang on to my knitting? I'll be back soon."

"I'll check out your alpaca yarn," Adalyn said.

Lucy smiled. "It's wonderful. You'll be knitting with it before long."

She went with the nurse to the recovery room.

"Alpaca yarn, Adalyn?" her mother asked.

"You should feel it. It's gorgeous."

She smiled. "You're right. I might try knitting again after all."

The ER waiting room at Southern Maine Medical wasn't crowded when Colin arrived with Emma. A few people with minor ailments sat far apart from each other. Faye and Lucas Sharpe and Finian Bracken were in an ER treatment room with Timothy. Colin checked with the receptionist to find out where to go, but before she could respond, Finian came through the ER doors into the waiting room.

Emma surged to him. "Finian, what's going on? How's Dad?"

Colin had never seen their Irish friend look so helpless. "I'm sorry, Emma. Your father went into cardiac arrest. There was nothing anyone could do. He died just as we got here."

She stared at him. "What?"

Finian had a soul-deep sadness in his eyes. "Timothy's gone to God, my dear friend. Your mother and brother were at his side."

Colin put an arm around Emma's waist as she absorbed the news. He'd seen it happen before. Timothy hadn't been in the water long enough for hypothermia to get him, but the shock of the cold on his already weakened system had sent him into cardiac arrest.

"The anointing of the sick...the sacrament..." Emma couldn't get the words out.

Finian Bracken gave a solemn nod. "He received the sacrament, Emma. He was at peace on his final journey."

"Strength, peace and courage." She looked up, her green eyes soft with tears and love. "He was a man of faith, Father. In his own way. Thank you."

"He had a heart condition," Finian said. "Your mother knew. They didn't want you and Lucas to worry any more than you already did. She asked me to tell you."

She nodded. "I understand."

Colin could feel her steady against his arm. "Emma, I'm so sorry."

She kept her gaze on Finian. "Granddad? Does he know?"

"Not yet. They're waiting for you. It's late in Dublin."

"He knows," she said quietly. "The banshee..."

Finian looked out the windows at the Maine summer afternoon, but it was as if he was seeing his homeland, the green hills of the Ireland he'd left months ago. "The banshee your grandfather heard was keening for Timothy. His son." Finian shifted back to Emma. "I'll wait inside the doors and take you to your mother and brother when you're ready."

She watched him go through the double doors, back into the ER. Colin ached for her. "I'm glad you were with him," she whispered. "I'm glad he didn't die out there in the water, and Mom and Lucas got here in time—and Finian. Dad's at peace. I believe that. But, Colin..."

He took her hand and drew her to him. "I know, Emma. I know, babe."

She sobbed into his chest. "I didn't get to say goodbye."

27

Oxford, England

I'll burn the bloody painting.

Just like Clementine Churchill did with the portrait Winston so hated, depicting him as an old man…an authentic painting, likely brilliant, done by Graham Sutherland. Lady Churchill, ever devoted to her husband, had it destroyed.

I'll burn the fake Fletcher Campbell painting. I don't want any reminders of that murderer Rex in my home.

I enter the drawing room. I'm weak. My sister is in the kitchen, making tea, eager to fuss over me. I'm pleased she's here. She knows this place never felt like my home. Now it never will. It's the Blackwood home, and there are no Blackwoods to take it. Modest as it is by Oxford standards, it holds their family history. That meant so much to Graham. He'd take out that old game-hunting rifle and see the worn spots where his father and grandfather had used it. Continuity from one generation to the next. But there would be no more Blackwoods here.

I touch the painting that has caused so much trouble.

"Stefan… I'm so sorry…"

Shot with Graham's rifle. The Blackwood rifle. Stolen by that monster Rex.

The river scene was a pleasant one. There was no denying that. Fletcher had guided Rex, and probably Ophelia, too, but it was missing his spark, his genius… I can see that now. If only I'd asked questions sooner. Done something sooner. The painting would never be worth what Graham had paid for it…

No.

I'll burn it first chance I get. I'll get my sister's help. We'll drink wine and be done with it.

It'll be cathartic. A new beginning.

Dear Graham, wanting to help a friend…trusting, believing he wouldn't be cheated…

I hear the kettle ding. Tea and biscuits soon. Then we'll get the dog. I'll scatter Graham's ashes on my own, once they arrive from the US. The pup and I will find a spot on the river Graham so loved. We had a short time together, but it was good. He was kind and frugal, leaving no debts, perhaps little mark on this world—but didn't kindness always leave a mark?

I take the painting off the wall and set it in the entry, turned around so that I don't have to see the scene.

I wish I had my husband back. I wish we'd had a chance to have children together.

When the time is right, I'll return to London, and to work, I don't know where—somewhere nice. I'm young. I'll put evil Rex behind me. If Adalyn wants to get in touch, I'll respond, but I won't seek her out. She's young. She needs to create her own life and not get dragged down by these past weeks.

Graham left me a bit of money, and this house, which will sell easily. His life's work was international diplomacy and policy. I'll make a donation in his name to that work, and transfer anything of interest in the think tank to let someone else continue its mission.

My sister calls me for tea.

I have a chance at a new beginning for me.

A new life.

I kick a hole in the painting as I head out to the patio for tea, biscuits and planning our fire and wine.

28

Oliver didn't resist in the slightest when Henrietta snuggled with him on the couch in the drawing room at the farm, with glasses of his lowlands single malt on the table in front of them. She liked it better than he did. Made a change. "Why do you suppose Rex didn't throw the Rigby into the river after he shot poor Stefan Petrescu?" she asked.

Oliver should have known she was still thinking about the case. The police had completed their thorough search of both the Blackwood house and the Campbells' Oxford cottage. They'd discovered the Rigby in Graham's gun cabinet. "Rex was arrogant enough to think the police would never test Graham's rifle as the murder weapon."

"Hmm. It would have caused more questions if it'd turned up missing, I suppose. Rex had access to the Rigby and knew how to use it, and that's what he did."

"Graham's father and grandfather were keen game bird hunters."

Henrietta raised her head from Oliver's shoulder, some of her curls sticking out, others matted down. "And how do you know?"

"Oxford's my old stomping grounds."

"Everyone was taken in by Rex's charms and sympathetic to his position as his reckless parents' only child. He was stuck caring for them, but he never let anyone think there was a problem—beyond flagrant infidelities, obvious overspending and then severe illness. He made it look easy, as if he didn't have a care in the world and could manage whatever happened." Henrietta resumed her snuggling position. "He knew how to put it on."

"He'd watched his parents long enough," Oliver said.

"He never grew up, did he? He lived in something of a bubble, and when it burst, it burst badly."

Oliver thought that was a perfect description. Jolie Romero and the Blackwoods hadn't realized how much Rex had at stake with his mother's death and father's mental decline. No more paintings meant no more money. "Do you think Graham didn't go home with Verity because he suspected Stefan's death had something to do with her concerns about the Campbell painting?"

"He considered the Campbells friends," Henrietta said.

"Perhaps he felt a bit sorry for Rex."

"Rex must have been angry at his parents for the situation in which he found himself—caring for his dying mother, caring for his father on his long goodbye, utterly broke. They used him," Henrietta added with a sigh. "He had no money, and he still had his father's care to see to. What if he'd had to get a job? He had no skills."

"He managed to kill two people and almost killed more."

"A pathology not a job skill," Henrietta said firmly.

"I wonder if he knew all along his parents hadn't saved a penny."

She gazed at the quiet room. "One does, don't you think? Deep down, one knows."

"I suppose," Oliver said. "We are extremely fortunate, Henrietta, to have what we have. I'm no saint, but Rex…"

"Rex would have been no use to MI5, that I can say." She

raised her head, her eyes luminous in the evening light. "If all this disappeared, we'd figure things out."

"Stefan knew the painting was a fake but he gave Rex a chance to put things right. He probably had no idea Rex was behind the whole thing. Rex felt he had no choice but to kill him. Daring, waiting for him in the dark. I suppose he'd have found another way if Stefan hadn't stopped for his routine comfort break."

"Poor man."

Henrietta settled back down, her head on Oliver's shoulder. He brushed his lips on her hair. She'd been there all the time, in and out at her great-aunt's house, lonely, fierce, intelligent. This incredible woman.

But she was contemplative, sorting out the past days in her mind. "And Timothy Sharpe," she said, her sadness palpable. "Rex didn't kill him but he would have. He was flailing around for someone to take the blame. Life had been good for him and then it wasn't. It was bloody rough, and he did the only thing he knew how to do—figure out how to live off his parents."

"He even set up Fletcher, his own father. It's lucky he didn't shoot someone."

They picked up their glasses and toasted their friend's departed father.

"Best to leave Yank and Emma and Colin to recover and grieve," Henrietta said, sipping the whiskey.

Oliver cupped his glass in his palm. "And us, Henrietta?"

"We're together. It's destiny, I suppose." She smiled, taking his glass from him and setting it and hers on the table. She returned to him, her curls hanging in her face, shadows in her eyes. "We're meant for each other, Oliver. Now, always."

He tucked a finger under her chin, kissed her and smiled. "This means I have to watch those Thor movies, doesn't it?"

She patted his knee. "You'll love them. I'll make popcorn."

He tucked her hair behind her ears. "Timothy Sharpe was a good man, Henrietta. That's enough, isn't it? To live your life as best you can, and at the end people know you were a good person."

She touched her fingertips to his lips. "Yes, my sweet, dear mythologist, best friend, lover, master of Alfred, ex–art thief and MI5 helper, it's enough." She got to her feet, her hair in her face as she looked down at him. "It's everything, Oliver."

"I love you, Henrietta. You know that, don't you?"

She grinned. "Yes, but it bears repeating. Often."

"And me? Can you—"

"Always, Oliver. I love you."

"It's not just because I do all those martial arts and am good in bed?"

"Well, there's that." She laughed, color rising in her cheeks. MI5 though she was, she still could blush. "Shall I make that popcorn?"

"Do I have popcorn?"

"You do. Ruthie and I saw to it."

"Put on the first Thor movie, then. Pop the popcorn. I'll refill your glass." He settled back in the couch, tasting the Scotch, watching Henrietta, wanting her in bed with him, now. He'd see if they made it through the movie. "We'll let Alfred be, though."

"It's settled, isn't it? He's Martin's dog."

29

Colin stood on the pier in Rock Point harbor with Finian Bracken, in the same spot where they'd met last June. They'd walked down from the church after Timothy Sharpe's funeral. Finian had led the service. Sam Padgett and several other members of HIT had attended, in support of Emma, but Yank was still recovering in the hospital. Lucy had come up, but was on her way back to be with her husband. She'd said, smiling through tears, that Yank was considering learning to knit as a way to relax. Colin would believe it when he saw his boss with knitting needles and yarn, but stranger things had happened.

A cormorant dove out in the harbor, quiet under a clear early-evening sky. Lobster boats were tied at their moorings. It was midtide, waves washing onto pebbles and mudflats. "You have doubts, Fin."

His friend stared at the water. "I am where I am called to be."

"You are. For now, not forever."

"You always speak honestly, don't you?"

"Sometimes I can be too blunt."

"There's no posturing with me because I'm a priest." Finian paused, glancing at Colin. "But I am a priest, Colin. If you wish to speak to me in that capacity, you know you can."

"Yeah. I do." He watched the cormorant reappear. Emma

loved to watch cormorants. He loved watching them with her. "What if I missed something, Fin?"

"Then you missed something. You did your best. It's all any of us can ask of ourselves." Finian paused, touched one of the lobster traps stacked next to him. "Being an FBI agent is your calling, Colin."

The cormorant dove again, unaware of funerals, investigations, grief. "It's a job."

"It's a job you're good at. You stop people from doing bad things or you find them and arrest them before they can do more bad things. You bring them to account."

"If it's a calling…" He turned to his friend. "Callings can change."

Finian smiled. "You're a stubborn man."

They left the cormorant to do its thing and walked up to Hurley's. Emma, Lucas and Faye were there. They'd persuaded Wendell not to risk the trip, given the strain of losing his only son, and he'd stayed in Ireland. All the Donovans were there. Mike had come down from the Bold Coast and was explaining a fine point about lobstering to his love and Nashville native, Naomi MacBride. Andy was arguing with Julianne Maroney and her feisty grandmother about something. Kevin was alone at the bar with a beer. He'd thought they'd gotten to Timothy Sharpe in time and he'd be okay. Colin had, too. So had the medical types, at first. He and Kevin, Mike, Andy, their folks—they'd seen such things in their lives on the coast.

But this was Emma, Colin thought, watching her with her mother and brother. They were telling family stories, about good times as a family—times he could imagine but hadn't shared.

Finian opened a new bottle of whiskey that Bracken Distillers had sent for today, with their condolences. Johnny Hurley himself poured the whiskey into glasses as Finian explained its complexities and sherry barrels and all the time, work and love that had gone into it. Johnny, a big man, rolled his eyes and grinned as he passed out the glasses.

"*Sláinte,*" Finian said finally, raising his glass.

Everyone gathered responded in kind. Colin had eased next to Emma and saw the tears streaming down her face as she said goodbye to her father.

Colin didn't know if he wished he'd had more whiskey or less whiskey. It was late when he and Emma returned to the house, and she had flour and butter out on the counter. "I don't know what kind of pie to make. I'm saving Dad's wild blueberries for winter." She dug out a wooden rolling pin that had belonged to her paternal grandmother. Colin hadn't owned one in his life before Emma Sharpe. "Chocolate pie?"

"What kind of chocolate do you need?"

"Bittersweet would be best."

He shook his head. "Don't have any."

She sighed. "I didn't think so. I should abandon this effort, shouldn't I?"

"The church ladies did make sure we had plenty to eat."

"I haven't had so many dabs of casseroles in ages. So good. Dad…" She shoved the rolling pin back in the drawer, returned the flour bin to its shelf and the butter to the fridge. "Sister Cecilia's going to give me a painting lesson tomorrow. We're meeting on the porch at the offices. Lucas closed them until Monday."

"Painting sounds good," Colin said. "For both you and Sister Cecilia."

"She feels empowered because she was able to help find

Tamara's car." Emma pushed on the fridge door, as if she wanted to be sure it had shut properly—but it had. "She assured me she's not interested in switching careers. She's where she wants to be."

He heard something in her voice. "Emma…"

"I need to go to Ireland, Colin. I need to see Granddad."

He nodded, taking her into his arms. "I know," he whispered. "I know, babe."

"Mom and Lucas approve. I can take the time."

"I'll go with you if you want me to, but I think you need to do this alone." He kissed her softly, felt her warmth, her fatigue. It'd been a long, difficult few days. "So, a pie…it can wait?"

She draped her arms over his shoulders. "Once the rolling pin's back in the drawer, that's it. The mood has passed." Her eyes connected with his, and he saw the pain, the grief, the love. "Colin…"

He lifted her, swept her up and carried her to the front room and up the stairs. He laid her on their bed. He remembered when it was his bed. When this was his house. When he'd only dreamed of having a woman in his life he could love as much as this woman. But he'd never imagined her, never imagined the depths with which he could love.

"I'm sorry, Emma. I wish I could have gotten to him sooner."

"It might not have made a difference, and it wasn't to be. You were with him in the end, and Finian, Mom, Lucas." She drew him to her. "Make love to me tonight, Colin."

"All night, any night." He kissed her, felt the tears wet in her hair. "You'll go to Ireland, and you'll walk the Irish hills with your grandfather."

"I'll come home to you. I'll find you."

"We'll always find each other."

★ ★ ★

The next morning, Colin returned to Boston with Emma, and he visited Yank in the hospital while she packed for Ireland. He set a vase of coneflowers on Yank's bedside table. "Sister Cecilia picked them for you at the convent."

"Sweet of her. For a second I thought you might say you picked them."

"I thought about it. That count?"

"No." But Yank grinned, sitting up straighter. He had an IV but no other tubes, and he looked good for a man who'd been shot and lost a lot of blood. "I get to go home tomorrow. I'm off the heavy pain drugs. I can see why people get stuck on them."

Colin nodded to a get-well card. "It's from the director herself?"

"She called, too."

Mina Van Buren was relatively new to the job, but she'd earned the respect of Matt Yankowski and his small team— and they hers, even if she'd shut them down in a heartbeat if she had to. She'd sent Emma a card, too, with her condolences on Timothy's death.

"I'm sorry I couldn't be there yesterday for the funeral," Yank said.

"A bullet in the shoulder will slow you down. Not for long, though."

"Yeah. Lucy won't want me hanging around the apartment for long. I should have kept a closer eye on Rex. He gave his father the gun. An old man with Alzheimer's. Emma could have shot him. He could have shot himself."

"I suspect Rex would have been fine with that."

"No more bills for his father's care." Yank sighed, waved a hand. "Doesn't matter now. HIT isn't going anywhere. Mina Van Buren told me so herself."

"That's good, Yank," Colin said.

"She said I have work to do."

There was more. Colin could feel it.

"She said to tell you that you have work to do, too."

30

Iveragh Peninsula, Ireland

They stopped on a grassy lane with a view of Skellig Michael
out in the Atlantic, glistening under the blue summer sky.
"Skellig means 'rock in the sea,'" Emma said. "Appropriate,
don't you think?"

Her grandfather nodded, his gaze riveted on the spectacular sight. Emma had visited Skellig with him once, when
she'd worked for Sharpe Fine Art Recovery in Dublin, between the convent and the FBI. More than a thousand years
ago, early medieval monks had created a monastic Christian
retreat on the small, rocky island. It had lasted from as early
as the sixth century into the thirteenth century. Hundreds of
years. As forbidding as the island seemed nine miles into the
rough Atlantic, its geography and the monks' clever place-
ment of their site actually somewhat protected them from the
fiercest weather.

"Scenes in a couple of *Star Wars* movies were filmed on
Skellig Michael," Emma added. "Luke Skywalker retreats
there. It's a remote planet in the movies."

"I saw the first *Star Wars* when it came out forty years ago.
Skellig is a sacred place, at least to me. I remember when it
was put on the UNESCO World Heritage List."

"Skellig Michael is irreplaceable."

Her grandfather sighed, shifting to Emma. It was a warm

day for their hiking, and he'd tied his windbreaker around his waist. "I'll never go to Skellig again. It's not the treacherous steps, or your father. My son. Tim." He smiled, tears in his eyes, and winked at her. "It's the damn boat ride out to the island."

Emma laughed through her own tears, and they resumed their walk. It was their third day of wandering on the Iveragh, Ireland's largest peninsula and one of its most beautiful areas with its mountains and hills, isolated lakes and valleys, its endless green fields and its breathtaking sea views. They covered about ten miles a day, most of it on the Kerry Way, a network of marked trails, roads and lanes that extended around the entire peninsula. They'd meet other hikers, more in some spots than others, but today they were on one of the quiet stretches.

After another hour, they came to the bed-and-breakfast where Emma had reserved two rooms for the night. It was known for its breakfasts. She liked starting a day of hiking with a good breakfast. Hiking filled up the days. There was always something to see, a wrong turn to avoid, a route to sort out. It was the evenings that were difficult. They'd take showers, and her grandfather would take a nap, and they'd find a pub for dinner.

Emma looked at her phone. She had no messages. It was just noon in New England. Colin was back at work; Yank was out of the hospital. Lucas would reopen the offices next week. Her mother was seeing friends, revamping the yard. In the evening, right before bed, Emma sent her husband, her mother and her brother a log of what she and her grandfather had done that day. What they'd seen, where they'd stayed, what they'd had to eat. She'd add a couple of photos.

She went into the bathroom. It was downright prehistoric but spotless. It didn't have a shower, but it had a handheld spray that worked fine. She didn't do a soak. She pictured Colin sitting on the edge of the tub, chatting with her, looking at her in that sexy way he had.

She put up her hair, dressed in jeans and a T-shirt with a lightweight leather jacket and kicked the mud off her hiking shoes. When she met her grandfather in the entry of the quiet little house, he smelled like aftershave and the ends of his thinning gray hair were damp. His eyes sparkled with warmth and energy, more so than they had since she'd arrived in Dublin and whisked him to the southwest coast.

They walked to a small pub. Tourists and locals were crowded at the wood bar and scatter of tables. A fiddler was playing lively Irish folk tunes. "Dad loved his Irish music," Emma said.

"That he did." Her grandfather put out his hand to her. "Dance, kid?"

She took his hand and smiled. "Dance."

★ ★ ★ ★ ★

AUTHOR NOTE

I wrote much of *Impostor's Lure* during a cold New England winter. I'd be imagining 90-degree weather in Boston when it was struggling to get into the single digits on my Vermont hilltop. What fun! Of course, I did do some research and thinking on a beautiful late-summer visit to Ireland. I also ran the Dingle Half Marathon on a rainy, windy day. It ended at a pub. Perfect.

So many people helped get this book out of my head and into your hands. Many thanks to my niece, Sarah Stilwell Josti, for her help with medical research as she, her husband and two little ones welcomed baby Eliza. Thanks, too, to our Irish friend John Moriarty, who not only answered my obscure questions but reminded Joe and me that he has Redbreast 21 in the cabinet.

As always, thanks to my editor, Nicole Brebner, and the entire team at MIRA Books, and to my agent, Jodi Reamer at Writers House. Special thanks to my husband, Joe, and our gang—son Zack, whose design for our limited-edition Bracken Distillers glasses has gotten rave reviews from readers, and daughter Kate, her husband, Conor, and their three little ones. Nothing like a visit with the grands to perk up this writer's life!

Regular breaks in my writing days are calls with my mother, who at eighty-three is slowing down but still loves to watch birds at the feeders outside her kitchen window.

For information on my Sharpe & Donovans and all my

books, giveaways and events, please visit my website. Be sure to sign up for my newsletter! We keep it fun, informal, and focused on what readers tell me they want to know about my books and what I'm up to.

Until next time,
Carla
CarlaNeggers.com